A LIVING LEGEND

All eyes turned to the old man who was walking toward them, supporting himself on a silver-headed cane in his left hand. "I think I'll deal myself a hand of this little fracas if y'all don't mind."

"Step away, old-timer," Fletcher said. "This isn't your fight."

The old man smiled. "Damn it all, Buck. I'm but thirty-seven years old. Younger than you, a lot better looking, and I must say, when you get right down to it, a whole heap better mannered."

Jesse, his eyes ugly, snarled: "The man is right. This ain't your fight, Doc."

Doc! Fletcher knew why the old man had seemed so familiar. The last time he'd seen Doc Holliday had been in Deadwood, ten years before. But the little gambler's tuberculosis was now far gone and the disease had aged him terribly.

Grief and fear spiked in Fletcher as he heard Doc say: "Jesse Taylor, Buck Fletcher is my friend. You know I can't walk away from this."

"Then so be it, Doc," Jesse said. His shotgun came up fast.

Fletcher drew, but his gun still had to clear the leather when Doc fired, skinning his Colt from a shoulder holster with lightning speed.

Ralph Compton

Vengeance Rider

A Ralph Compton Novel
by Joseph A. West

BERKLEY
New York

BERKLEY
An imprint of Penguin Random House LLC
penguinrandomhouse.com

ISBN: 9780451212207

Signet mass-market edition / June 2004
Berkley mass-market edition / November 2020

Printed in the United States of America
9 11 13 15 17 16 14 12 10 8

Cover art by Hiram Richardson
Cover design by Steve Meditz

The Immortal Cowboy

This is respectfully dedicated to the "American Cowboy." His was the saga sparked by the turmoil that followed the Civil War, and the passing of more than a century has by no means diminished the flame.

True, the old days and the old ways are but treasured memories, and the old trails have grown dim with the ravages of time, but the spirit of the cowboy lives on.

In my travels—to Texas, Oklahoma, Kansas, Nebraska, Colorado, Wyoming, New Mexico, and Arizona—I always find something that reminds me of the Old West. While I am walking these plains and mountains for the first time, there is this feeling that a part of me is eternal, that I have known these old trails before. I believe it is the undying spirit of the frontier calling, allowing me, through the mind's eye, to step back into time. What is the appeal of the Old West of the American frontier?

It has been epitomized by some as the dark and bloody period in American history. Its heroes—Crockett, Bowie, Hickok, Earp—have been reviled and criticized. Yet the Old West lives on, larger than life.

It has become a symbol of freedom, where there was always another mountain to climb and another river to cross; when a dispute between two men was settled not with expensive lawyers, but with fists, knives or guns. Barbaric? Maybe. But some things never change. When the cowboy rode into the pages of American history, he left behind a legacy that lives within the hearts of us all.

—Ralph Compton

One

The horse was gone . . . and with its loss came the death of hope.

Tiny McCue lay dead in a pool of his own blood, his small, thin body shot to doll rags, the tracks of the six riders who had murdered him pointing due south.

Buck Fletcher took off his hat and wiped his sweaty brow with the back of his wrist, still desperately grappling to believe what he was seeing. His face bleak, he kneeled and looked more closely at Tiny's body.

Judging by the hole it had made, the little puncher had been shot in the back by a rifle at long range; then another six bullets had been pumped into his chest while he lay helpless on the ground.

The thong was still over the hammer of Tiny's Colt. The man never even had a chance to draw.

Fletcher rose, a sigh escaping, unbidden, from his lips. Tiny had not returned to the ranch after he'd left to exercise the bay thoroughbred, a chore he performed regularly. That had been two days ago.

At first Fletcher had not been too concerned, thinking that Tiny had stopped over at one of the surrounding ranches, something he did now and then to swap lies with other punchers.

But when another day went by, he'd grown worried. The Black Hills country was beautiful, but hidden within its rugged splendor it harbored a hundred different ways to kill a man and sometimes all it took was a momentary lapse in concentration, a thoughtless choice or just some mighty bad luck.

It looked like Tiny had run into all three.

Fletcher had set out earlier that morning to search for the man, and after three hours of following tracks this is what he'd found.

Around him the magnificent, uncaring land was bathed in morning sunlight, and the blue shadows were slowly washing from the arroyos and canyons of the surrounding hills. Jays quarreled noisily among the branches of the yellow aspen and higher up the slopes, green arrowheads of spruce stirred in a warm, southern breeze and, towering above the trees, rose soaring, fantastic spires of gray rock. The sky was a clear, brilliant blue, streaked here and there with hazy smears of white cloud, and the air smelled of pine and wildflowers.

All this Buck Fletcher experienced without joy. A dull rage burned in him, changing the color of his eyes from the same blue as the sky to a hard, gunmetal gray, and his mouth under his sweeping dragoon mustache tightened into a thin line.

Six men had come here, to his range on Two-Bit Creek in the Dakota Territory, and killed his hired hand. And they had taken the horse that meant the difference between life and death for Fletcher's six-year-old daughter.

Slowly, with deliberate motions, Fletcher rolled a smoke, a scalding anger building in him.

He had not taken up his guns for almost ten years now, and had thought to never do so again.

But he vowed to himself that he would take them up once again and exact a terrible vengeance.

He had been wronged and he would bring about the reckoning.

Fletcher lifted Tiny's body onto the back of his horse. He was stepping into the stirrup, preparing to swing into the saddle, when the puncher's hat fell to the ground. Fletcher picked up the hat and made to jam it back on the man's head. But something caught his eye; the corner of a twenty-dollar bill sticking out of the band.

There was a total of eighty dollars neatly folded into the hatband, and a picture of a buxom woman in corsets torn with loving care from a drummer's catalog.

Fletcher shook his head. It was little enough to show for fifteen years as a puncher and a dozen drives up the dusty, dangerous trails from Texas. Little enough to compensate a man for the rheumatisms that plagued him every winter and the pain from the Kiowa arrowhead of strap iron buried deep in his lower back, too dangerously close to the spine to be removed.

Sometimes, especially when the red wheat whiskey was on him, Tiny was a talking man, and Fletcher recalled him once saying that he had an older sister back to Laredo, married to a man who traveled in hardware. He would get his wife to send the woman the eighty dollars, plus whatever Savannah considered a fair amount for the puncher's guns, saddle and horse.

It was not much of a legacy as legacies go, but it was all there was, that and the month's wages still owing to him.

After a careful study of the woman in the corsets, Fletcher folded up the scrap of paper and shoved it into

Tiny's shirt pocket. It might bring the little rider some comfort to be buried with it.

Fletcher swung into the saddle and headed north toward his ranch on the Two-Bit. His buckskin gelding, made uneasy by the smell of blood and the nearness of death, tossed his head, jangling the bit, and once the horse shied as a jackrabbit burst from under his feet and zigzagged its way across the buffalo grass.

Ahead of Fletcher rose the looming bulk of Dome Mountain, a great bulge in the earth's crust cut through by deep gorges and ravines, and further east he could just make out the smoke-colored cottonwoods lining the banks of Lost Gulch.

The sun had climbed higher in the sky and the morning was already hot, heralding another stifling day.

Fletcher rode through a tree-lined valley between a pair of saddleback hills, where he briefly let the buckskin drink at a clear, shallow stream bubbling up from some tumbled granite rocks, then swung west, toward his ranch.

As he left the hills and crossed the flat, he came across more and more of his own cows, young stuff mostly, Texas longhorns crossed with his Hereford bull, each bearing his FS Connected brand on the left shoulder.

He'd sold twenty steers earlier in the spring, fresh beef for the miners in Deadwood, and the five hundred dollars the cattle had brought him now resided in a money belt at his cabin.

This was seed money, and Fletcher had hoped he would soon see it grow to the ten thousand dollars he so desperately needed. But with the death of Tiny McCue and the theft of the fast, game Star Dancer, that hope seemed all but gone.

Grimly, Fletcher set his jaw. No, it was not gone. He

would take time to bury Tiny decent, then get the horse back—or die in the trying.

His daughter Virginia, with her blond hair and her mother's laughing green eyes, had no one to depend on but him. And if she asked it, Fletcher would move Dome Mountain itself for Ginny, even if he had to take the peak apart rock by rock with his bare hands and reassemble it somewhere else at a place of her choosing.

In the past, during his wild, violent and ofttimes lawless years, Fletcher had never imagined that one day he would wrap his Colts in a blanket and settle down to the life of a rancher with a woman and child he adored. But now that it had happened, he could envision no other life. He would grow old with Savannah and see Ginny . . .

But what of Ginny?

That question hit Fletcher like a blow to the stomach. Yes, what of Ginny now that Star Dancer was gone?

He had already made up his mind on that score. It was six against one, but he would bring back the horse. He had to.

A thin column of smoke, straight as a string, rose from the chimney of the cabin as Fletcher rode up, and the smell of newly baked soda bread hung fragrant in the air. Savannah's paint stomped at flies in the corral beyond the house and, nearby, the stream Fletcher's father had diverted from the creek twenty years before tumbled over a bed of sand and mossy pebbles, chuckling in amusement with a humor all its own.

But as Fletcher reined up outside the cabin he noted that the stream level was much lower, as was that of the creek. No rain had fallen since the end of March and out on the range the buffalo grass was already showing patches of brown, frizzled by the long winds blowing hot and dry from the south.

Normally, for Fletcher, this would have been a worrisome thing, but right now he chose not to dwell on it. There were other, more pressing matters at hand.

The cabin door swung open and Savannah stepped outside; the sight of her, as it always did, taking Fletcher's breath away.

His wife's auburn hair was loosely pulled away from her face, tied with a pink ribbon at the back of her neck, and her emerald eyes were bright with welcome. Savannah's teeth flashed white as she smiled, her mouth a little too wide for true beauty, tiny, arched lines showing at the corners of her lips. She wore a dress of pink gingham that matched the color of the bow in her hair and showed off the generous curves of her body. She was, Fletcher decided, not for the first or the last time, a right pretty woman, a woman a man would never tire of coming home to, a woman like no other he'd ever known.

And he wondered, as he many times did, what she had ever seen in him.

He knew himself to be a big, homely man who was not at all skilled in the social graces and whose pleasures were few and simple. He was now, at forty, showing traces of gray in the dark hair at his temples, and the wrinkles around his eyes and mouth were etched deep from exposure to all kinds of weather and from life and the living of it, a life recently good but before that almighty hard. What he did not know, and could not see, were the things Savannah admired in him. She loved his fumbling, always half-embarrassed kindness and the genuine good humor that crept into his eyes when she, sometimes thinking him a little too demanding, harkened back to his service in the War Between the States and addressed him as "Major Fletcher," snapping to attention as she gave him the palm-forward salute of the Union horse artillery.

But most of all, she admired Buck Fletcher's genuine

quality of empathy. He had the instinctive awareness and deep regard for another's feelings that was, and remains, the mark of a true gentleman.

Courage, determination, the will to endure, Savannah saw these and other attributes in her husband—most of which he could not guess at, and if she had ever uttered them aloud it would surely have embarrassed him horribly.

Despite the morning heat, Savannah looked as cool as the sprig of mint in an iced julep glass, but now her cheeks drained of color as she saw the double burden Fletcher's horse was carrying.

"Tiny is dead," Fletcher said, replying to his wife's unspoken question. "They killed him and took Star Dancer."

Savannah's face was stricken, understanding the consequences of the stolen horse as keenly as did her husband.

Fletcher swung out of the saddle and, spurs chiming, stepped toward his wife. "I plan to bury Tiny decent and go after them."

"How many?" Savannah asked.

"Six. Maybe more."

The woman nodded. "I'll sack you up some supplies."

Fletcher had expected nothing less. He knew Savannah would not plead, would not beg him to let it go and have the law handle it. She accepted what had to be done. Like all frontier women, his wife knew that in this harsh, unforgiving land a man was expected to make his own way, right his own wrongs. With the spring roundup so close, there could be no asking the surrounding ranchers for help, nor, she understood well, would her husband ask for it.

They needed the horse back and now Buck had it to do. That was the beginning and the end of the story. There would be no discussion. No argument.

"How is Ginny?" Fletcher asked.

Savannah's face changed, lit up by a smile. "She was up

today for a couple of hours. She even helped mix the bread dough." The woman's eyes sought those of her husband, seeking an answer to a question she'd not yet asked.

Now she asked it. "Ginny's getting stronger, Buck. Isn't she getting stronger all the time?"

Fletcher saw the pleading in his wife's eyes, knowing the answer she wanted. Savannah had asked him the question but he chose to step carefully around it.

"The doctors at the Swiss clinic . . ." he hesitated, trying to frame his words, ". . . they'll make Ginny better." He forced a smile. "You'll see."

Savannah bit her lip. For a few moments she stood in silence, looking at her husband. She had hoped to hear comforting words that never came, hoped for a reassurance he could not bring himself to give. Fletcher realized she was disappointed, but he had never lied to her and now was not the time to start.

Finally Savannah turned and glanced back toward the window of the cabin. "Buck, find Tiny a place further along the creek. I don't want Ginny to know."

Tiny McCue, with the cowboy's almost superstitious dread of tuberculosis, had seldom come near the cabin where Ginny lay. But the child had often watched him from the window as he worked, something of interest to see in a still, unchanging land.

But Savannah was right. Better Ginny did not know. They would tell her Tiny had moved on, as several hands had done in the past.

Fletcher had wanted to first go inside and see his daughter, but now he led his horse into the barn behind the cabin. He lit the fire in the forge and began to heat an iron rod, the rusty handle of an old branding iron. That done, he made a headboard of rough pine slats, and took the red-hot iron and wrote on the board. He had to reheat the iron several times before the marker was finished, precious time he knew he could ill afford.

But Fletcher had seen too many dead men tumble into unmarked graves over the years, and he would not make Tiny another.

All in all, Tiny McCue had been only a fair hand, and a sometimes sour and unwilling one at that, but every man should leave something behind to mark his passing.

Fletcher grabbed a shovel, then led the buckskin to the base of a hill about half a mile from the cabin. The ground was dry, hard and dusty, but he buried the little puncher deep enough to discourage marauding coyotes and covered the grave with as many loose rocks as he could find.

When Savannah joined him, they said the prayers they knew, then Fletcher hammered the marker into the grave with the back of the shovel. It said simply:

Tiny McCue
A good rider
1886

It was not much to say about a man, but it was enough. Some Fletcher had known, better men than Tiny, had gone to their Maker with much less.

When Fletcher and Savannah returned to the cabin Ginny was asleep. The child lay on a cot in the main room of the cabin, the arcs of her long eyelashes dark on her pale cheekbones, her corn yellow hair spread like a halo across the pillow.

The consumption had come on her a year before, and already the disease had exacted its toll. Ginny was very thin and her face had taken on the strange luminosity often seen in victims of advanced tuberculosis, an inner glow like the light artists paint into storybook angels.

But this light was not light, it was darkness. It was, Fletcher knew, the pallid shadow of death. The sand was fast running through the hourglass and Ginny's time was growing short.

"She'll die, as we all must die," Dr. Jacob Anderson had told Savannah and Fletcher a few months before. "All I can tell you is that you should prepare."

Savannah, desperate, willing to clutch at any straw, begged Anderson to tell her if he knew of any other doctor wise in the ways of the disease who might save her child.

The physician tugged at his beard and shook his head. "Not in this country. But there is a mountain clinic in Switzerland, very exclusive, very expensive, and I'm told the doctors there are doing wonderful things." The old man looked around their spare cabin, his eyes bleak. "Ginny would have to stay there for a year, maybe longer, and the cost . . ." he shook his head, ". . . ah . . . the cost."

"How much?" Savannah asked, hope flaring in her eyes.

"At least five thousand dollars."

"I'd want to go with her," Savannah said.

"Then double that amount." Anderson glanced around the cabin again. "Do you have that kind of money? Ten thousand dollars is a great deal."

It was Fletcher who spoke. "We'll get it, Doc. Somehow we'll get it."

Anderson shrugged. "I can write the letters, make the necessary arrangements. But it will have to be soon."

"How soon?" Fletcher asked, fearing the physician's reply.

The doctor's eyes were level, his voice calm, matter-of-fact, professional. "Mr. Fletcher, without the Swiss clinic, your daughter will be dead in six months."

* * *

Now Fletcher leaned over and gently kissed the sleeping child on the cheek. The girl stirred and muttered something he did not understand, then slept again.

Fletcher turned to his wife, his eyes red. "Take care of her, Savannah."

"I will, Buck. Until you come home."

Fletcher quickly brushed the back of his big, work-roughened hand across his eyes and Savannah, knowing well her husband's touchy masculine pride, said: "You must have gotten dirt in your eyes, Buck."

Fletcher nodded, accepting what she was giving him. "Probably when I was digging Tiny's grave."

Savannah nodded. "It's so dry and dusty out there."

"Yeah, it's dusty."

Fletcher was wearing his guns, a blue, short-barreled Colt in a crossdraw holster at his waist, another with a seven-and-a-half-inch barrel on his hip, both in .45 caliber.

He and Savannah stood, wordlessly looking at each other for a few moments, then the woman seemed to make her mind up about something. She stepped to the pine chest that Fletcher had made for her, opened a drawer and brought out the money belt.

"You better take this," she said. "You may not have time to come back home before the race."

Fletcher hefted the belt in his hand, the twenty-five gold double eagles heavy. "I'll have to find a jockey now Tiny is gone."

"You'll find one." Savannah managed a smile. "I imagine there are plenty of skinny boys in Arizona who know how to ride a racehorse."

"I reckon."

They stood close, each unwilling to say the words of good-bye. Finally Fletcher said: "Well, I guess I got to be getting along."

Savannah nodded. "Wait," she said.

She stepped to the chest again and from another drawer brought back a small pile of bills and coins that she thrust into his hand. "There's forty-seven dollars and thirty-five cents there, Buck. You may need it."

Fletcher shook his head. "Savannah, that's all the money we have. I can't take it."

"I'll make out." She stood on tiptoe and kissed Fletcher on the mouth. "Now," she said, her voice breaking, "leave before I become a silly woman and make a complete fool of myself."

"Savannah," Fletcher whispered, holding her close, "I'll be back and I'll have the ten thousand dollars. I promise you."

"I know you will."

Savannah stepped out of her husband's arms and took a bulging canvas sack from the table. She handed it to him. "There's a loaf of sourdough bread, some bacon and a couple of cans of peaches." She smiled. "And an extra sack of tobacco."

Fletcher smiled. "I guess you know how I get without my tobacco."

"Only too well."

When they stepped out of the cabin, Fletcher swung into the saddle and Savannah stood at his stirrup. "Take care of yourself," she said. "Come back to us, Buck."

"Depend on it."

He swung his horse south and, behind him, Savannah raised her arm and called out: "*Vaya con Dios*, Buck Fletcher."

Fletcher turned in the saddle and touched the brim of his hat, words failing him.

Ahead lay the long miles and six murderous outlaws he

would hunt down and kill or see dangle from the end of a rope.

And behind, he was leaving the woman and child he loved, maybe forever.

Fletcher rode on, away from his home on the Two-Bit, a hurting in him that clutched at his belly and would not let him go.

Years before, a wild-eyed preacher had told him about hell and at the time Fletcher had paid him no mind. But now it all came back to him.

"A place of blazing fire, of terror, of vengeance, and of screams and torment," the man had said.

"So be it," Fletcher whispered, as he rode into the white heat of the burning morning.

He was bringing hell with him. That too was part of the reckoning.

Two

When Fletcher splashed across a foot of water in Bear Butte Gulch, the sun had risen high above Bear Den Mountain and the day was still and hot, the dry south wind no longer blowing.

Sweat trickled down Fletcher's cheeks and under his shirt. Around him brooded silent, pine-covered hills, and his eyes reached out across the far, hazy distance only to see land and sky melt together, forged into a single shimmering, molten mass by the relentless hammer of the sun.

A mile to his east squatted a small log cabin, the home of a widow woman and her two children. She had come here with her husband three years before to farm this land, hoping to coax crops from the thin, rocky soil, and had failed.

After two years, drought, insects and grinding, endless toil had done for the man. He'd been plowing when a terrible weight, heavy as an anvil, had crushed his chest, numbing his left arm, twisting half his face into a grotesque mask. He clung to life for a few days and then died.

The woman, trying to succeed where her husband had failed, remained.

Fletcher glanced over to the cabin and shook his head. He did not give much for her chances. This was a harsh, relentless land that had no mercy on the weak. A woman alone, without a man's strong back to help her, had little hope of surviving.

Once, Fletcher had ridden over there and asked if there was anything he could do to help. But the woman was proud, a stiff-necked, Yankee kind of pride, and she had refused. She had been polite enough, but firm and unyielding, and Fletcher, admiring her spirit, had not pressed the matter.

The smoke that rose from the cabin's chimney told him she was still there. Good luck to her, he thought. And he wished her well.

Without rain, the tracks of the six raiders still scarred the buffalo grass, heading due south, seemingly in no great hurry, confident of their guns and numbers.

Fletcher reined up under the shade of a cottonwood on the bank of Elk Creek at the southern limit of grassy Windy Flats and built himself a smoke, trying to think the thing through.

He had no idea why the men had stolen the horse. If they intended to sell him, they would have to do it soon, though there were few around these parts who could afford to buy a thousand-dollar thoroughbred. With six of them sharing the loot, to sell Star Dancer for anything less would hardly bring them riding wages and such little profit was a small enough reason to kill a man.

Did they intend to keep him? That was a possibility, though the big three-year-old was high-strung and most times nigh impossible to handle. He was no cow pony and no day-to-day riding horse either.

Fletcher shook his head, his thoughts getting him nowhere.

Careful of fire, he stubbed out his cigarette on the side of his boot and pitched the dead butt into the water of the creek.

He swung his horse around and followed the tracks again, pointing straight as an arrow toward the lower reaches of the Cheyenne and the Nebraska border.

Mindful that the outlaws were two full days ahead of him, Fletcher rode through all of the searing day and considered making camp only when the night birds were pecking at the first stars and a waxing moon rose to cool a land scorched by the sun.

Around Fletcher the hills lay still, each surrounded by silence, broken now and then by the calling of the coyotes out in the darkness.

Once, he had been a man who loved solitude, finding no quieter and more untroubled retreat than in his own soul. But now, as he sought a place to make his fire, there was an aching loneliness in him, memories of Savannah and Ginny echoing in his mind like the failing notes of a faraway bugle.

He knew the separation was none of his doing, but that did little to make the hurting less.

Fletcher made camp near the ruin of a stone cabin he figured had been destroyed in some long-forgotten Indian raid years before. The cabin stood at the base of a flat-topped hill, close to the aspen line, and a narrow, sluggish stream ran nearby, lined by a few struggling and dejected willows.

Only one wall of the cabin still stood, and Fletcher built a small fire at its base, then stripped his horse and rubbed down the buckskin's back with a piece of coarse sacking he carried in his saddlebags. He led the horse to the stream to drink, then staked him out on a good patch of buffalo grass.

Only then did Fletcher himself drink. He splashed water on his face and chest and ran a wet comb through his thick hair. Then he filled his coffeepot and settled it on the glowing coals of the fire.

While he waited for the coffee to boil, he leaned his back against the wall of the cabin and began to build a smoke.

Beyond the glow of the fire, the darkness was gathering around him, the movement from day to night now complete, yet done so gradually and easily, Fletcher could scarce recall when the light had passed.

He lit his cigarette and dragged deep, liking the harsh taste of the tobacco.

"Hellooo the camp!"

A man's voice came from out of the shadows and Fletcher rose to his feet, stepping from the arc of the firelight, his hand close to his Colt in the crossdraw holster.

"Come on ahead," he yelled, "but I'd take it as a real courtesy if you keep your hands well away from your belt buckle."

The man chuckled. "Don't wear no belt, sonny. But I'll keep my mitts away from my suspenders if'n that sets right with you."

Fletcher's fist closed on the walnut handle of his Colt. "Step slow and easy, mister. I'm not what you'd call a trusting man and tonight I'm a might tetchy to boot."

The man chuckled again and then emerged slowly from the darkness. He was maybe seventy years old, dressed in the plaid shirt, canvas pants and mule-eared boots of the gold prospector, and he led a small burro burdened with pick and shovel and the other tools of his trade.

"Smelled your coffee," the old man said. "Don't have none myself. Fresh out this morning."

"There's plenty," Fletcher said, relaxing some, his hand dropping from his gun.

"Name's Salty Higgins," the old man said. "Prospected in these parts, man and boy, nigh on fifty years." Higgins smiled behind his long, gray beard. "I been to Denver, blew my poke, now I'm back to the diggings again and as broke as ever was."

"Easy come, easy go, I guess," Fletcher said, a statement he was to make again but in a different time and place.

Higgins nodded. "You could say that. At least the go part is easy. When it's about money, it's the come part that's tough."

Fletcher inclined his head. "There's a stream over there where you can water your animal." He jutted his chin toward the burro. "But when you strip the pack off him, I'd take it as a kindness if you'd steer well clear of your Henry."

The old man laughed. "Dang it all, sonny, you said you wasn't a trusting man an' I'm beginning to see clear that you wasn't just makin' that up."

Fletcher nodded. "I've lived this long by stepping easy and being real careful."

Salty Higgins saw to his burro and returned to the fire carrying a tin plate and cup. Fletcher filled his cup and Higgins set it on the ground beside him. He reached into his shirt pocket and found a battered, yellowed meerschaum pipe. He lit the pipe, then lifted the cup to his mouth, smacking his lips in appreciation. "You make good coffee, sonny."

"I get by," Fletcher said.

The old man nodded, giving Fletcher a sidelong glance. He opened his mouth to say something, changed his mind and sealed his lips with the rim of his cup.

"You got something on your mind, old-timer, say it," Fletcher said, smiling, so there was no implied threat behind the words.

Higgins laid down his cup, slow and careful. "Well, I mean no offense mind, but I've been studying on you some. You could say that's a habit with me, studying on folks I mean."

"Strange things, habits." Fletcher shrugged, building another cigarette. "Seems to me, most folks don't even know they have them."

"Maybe so. But I guess I know all the ones I got, both good and bad." The old man tasted his coffee, blew on it, then tried it again. "Hot," he said. He laid the cup beside him. "Anyhoo, what I was going to say is that it could be you're an old-timey gunfighter by the name of Buck Fletcher. And it could be, a spell back, ye rode with John Wesley Hardin and the Taylor boys and them wild ones down to Texas a ways." The old prospector made a show of carefully studying the glowing coal of tobacco in his pipe. "I ain't saying it as a natural fact, but it could be you did."

Without looking up, Fletcher sliced bacon into his small frying pan and set it on the fire to cook. "How do you know these things, Salty?" he asked finally.

The prospector shrugged. "Could be that back in the spring of '74, I was passing through Comanche, Texas, when John Wesley shot a deputy by the name of Charlie Webb. But it could be that Webb got a bullet into Wes afore he died. And it could be that it came about by and by that Wes's brothers Joe and Bud, along with a mean one named Tom Dixon, was took and hung.

"And could be I saw with my own eyes how John Wesley escaped—on the back of a sorrel hoss rode by a big, homely man who was hell on wheels with a gun and shot his way out of town. Could be that man was Buck Fletcher." Higgins nodded to himself. "An' it could be that man was you."

Fletcher turned the bacon with the blade of his pocketknife, a beautiful ivory-handled folder made in Sheffield, England, the gift of a Confederate colonel he'd captured at Antietam.

Once the bacon was crisp he placed it to the side of the pan and fried two slices of sourdough bread in the smoking fat. He made a sandwich of the bread and bacon and passed it to Higgins, Western etiquette dictating that the guest must always be served first.

Fletcher sliced more bacon into the pan and only then did he speak.

"Maybe you're right, Salty. Maybe I am Buck Fletcher and maybe all that riding I did with Wes and them wild ones happened so long ago I can scarce remember." He shook the bacon to fry it evenly. "But I recollect that Wes was all right. Maybe a mite too quick on the trigger was all."

Higgins chewed his sandwich thoughtfully. "Y'know, one time I had me a big poke an' I bought me a steak sandwich in Delmonico's over to New York." The old man smiled, his milky blue eyes glinting in the firelight. "It weren't a patch on this."

Fletcher nodded, acknowledging the compliment, and built his own sandwich.

"See," Higgins said, "a sandwich like this, it slicks up a man's skin an' protects him from the cold, and the bacon fat greases his joints and saves him from the rheumatisms. That," he added, talking around another huge mouthful, "is something to remember."

After the two men had eaten, Higgins lit his pipe and Fletcher rolled a cigarette. Once they were both smoking, Higgins said: "Could be I got something else to say."

"Then say it," Fletcher said. He felt drowsy and relaxed. The moon was splashing silver paint over the surrounding hills and the fire crackled, a burning stick now and then shifting, sending up a small, bright shower of sparks. The coyotes were calling out to each other again and, fairly close, a sleepless owl questioned the deepening night.

"Could be I heard—"

"Say it straight out, Salty," Fletcher interrupted. "I'll take no offense."

The old prospector nodded. "So be it. I heard tell the last time I was in Deadwood that Buck Fletcher had himself a wife and a young 'un and a spread up on the bend of the Two-Bit."

"You heard right," Fletcher said, only mildly interested in what the old man was saying.

"All the talk in the saloons was how you'd hung up your guns and had bred a racehoss so fast he could run from sunup to sundown in less than half an hour."

The drowsiness left Fletcher instantly and he leaned forward with a start. "What do you know about the horse?"

Higgins shrugged. "Only this—I think I saw him two days ago."

"Where?"

"South of here. A big, lanky bay with a white star on his forehead. Steps real high an' lively, ain't that right?"

"That sounds like Star Dancer," Fletcher said, excitement building in him. "Where did you see him?"

"Right near Harney Peak, north of the Cheyenne. There were six men with him, mean ones."

"Salty, how did you come across them? It seems to me they wouldn't be keen to welcome strangers."

"I'm a coffee-drinking man," Salty said. "But I never seem to have any, maybe because I drink it up so fast. I smelled their coffee, just like I smelled yours, and walked into their camp." The old prospector smiled. "I wasn't exactly told to make myself to home, but they didn't shoot me either."

"Recognize any of them?" Fletcher asked.

"Sure thing. I knew Bosco Tracy right off, him and his no-account brothers Luke and Earl. Two others I'd never seen afore, but the other one I recognized." The old man leaned over and spat. "He was Port Austin."

Fletcher eased back against the wall, his fingers going to

his shirt pocket for the makings, remembering things he'd been told.

The Tracy brothers were mean all the way through, cold-blooded killers who would cut any man, woman or child in half with a shotgun for fifty dollars. But for sheer badness they didn't hold a patch to Port Austin.

A few years back Austin had come up the Chisholm Trail with a herd from Texas to Abilene; then, after brushing off the dust of the long miles, decided honest work was about as welcome as a wart on a whore's butt. To make his point, he robbed a general store in Hays and made his getaway by outdrawing and killing a deputy sheriff. A month later he killed Quirt Lawson, the lightning-fast Newton gunfighter who was said to have six dead men to his credit.

On Christmas Eve '79, angry at the inflated Festive Season price a young soiled dove tried to charge him in a brothel in Wichita, Austin stabbed the woman to death and later decorated the bridle of his horse with her long, red hair.

In the months that followed, he robbed banks all over Kansas and beyond, but he really didn't come into his own until he hooked up with the Tracy boys.

The last Fletcher heard, Port Austin had carved eight notches on his gun butt, and the number had probably grown since. He was poison mean and fast as a rattlesnake with his Colt. Fear didn't enter into this thinking, but neither did mercy or compassion or any other human emotion.

Austin was a born killer with ice in his veins and he thought no more of shooting another human being than he would a rat. If evil truly existed, shackling the mind and perverting the conscience, then its personification was Port Austin.

Higgins raised an eyebrow. "Now you're doing some thinking your ownself, Buck."

Fletcher nodded, his face revealing an uncertainty not

unmixed with a measure of apprehension. "I was studying some on Port Austin."

The old man nodded. "He's a handful all right. They said he's the best with a Colt's gun as ever was."

Letting that remark slide, Fletcher asked: "Salty, did they tell you where they were taking the horse?"

The old man shook his head. "Not directly. But, like I said, I'm a studying man and I keep my ears open. If a feller just sets quiet and listens, he can learn a thing or two."

"What did you learn?"

The prospector extended his cup and Fletcher filled it. "I heard them cussin' and discussin' about how they'd staked out your ranch for three, four days afore they killed your hired hand. Bosco said it was just as well, because he was getting a tad impatient and favored just riding in there and taking the horse. Ol' Port, he said he'd gun all he found in the cabin so there was no witnesses."

Fletcher swallowed hard. During the past days he'd been spending a lot of time on the range, and if Bosco Tracy and Austin had found Savannah and Ginny alone, he would have murdered them both without giving it a second thought.

A coldness in his belly, a stunned note of disbelief in his voice, he asked: "They knew it was my horse, Buck Fletcher's horse?"

Higgins nodded. "Sure they knew, but they didn't give a damn. Buck, you've been out of the limelight for nigh on ten years. Folks forget what you were an' what you done in the olden days. Bosco and Port Austin and the others are a different generation. Hell, them boys have read the dime novels and filled their heads with all kinds of rattlebrained fancies. They hang their guns low on their thighs and strut around and think themselves . . ." The old man stopped and motioned to the south with the stem of his pipe. "Here, what was the name of that youngster who caused all the trouble down there to Lincoln County in the New Mexico Territory a few years back?"

Fletcher thought for a few moments then replied: "William Bonney, as I recollect. The newspapers called him Billy the Kid. Or he did."

Higgins nodded. "Yeah, that's him. Well, Bosco and Port Austin and them, they think themselves to be just like Billy the Kid. They want to get their names in the newspapers and become known as famous bad men."

His mouth tightening into a grim line, Fletcher said: "All that newspaper ink didn't do Bonney much good. He's dead."

Higgins shrugged. "I guess Bosco and Port figure that won't happen to them. Or maybe they just don't give a damn. Boys like that want to live fast and wild. That's why they stole your hoss, to get money for women and whiskey, two things that's a big part of living." The old prospector smiled in his beard. "For any man."

Fletcher's ego was badly bruised, even as he told himself that his gunfighter days were long gone and that a man's sense of self-importance just laid out the perimeters of his own limitations.

But, looking at Salty Higgins with unhappy eyes, a bitterness rising in him, he asked: "I guess my being over-the-hill and all, they figured I wouldn't come after them?"

The old prospector grinned. "Hell, Buck, they knew from the git-go you'd come after them. But like I tole you, they don't give a damn. There ain't a single one of those boys who don't figure he could take you in a gunfight."

"Are they that good?"

Higgins shrugged. "I don't know, except for Port an' maybe ol' Bosco his ownself. But the rest sure reckon they are."

Fletcher rolled a smoke. The south wind was stirring

again, making the flames dance. The glow painted red the hard planes of his face, giving him the expressionless, wooden look of a cigar store Indian.

Picking up a burning brand from the fire, Fletcher lit his cigarette, his great, beaked nose and high cheekbones flaring orange for an instant.

"Where will they try to sell the horse, Salty?" he asked finally, tossing the twig back into the flames.

"Not around here, that much I know."

"Where then?"

"Arizony. They said they were selling the hoss to a gambling gent down there."

"Long ways to take a horse."

Higgins nodded. "Maybe so, but I heard tell that Texas John Slaughter is organizing a big hoss race on the Fourth of July down at his ranch in Cochise County in the Territory. They say the purse is ten thousand dollars, winner take all. Maybe the sporting gent plans to enter your hoss in the race and bet heavy on him on the side."

The old man smiled. "If that's the case, he's taking a chance. I don't know if your Star Dancer is as fast as they say, but ol' Texas John has an American stud he calls Big Boy an' folks tell me that sorrel can't be beat by anything on four legs."

All this Fletcher already knew. Slaughter was charging five hundred dollars to enter a horse in the race—the twenty-five double eagles that now weighed heavy in his money belt.

Higgins shrewd old face lit up as a thought hit him. "Buck, was you thinking of entering your hoss in ol' John's race your ownself?"

Fletcher nodded. "Thinking about it." He decided not to mention Ginny, since that might elicit sympathy or, worse, pity, a thing his already battered ego could not abide. "I figured to use the prize money to buy another Hereford bull and maybe make some improvements at my ranch," he said, skirting the truth to head off the old man's questions.

Higgins nodded. "Ten thousand is a lot of money."

Fletcher pitched his half-smoked cigarette into the fire. "Salty, I don't suppose Bosco mentioned the name of the gambling gent?"

The old man shook his head. "If he did, it was out of my hearing."

"If I find out who he is, that gambler and me will have words," Fletcher said, his eyes glittering hard in the firelight.

"Buck," Higgins said, a slight smile on his lips, "something tells me I'd hate to be in that sporting gent's shoes when you catch up to him."

Fletcher rose to his feet, stretched and yawned, and said: "I got to find my blankets, Salty. I want to be on the trail come sunup."

The old man, with considerably less ease than that just shown by Fletcher, also stood, his joints creaking. "Wait, Buck, I got something to give you."

Higgins reached behind his head and untied the rawhide thong of the necklace he wore around his neck.

"I want you to have this, Buck," the old man said. "It was give to me by an Apache woman a few years back." The necklace gleamed in the firelight as Higgins held it out to Fletcher. "The beads are red jasper and turquoise, and the Apaches say wearing it will bring you closer to the Great Spirit and he will send you luck."

Fletcher shook his head. "Salty, I can't take this. You don't owe me a thing."

Higgins reached out, took Fletcher's hand and laid the necklace in his palm. "Call it my way of helping you get your hoss back, Buck. See, I know the real reason you need that ten thousand and it ain't for no Hereford bull. On account of how I'm a listening man, I heard about your daughter my ownself back to Deadwood a spell ago. I'm too old and stiff to ride with you, but, small as it is, this is help I can give."

It was not in Fletcher's nature to deeply hurt a man, and to turn down the old prospector's gift would be to wound him terribly.

When a man drinks at a stream, he should always remember the source, and this Fletcher did now. He tied the necklace around his neck and said: "Thank you kindly, Salty. I'm not likely to forget who gave me this."

Pleased, Higgins smiled. "Now I got to turn in my ownself." He slapped his leg. "And, dang it all, I'll have me some coffee in the morning."

Within minutes both men slept, and around them the quiet hills were silvered by the moonlight, their chasms and arroyos in deep blue shadow. The pines stirred in the faint southern breeze and the buffalo grass rippled like waves on an inland sea. The campfire guttered down until there was only a dull, crimson glow at the center of a pyramid of gray ash and black-charred wood. At around two in the morning rose a last, frail wisp of smoke, at once taken by the wind to disappear like a ghost.

Fletcher and Higgins slept on. Once, toward daybreak, Fletcher stirred and called out in his sleep, dreaming of men and guns, and running among them, lost in the flame-streaked powder smoke, Savannah and Ginny begging him to help them.

Wildly, he reached out a hand . . . and felt only the big, calloused paw of Salty Higgins.

"Well, howdy-do your ownself," the old prospector said. "I must say, that's a right friendly way to greet a man in the morning."

Fletcher jerked his hand away like he'd touched something red-hot and opened his eyes. Higgins was looking at him, a wide grin stretching from ear to ear.

"I was dreaming," Fletcher said. "I do that sometimes."

Higgins nodded. "It's good for a man to dream. It's kinda like hitching your wagon to a star and traveling wherever you please."

Fletcher rose to a sitting position, put on his hat, and then his fingers automatically reached for the tobacco sack in his shirt pocket.

"Coffee's almost biled," the old prospector said. "An' it's nearly sunup."

Half an hour later, as the night brightened into morning, Fletcher took his leave of Salty Higgins and followed the horse tracks south.

Ahead of him lay the bend of the Cheyenne, to his east the Badlands—and in between a world of danger.

Fletcher rode alert in the saddle, Colts loose in their holsters. His gunfighter's instincts had been dulled by the years, but once again were being honed to a razor-sharp edge.

There was some kind of showdown coming . . . and the coldness in his belly from the knowing of it was just as certain as the warmth of the rising sun on his face.

Three

At noon, Fletcher stopped at French Creek, a few miles north of the Cheyenne, in a grove of mixed willow and cottonwood. The trees grew on each side of a stream branching off the shallowest part of the creek, the willows trailing their branches in the water.

Steep hills rose on each side of the grove, the slopes covered mostly in spruce, their crests rawboned pillars of gray rock like the battered towers of an ancient citadel.

The day was hot, but among the trees it was much cooler and the stream made a pleasant bubbling sound as it ran over a bed of sand and pebbles.

Fletcher gathered enough dry sticks to light a small fire, then filled his coffeepot from the stream and placed it on the coals. That done, he stripped the saddle from the buckskin and let him graze on the lush, plentiful grass growing along the bank.

Fletcher calculated that the thick canopy of leaves overhead would shield him from the aim of any rifleman hidden higher up the slopes of the surrounding hills, and the trees would slow anyone coming at him head-on, either on horseback or on foot.

He smoked a cigarette and drank coffee, then stretched

out under a tree, tipping his hat over his eyes. He dozed off and on for an hour, rose and threw the dregs of the coffee on the fire.

Suddenly Fletcher dropped the pot and yanked the Colt from his crossdraw holster. He swung around as he did so, as though drawing down on somebody creeping up behind him. He reholstered the gun, drew again. And again. And again.

His frustration growing, Fletcher finally shoved the Colt back into the leather. He shook his head slowly, his face gloomy. Unlike riding a horse, a thing a man learns and, once learned, never forgets, the ability to draw a gun fast and shoot accurately is a perishable skill.

To remain quick and smooth on the draw, a man needs constant practice, and Fletcher had not picked up a Colt in a decade. Now, at forty, his years were catching up with him, blunting his reflexes. Right now he was as slow as an old hound dog in August, no match for the young, Colt-slick Port Austin. And maybe even Bosco Tracy, a man known to be fast and accurate with a gun, could shade him.

It was a worrisome thing, and the knowledge of it flooded Buck Fletcher with doubt and filled him with rapidly building unease.

He took time to roll a cigarette, drew the smoke deep into his lungs, his hands just a mite unsteady, and thought the thing through.

Finally, as the cigarette burned, forgotten, down to his fingers, he had made up his mind. He would stand up and take the hits and keep on shooting back as long as his legs supported him.

His decision was a consolation of sorts, yet no consolation at all.

Maybe, Fletcher reflected, a small, wry smile playing around his lips, he needed a miracle. But miracles are not made in heaven. Men who use the courage and intelligence God gave them create their own miracles, and this Fletcher knew.

So be it. If a miracle was needed, he would shape his own.

He ground out the cigarette under his boot heel and quickly saddled the buckskin. He took to the trail again, the sun now slanting over his right shoulder. After three miles the horse tracks of the outlaws veered off to the west, sloping up toward a line of yellow aspen growing along the bases of several high, hump-backed hills.

Fletcher followed the tracks until they vanished among flat slabs of granite and tufted grama grass littering the lower slopes. To his left, a line of massive, tumbled boulders stretched away to the south until they were lost to sight over the brow of a hill just ahead of him. Squirrels and jays rustled in the branches of the aspen, and the ground between their slender trunks was covered in a carpet of bluebells, harebells and tiny, pink, wild roses.

Fletcher took off his hat and wiped the sweat from his brow with his forearm. He could no longer see the tracks. Had this been a deliberate move on Bosco Tracy's part to throw him off the trail?

He shook his head, dismissing the thought as quickly as it had come to him. If the outlaw took his pursuit as lightly as Salty Higgins had said, why would he bother to cover his tracks?

Then why ride up this way? Certainly there was shade among the aspens, but their crowded trunks made it no place to take horses. In fact, the entire going here was a lot rougher and slower than down in the flat basin country.

What was Tracy up to?

Suddenly uneasy, Fletcher settled his hat back on his head, then stood in the stirrups, his great beak of a nose lifted as he read an odd message in the wind. There, he smelled it again . . . a fleeting, elusive whiff drifting past, tattered by the breeze.

But Fletcher now recognized the odor. It was wood smoke.

Could it be that Bosco, Austin and the others were close by, waiting for him?

Fletcher reached down and slid his Winchester from the boot under his left knee—just as a rifle shot hammered from the aspens, the thundering echoes rebounding among the surrounding hills like great boulders being thrown down an iron canyon.

Another shot rang out and something tugged at the collar of Fletcher's shirt. He threw himself off the buckskin, rolled, then came up on one knee, his rifle jumping up fast to his shoulder. He saw a puff of gray gunsmoke drift from the aspens just ahead and above him. He fired—once into the smoke, two more quick rounds close to the right and left of it.

Something crashed among the trees and he heard a man's startled curse. Fletcher cranked another round into the chamber then fired into the aspens where he'd heard the man's voice, dusting three more shots into the general area as fast as he could work the lever of the Winchester.

The man's voice called out to him, shrill and scared. "Don't shoot no more you son of a bitch, you've killed me!"

Slowly, taking care, his eyes alert for any movement, Fletcher rose to his feet. "You, in the trees!" he yelled. "Come out of there real slow and careful like. I want your hands empty and up high where I can see them real good."

"You son of a bitch, you've shot me all to pieces. I can't walk."

Fletcher, feeling not a shred of sympathy for this or any

bushwhacker, yelled: "Then crawl out of there on your belly, damn you."

Slow moments passed. It was very hot up here, the air sluggish and still. Beside Fletcher a lizard crawled along the side of a rock then stopped, its tiny mouth gasping.

"You're a son of a bitch!" the man yelled.

"Maybe so," Fletcher hollered back. "But I've been called worse."

"Are you Buck Fletcher?"

"That I am."

"You're a damn son of a bitch."

The undergrowth among the aspen rattled and a young, yellow-haired man staggered out, dragging a bloody leg behind him. He had a Colt in each hand and now he cut loose, triggering shots at Fletcher, the big revolvers bucking in his fists, muzzles flaring orange behind a thickening wall of smoke.

Fletcher laid his rifle sights square on the gunman's chest and fired. The man staggered and Fletcher fired again, and again. Slowly the bushwhacker sank to his knees, then sprawled facedown on a slab of broken, grass-tufted rock at his feet.

Warily, Fletcher cranked another round into the chamber of his Winchester and stepped to the side of the fallen gunman.

He turned the man over with the toe of his boot and, for the first time, got a look at the bushwhacker who had tried to kill him.

No man this, but a well-grown, overconfident boy, probably no more than eighteen. His blue eyes were open, wide and scared, freckles scattered across an upturned, pug nose.

"You've killed me," the boy gasped, blood pink and frothy on his lips, hemorrhaging from destroyed lungs.

Fletcher nodded. "You didn't give me much choice."

"You're a real son of a bitch."

"You've called me that before," Fletcher said, his voice cold, unforgiving, not yielding an inch. "Better you quit cussing and make your peace with God. Your time is close."

The boy coughed, his back arching high as pain slammed at him. Then, as the spasm passed, he said: "Bosco and Port an' them others, they told me you'd be easy, that you was just a tired old man."

"They told you wrong." Fletcher kneeled beside the boy, the pent-up bitterness slowly beginning to drain him. "What's your name, son? Maybe I can tell your folks."

"It's Clem, Clem Taylor." The boy grabbed the front of Fletcher's shirt. "Bosco said once you was dead, he'd give me fifty dollars to spend on whores and whiskey. I've drank whiskey plenty of times, but I never sparked me a girl, not even once. Hell, and I've never even had me fifty dollars in my whole life." The light was fast fading from the boy's face and his eye sockets were shading dark, lips peeling back from his teeth.

"Listen, mister," he whispered, "don't leave me here to the coyotes. Take me home where I can be laid to rest decent."

"Where is home, boy?" Fletcher asked.

"South of here . . . on the north bend of the Cheyenne . . ." Taylor was struggling, trying to form the last words he would ever speak. "Town . . . town called Blue's Stand . . . the sheriff . . . the sheriff . . . he'll . . . promise me . . . promise . . ."

The words died with Clem Taylor. His eyes were still wide open, only now they were staring into infinite nothingness.

Fletcher stayed where he was for a few moments, the killing of this boy weighing heavy on him. During the War Between the States he'd killed his share of boys like this, boys even younger in butternut or gray, and he'd hoped to never in his life do it again.

But a man should not shed fresh tears over old griefs and Fletcher forced himself to accept that what was done was done.

He rose to his feet, then scouted the area. The horse prints paralleled the aspen line for a way, then headed back down from the hills to the flat. He figured the prints were a couple of days old and that Clem Taylor had been laying up here for him that whole time.

Fletcher calculated that Bosco and the others had led him here, where the boy could get a clean shot at him. And he had. But the youngster had gotten overexcited or just wasn't good enough.

Either way, Clem Taylor was dead before he even got a chance to live, and Bosco Tracy had killed him as surely as if he'd put a bullet in his brain.

Fletcher walked back to Taylor's body. He owed this boy nothing, yet the thin whisper of his conscience was starting to nag at him, and he knew if he rode away from here now it would never let him be.

Cursing himself for a softhearted fool, Fletcher stepped into the aspens and after a few minutes' search found the boy's camp. Taylor had kicked his fire apart when he'd seen him coming, but not before Fletcher had caught the fleeting tang of wood smoke in the air that had saved his life.

The youngster's horse was tethered nearby, and Fletcher led the animal through the trees and back to where the body lay.

Taylor's horse was a half-broke mustang paint, a beat-up, ten-dollar saddle on its back, and it balked and reared at the smell of blood. But the closeness of Fletcher's buckskin helped calm the animal, at least long enough for him to hoist the boy facedown across the saddle.

He had never heard of a town called Blue's Stand on the Cheyenne—or anywhere else for that matter—but now he had to find it.

The day was hot. The burning sun had slapped its smoking brand on the swelling rump of the colorless sky and Fletcher smelled the rankness of his own sweat. He rode his buckskin, the mustang on a lead rope trailing behind him. Flies were already buzzing around the dead youngster's head, attracted by the drying blood, buzzing their excitement.

Fletcher hoped Blue's Stand was close.

In a couple of hours the body would smell even worse than he did. A whole heap worse.

Four

Under a blazing sun, Fletcher rode into Blue's Stand just before noon.

The town had been easier to find than he'd expected, settlements of any kind being few and far between in the vast, open range country north of the Cheyenne.

In the distance, two hundred miles to the west, soared the peaks of the Rockies, marking the Continental Divide, and beyond the mountains desert and plains stretched long and flat all the way to the sea.

Blue's Stand was a dusty, one-street cow town, ramshackle, false-fronted buildings lining both sides of the road. A narrow tributary of the Cheyenne crossed by a rickety wooden bridge delineated the boundary between the respectable part of town and the red-light district, identified by a faded, crudely painted sign that said: HIDE PARK.

Fletcher rode past a huddled collection of tarpaper shacks, most of them fallen into ruin, used by the girls on the line. There were three saloons, the grandest of which, boasting of a tall false front that bore the name CATTLEMAN'S REPOSE, seemed to have drawn an early crowd.

A piano dropped off-key notes into the hot, still air like pennies falling into a tin bucket, and from somewhere beyond the batwing doors a man roared and a woman laughed, loud, shrill and fraudulent.

Unseen, Fletcher crossed the bridge, the hooves of his horses sounding hollow above the slow-moving creek, and headed for the business district, if such description fitted a scattering of buildings that had been hurriedly thrown together with warped timbers held together by a lick of paint and starry-eyed hope.

Beyond these were half a dozen decayed gingerbread houses that baked in the relentless sun and gathered what was left of their shabby dignity around themselves like impoverished but proud dowagers. These would be the homes of the town's respectable businessmen: the banker, the livery stable owner and the man who ran the general store. And the saloon bartenders would reside here, the occupation of mixologist then considered by Western men to be every bit as prestigious as that of doctor, preacher or lawyer.

Cattle pens shouldered against a single railroad track, a spur to the main Union Pacific line far to the west. But the rails were rusted, weeds growing between the ties, and no train had passed this way for many a year.

On a shallow rise behind the town was a surprisingly large Boot Hill, bordered by a tall, wrought-iron fence, a flock of cantankerous crows quarreling raucously among the oaks that spread their branches over the mossy graves.

Fletcher reckoned that Blue's Stand had once been a booming place, roaring with lanky punchers, bearded miners, painted whores, white-fingered gamblers and wary, hard-eyed horsemen, lean as wolves, drifting in from whereabouts unknown, easing out again in the dark of night by moonlit trails.

But now this was a dying town, the buildings already fading to smoke gray like ancient ghosts. Soon, unlamented, it would vanish forever and only a few creaking, sagging walls and some scars on the prairie grass would mark its passing.

The West was full of such towns. Bypassed by the railroads and stage lines and the dusty longhorn herds up from Texas, they withered and eventually blew away in the long winds off the plains, the residents moving on to new places with nary a backward glance.

After Fletcher crossed the bridge and rode along the street, he finally began to attract attention.

A few townspeople stood on the boardwalks and watched him ride past, his buckskin's hooves kicking up puffs of tan-colored dust with every step. The faces of the onlookers were solemn, wide eyes blank and unrevealing, like so many painted dolls.

Fletcher reined up outside the Mercantile Bank, a low, sod-and-timber building with a single barred window to the front. A man with a huge belly, sweating in a black broadcloth suit and high celluloid collar, stepped to the edge of the boardwalk.

"What's going on here?" he asked. "And who is that dead man and who are you?"

Fletcher ignored the banker's questions, just as he ignored the pompous, arrogant tone of his voice. "Sheriff?" he asked.

The fat man's face flushed and he opened his mouth to speak again, but then he caught the coldness in Fletcher's eyes and thought better of it. He turned to a skinny boy in patched overalls who was tormenting a tiny kitten he'd tied to the boardwalk and snapped: "Ephraim, go get Lem Hall."

The boy gave the banker a sulky, insolent look and the man yelled: "Now!"

Slowly, to show he wasn't in the least bit intimidated, the boy rose to his feet and swaggered away, whistling through his teeth. He stepped into the general store and a few moments later Hall, a gray-haired man in a white apron appeared, dusting flour from his hands.

The man looked down the street at Fletcher, then quickly ducked inside again. When he reappeared he had removed the apron and was wearing a tin star on the front of his collarless shirt, a Colt belted around his waist.

Taking his time, the sheriff walked toward Fletcher, nervously rubbing the palm of his right hand against his pants.

Fletcher watched him come, coolly taking his measure. This skinny storekeeper was no gun-handy cow-town lawman. Obviously the man was a political appointee, entitled to charge for every stray dog he shot within the city limits and to skim off his share of the fines levied on what remained of the Hide Park whores and gamblers.

The man walked past Fletcher without a word and stopped at the mustang. He waved away the cloud of flies buzzing around the dead man and grabbed the head by the hair, yanking up the face where he could get a good look at it.

Hall let the head fall and turned to the gathering crowd on the boardwalk. "I know this boy," he said. "It's young Clem Taylor."

A woman in a blue sunbonnet gasped as her breath caught in her throat and an angry murmur ran through the crowd.

Fletcher turned in the saddle to face the sheriff. "He was old enough to use a gun." He jerked a thumb over his right shoulder. "He tried to kill me back there in the hills."

"So you say," the banker snapped, his piggy eyes ugly.

Fletcher looked at the man, his words falling like chips of ice. "Mister," he said, "if you open your mouth again, be damn sure you don't call me a liar."

The banker was a bully, all threat and bluster, a man long used to seeing lesser men step aside for him. But now the chips were down he reached inward to get a hold of courage, but found only empty space where his guts should have been. He opened his mouth to speak, gasped once or twice like a stranded fish, and lapsed into silence.

Hall, seeing this, did what he could to save the banker's face. "Here," he said, stepping up to Fletcher's stirrup, "we'll have no threats of gunplay. One dead man is enough for today."

The sheriff turned to the crowd on the boardwalk. "Some of you men carry this boy to Sam'l Jenks. He'll know what to do."

"Undertaker?" Fletcher asked.

Hall nodded. "That, and other things. He's also the town baker; makes a real nice soda cracker pie."

After the boy's body was carried away, Fletcher swung out of the saddle. "Now what?" he asked the lawman.

"Come with me to my office," Hall replied. "We got to talk things through."

"You arresting me, Sheriff?" Fletcher asked, his cold eyes boring into Hall.

The lawman shook his head. "Let's just say you're helping me with my inquiries."

Fletcher walked with Hall to the general store, a murmur of muted voices following him; most speculative, a few angry. Out of the corner of his eye he saw the fat banker whisper something to the boy who'd returned to the boardwalk and was again teasing the kitten. The man pressed a coin into the boy's hand, and the kid nodded and quickly ran behind the bank and was soon lost from sight.

Fletcher thought little enough of it at the time, but he'd later come to realize that the small transaction he'd witnessed had major consequences on the rapid, violent succession of events that followed.

Hall's office was at the back of his store, and Fletcher

followed him past shelves of canned goods, piles of clothing and barrels of crackers, pickles and molasses to a small, windowless room furnished with a rolltop desk, a couple of chairs and an unframed Currier & Ives print pinned to one wall, showing Adam and Eve being driven out of paradise.

The sheriff unbuckled his gun, wrapped the cartridge belt around the holster and laid it gently on top of the desk. It was a small, careful gesture and Fletcher caught its significance. Hall was taking care not to do anything that might be construed as a threat.

Hall dropped into a chair and waved Fletcher into the other. The lawman studied the big, homely gunfighter for a few moments, smoothing his ragged mustache with the back of his hand. "Tell me about it," he said finally.

Fletcher obliged. As was the Western way, Hall had not asked his name, but now Fletcher gave it. Then, in as few words as possible, he told of the murder of his hired hand and the theft of his horse. Lastly he described how Taylor had bushwhacked him in the hills and how the dying boy had asked that his body be brought here.

"The kid was running with a rough crowd," he said. "Bosco Tracy and Port Austin and a few other hard cases. These are the men who stole my horse. Clem Taylor told me Bosco had promised him fifty dollars to kill me."

The sheriff absorbed all this in silence, then came back to the discussion from an unexpected angle. "I knew I'd heard the name Buck Fletcher before, and just now it all came back to me. Seems to me you ran with a hard crowd your ownself a few years back; Wes Hardin and Jim Miller and them. And I heard tell you wasn't too choosy on what side of the law you sold your gun."

Fletcher shrugged, taking no offense. "In those days I never had much, didn't expect much." He smiled, his lips thin under his mustache. "It's the quality of a man's expectations that determines the quality of his actions. Sure, I sold my gun and you're right, I was never too particular about who was paying the money, just so long as he paid on time."

Leaning forward, Fletcher pinned Hall to his chair with his eyes. "But I tell you this, I never bushwhacked a man. When it came right down to it and the lead started flying, all my bullets hit a man in the shirt pockets."

Hall's smile was slight, without humor. "You're proud of that, Mister Fletcher?"

"I did my job and pride didn't enter into it. Pride is a rooster crowing on a dung heap. It doesn't amount to much."

Sheriff Lem Hall was a man who preferred to talk around things and he did it now. "If I had to," he said, "I mean if I was put to it, I'd arrest you, Fletcher."

Fletcher nodded. "Maybe you'd try, but you'd never make it to your gun. I have things to do, Sheriff, and I'm not about to let you hold me here."

"You don't think I'm much, do you?" Hall asked without a trace of bitterness.

"You don't scare me none, if that's what you mean."

"Well, if I had to, I'd arrest you or die trying. Call it professional pride—and that's not the squawk of a rooster on a dung heap."

Grudgingly, Fletcher gave this storekeeper turned sheriff a measure of respect. "Do you plan on arresting me, Sheriff?" he asked. Like Hall had done earlier, he kept his voice level, careful not to imply a threat.

Hall shook his head. "No, I believe every word you've told me, Fletcher. I believe you killed the Taylor kid in self-defense and I feel I've got no call to hold you here for the U.S. marshal."

"Then I'm free to go?"

The lawman nodded. "As a bird." But as Fletcher rose, he

added quietly: "Young Clem Taylor has brothers. That's something you ought to know."

Fletcher had been heading for the door. Now he turned. "I've done what the boy asked and brought him home," he said. "Someone else can tell his brothers."

"It's not that simple, Fletcher. Jesse and Rufus Taylor live in a dugout a couple of miles outside of town. They're wolfers and scalp hunters and God knows what else. They came into the Territory uncurried and wild from the Tennessee hills a few years ago, dragging young Clem along with them. Fletcher, men like that are born to the feud, so if I were you I'd step right careful. Them Taylors are long on revenge and mighty short on forgiveness."

"I'm not hunting trouble," Fletcher said. "All I want is a cold beer to cut the dust in my throat and I'll be on my way. I want my horse back."

Hall smiled. "There is no cold beer in Blue's Stand."

"Then what does a man drink around here?"

"Warm beer."

"It will do," Fletcher said.

"One thing more." Hall rose to his feet. "We still have the telegraph, about all that's left of the old days. I'll let the other lawmen down the line know about your horse. Maybe they can help."

Fletcher nodded. "I'd be right obliged."

He stepped outside and swung into the saddle. The big-bellied banker was still on the boardwalk and he watched Fletcher with hostile eyes as he rode past.

Fletcher ignored the man and recrossed the bridge, tying up his horse at the hitching rail outside the Cattleman's Repose.

The day had grown hotter and the pine-covered hills around the town lay still and listless under the fiery ball of the sun. The air was dry, smelling of the scorched brown grass that covered the bottomlands, and it held no promise of rain. Fletcher had seen how things were out on the open range and the signs did not bode well. The cattle were already suffering, trudging through choking clouds of their own gray dust like ghosts, tongues lolling from parched mouths as they explored the arroyos and rocky canyons in a ceaseless search for water.

He glanced at the searing white sky, shook his head with the rancher's inborn disgust of drought, and stepped through the doors of the saloon.

Inside it was cooler, but not by much, and Fletcher felt sweat trickle down his back as he walked to the bar, his spurs chiming.

The piano player had given up, surrendering to the heat, and sprawled asleep in a chair beside his battered instrument. Three men in patched and faded shirts and jeans, punchers working the grub line by the look of them, stood at the bar and an old, white-haired man sat alone at a table, a half-empty bottle of whiskey and a single glass in front of him.

Apparently the early morning crowd had left to doze away the hottest part of the day, and a couple of hard-eyed saloon girls in worn satin dresses stood together at the end of the bar, sharing a beer and their loneliness.

The old man at the table, dressed in a threadbare gray frock coat with a worn velvet collar, studied Fletcher with careful eyes as the big gunfighter stood at the bar and built a smoke. Fletcher took the man's unwavering look as an old-timer's idle curiosity and nodded in his direction. The old man ignored the gesture and looked away, pouring himself another drink, holding the bottle in a white, blue-veined hand that trembled slightly.

There was something vaguely familiar about the man, in

the way he held his head and the arrogant boldness of his gaze, but Fletcher couldn't pin him down in his memory.

He shrugged. He'd traveled a lot of trails, passed through a lot of towns and seen a lot of faces, and this old timer had probably been one of them. In the scheme of things, it really didn't matter a damn.

"What will it be?"

The bartender was small and portly, black hair carefully parted in the middle of his head, slicked down on each side, shiny and smooth with pomade. His mustache was a thin pencil smear across his top lip and dark half moons of sweat stained his striped shirt at the armpits. The bartender's brown eyes were impatient and uncaring, the look of a man who had worked at the same job for too many years and served too many people.

"Beer," Fletcher said.

"It ain't cold." The bartender shrugged. "Ain't nothing cold around here."

"I'll drink it warm."

"Suit yourself."

The man drew the beer then thumped the foaming mug on the bar. He waited until Fletcher fished in his pocket and laid a nickel on the counter, then quickly scooped up the coin and dropped it into the cash drawer.

One of the punchers, sour and nursing a hangover, turned, looked Fletcher up and down with bloodshot belligerence and opened his mouth to speak. Then he looked again, took in the way this stranger wore his guns and the hard coldness in his eyes and thought better of it. He turned away and gazed morosely into the bottom of his empty glass, saying nothing.

Fletcher tried his beer. It was warm and rapidly getting warmer, but it cut the dust in his throat and he quickly drained the glass and ordered another.

A girl uncoiled herself from the end of the bar and strolled toward him, her hips swaying, a painted, predatory smile on her lips. Fletcher watched her come and gave an almost imperceptible shake of his head. The girl stopped in mid-stride, surprised, then pouted and flounced back to her companion, muttering something about the dire shortage of sporting gents in Blue's Stand and the impoverished state of the local drovers.

The old man at the table had watched all this with keen interest and now he poured himself another drink, careful not to spill a single drop, and sat back in his chair, smiling slightly, his eyes on Fletcher.

It seemed the bartender had decided to be sociable, and when he laid Fletcher's beer in front of him he asked: "Passin' through?"

Fletcher nodded. "Heading south, all the way to the Arizona Territory maybe."

"Long ways," the bartender said.

"It's a fair piece," Fletcher acknowledged.

The old man was now sitting forward in his chair, attentively listening to this exchange. He gave Fletcher a long, speculative look, made up his mind about something, and slowly began to rise. But the sound of hard-ridden horses being reined to a rearing halt outside stopped him and his eyes swung to the door.

A few moments later two men, huge, shaggy and bearded, stomped into the saloon.

And Fletcher saw nothing but trouble.

Five

The two men stopped just inside the saloon doors and their eyes swept the room, taking in Fletcher, the old man at the table and the punchers standing belly to the bar.

The bigger of the two, red hair falling lank and greasy over his shoulders, beard hanging thick to his belt buckle, motioned with the Greener shotgun in his hands.

"Which one of ye brung in a dead boy today?"

Fletcher turned slowly until he was facing the men. "I guess that would be me."

The red-haired man nodded. "My name is Jesse Taylor an' the boy you killed was my brother." He hawked and spat on the floor, narrowly missing the toes of Fletcher's boots. "I'm here to even the score."

Trying desperately to step away from this, Fletcher said: "Your brother bushwhacked me, and him having nothing against me that either of us could remember. It was a no-account outlaw by the name of Bosco Tracy who put him up to it. He told the boy he'd pay him fifty dollars for my scalp. Clem shot first, but he missed, so as things turned out he didn't live to collect it."

The other man, and Fletcher guessed this could only be Rufus, was a smaller and meaner version of his brother. He carried a Winchester and his eyes were hard and rattlesnake cold.

"That don't make no never mind," Rufus said. "Clem wasn't much, on account of how he took after Ma's side, that Bible-thumping Hook Creek bunch, but he was kin and we've come to kill him as murdered him."

The railroad clock on the wall behind the bar ticked loud seconds into the room like water from a leaky pump dripping into a tin bucket. Wary, stepping lightly, the cowboys eased away from the bar and backed toward the far wall, out of the line of fire. The piano player woke and instantly figured out what was happening. His eyes wide and frightened, he ushered the two saloon girls behind the inadequate barricade of the piano, then squeezed next to them.

Fletcher tried again, hoping to make the whole thing go away. "I got no quarrel with you boys," he said. "I'm sorry for what happened to your brother but he gave me no choice. Now just turn around and walk on out of here. There's no need for more men to die."

Jesse shook his head, smiling, showing a few black stumps of teeth. "Big talk for a man standing alone. We're two agin one, so I reckon the only dead man here will be you."

It had come. Fletcher tensed, steadying himself for the draw, knowing how hard it was to shade a man with a gun already in his hands but seeing no other choice.

He caught the sudden, wild look in Jesse's eyes and his own vision narrowed, like he was looking at the brothers through a tunnel. The drumbeat sound of his heart was loud in his ears as the fingers of his right hand spread wide, ready.

"Here, this won't do. That man has friends heah."

The tense moment fractured into a million pieces, the words like rocks thrown through a pane of sheet glass.

All eyes turned to the old man who was walking toward

them, supporting himself on a silver-headed cane in his left hand. "I think I'll deal myself a hand in this little fracas, if y'all don't mind."

"Step away, old-timer," Fletcher said. "This isn't your fight."

The old man smiled. "Damn it all, Buck. I'm but thirty-seven years old. Younger than you, a lot better looking and I must say, when you get right down to it, a whole heap better mannered."

Jesse, his eyes ugly, snarled: "The man is right. This ain't your fight, Doc. Don't take sides or we'll leave you dead on the floor alongside of him."

Doc! Fletcher knew why the old man had seemed so familiar. The last time he'd seen Doc Holliday had been in Deadwood, ten years before. But the little gambler's tuberculosis was now far gone and the disease had aged him terribly. Doc looked to be at death's door, bent and frail, knocking loudly to be let inside.

Even as he faced the present danger, Fletcher's thoughts flashed to Ginny. Was this how she'd end up without that trip to the Swiss clinic? Like Doc? Old before her time, a pale, deathlike shadow of what she'd once been and might have become?

Grief and fear spiked in Fletcher as he heard Doc say: "Jesse Taylor, Buck Fletcher is my friend. You know I can't walk away from this."

"Then so be it, Doc," Jesse said. The man was all through talking. His shotgun came up fast.

Fletcher drew, but his gun had still to clear the leather when Doc fired, skinning his Colt from a shoulder holster with lightning speed. Hit hard by Doc's bullet, Jesse took a step back, colliding with his brother, who had swung his rifle on Fletcher. Jesse's shotgun roared. Too high. Buckshot slammed into the ceiling, scattering wood chips over Doc's shoulders.

Fletcher fired at Rufus as the man threw his rifle to his shoulder, then fired again. Rufus staggered, but his rifle barked and Fletcher felt the bullet tug at the sleeve of his shirt.

Stepping out of the thick, gray cloud of his own gunsmoke, Fletcher fired again, and this time Rufus pitched forward onto the floor, rolled and lay still.

Jesse Taylor, tall and terrible, his eyes wild, the front of his shirt where it showed under his coat splashed scarlet with blood, yanked the spent red hulls from his Greener. He fumbled in the pocket of his coat, found two more shells and thumbed them into the scattergun.

"Let it be!" Fletcher yelled. "It's over."

The man ignored him. The shotgun swung. Doc and Fletcher fired at the same time and Jesse, hit by both bullets, sank to his knees. His Greener blasted. Two barrels of buckshot blew a huge hole in the side of the bar at Fletcher's left thigh, splinters flying.

Fletcher fired, his bullet kicking up a puff of dust from the shoulder of Jesse's coat.

"Give me more shells, somebody," Jesse yelled, his wild eyes frantically sweeping the saloon. He was splashed in blood from collar button to belt buckle, but would not give up the fight.

Doc ended it.

Grasping his Colt in both hands, he sighted carefully and fired, his bullet crashing into Jesse's head just above the right eye.

The man screamed, not from fear, but from rage and defiance and the certain knowledge of his own death, then he sprawled his length on the floor.

Doc stepped to the fallen man and gingerly prodded him

with the toe of his polished, elastic-sided boot. "Dead," he said, to no one in particular. Doc shook his head in wonderment. "This fellow had sand. I have to give him that. Yes, rough and uncouth as he was, I do believe he had sand."

Fletcher, the old, familiar sickness in him that always followed a gunfight, stepped beside the fallen men, gunsmoke curling around him. "I gave them their chance," he said. "They could have walked away from it."

Doc shrugged, the smell of whiskey surrounding him like a haze. "Who cares? They're no great loss."

He looked at Fletcher, one eyebrow arching high up his forehead as he slid his Colt back into the leather. "A tad slow on the draw, there, Buck," he said. "You've eased up some."

Fletcher nodded. "I'm out of practice, I guess."

"You'd be dead if it wasn't for me," Doc said. "Something for you to remember."

"I'm not likely to forget, Doc," Fletcher said.

"Damn right you're not, because I won't let you."

The saloon doors crashed open and Sheriff Hall walked inside, flanked by two men carrying shotguns, tin stars on their chests. These were deputized citizens of Blue's Stand, but they looked determined and capable enough and the scatterguns weren't for show.

Hall took in the scene at a glance. He glared at Fletcher. "Tell me about it."

"It was self-defense, Hall," the little bartender interrupted, surprising Fletcher. "The Taylor brothers came at this man and Doc here took a hand."

One of the punchers, a gray-haired man in a black-and-white cow-skin vest, stepped into the middle of the room and nodded to Fletcher. "Hell, Sheriff, this ranny tried to back away from it, but they wouldn't let him. Seen that my ownself."

Hall's eyes swept the others. "Anybody disagree?"

No one spoke, and even the belligerent puncher held his tongue.

The sheriff thought this through, then said. "Doc, self-defense or no, you've overstayed your welcome. Go to the hotel and get your stuff. I want you out of Blue's Stand within the hour." He turned to Fletcher. "And that goes for you too."

Doc Holliday gave Hall an exaggerated little bow. "Believe me, Sheriff, leaving this dung hill you call a town will be no great wrench."

Fletcher stepped closer to Hall and asked: "Who sent the word to the Taylors? Was it the banker? I saw him give a boy some money, then the kid took off out of town."

Hall was kneeling, his hand on Jesse's chest. "Dead as dead can be," he said, shaking his head, as though bemused by the vagaries of human nature and the frailty of life. He looked up at Fletcher. "I don't know who sent for the brothers. I guess it could have been banker Loughlin. The boy you saw with him is his son."

Fletcher nodded. "Somehow that doesn't surprise me."

The sheriff shrugged. "Hank Loughlin cuts a wide path around these parts but you made him eat crow. You put the crawl on him, Fletcher, and that sticks in a man's throat."

Hall rose to his feet, his right knee cracking loudly. "What I said still goes. I want you two out of here. It's only a shade past noon and already I've got three dead men on my hands."

"Suits me," Fletcher said. He turned to Doc. "You helped save my bacon today. I'll remember it."

Doc shrugged. "You know, Buck, I studied on it for a while. I recognized you right off, of course, but I was ready to let it go, figuring your problems were none of mine and mine none of yours." He smiled. "Then I thought, what the hell, I have nothing to lose. Might as well deal myself into the game."

"Well," Fletcher said, "I'm mighty glad you did and, like I told you, I owe you one."

"I heard you say you were heading for Arizona," Doc said. "I think maybe I'll ride along with you."

Fletcher shook his head. "That's not going to happen, Doc. I'll be riding fast and far." He looked at the man, a bag of yellow skin and bone covered by a shabby suit several sizes too large for him. "Damn it, Doc, you shouldn't be riding; you need medical help."

Doc glanced around the room, at the closeness of the onlookers and the attentive Hall and his deputies. He stepped into a quiet corner and motioned Fletcher to come after him.

When Fletcher joined him, Doc said in a hoarse whisper: "Buck, I've won a lot of battles in my time, but I'm losing my last one. Fact is, I'm dying. I talked to a doctor in Dodge a while back and he told me I got three, four months."

Fletcher opened his mouth to speak, but Doc shushed him into silence. "I'm flat broke." He pulled his watch chain from the pocket of his vest. There was no watch attached to it. Doc Holliday's famous gold English repeater by George Edward and Sons of London, England, was gone.

"Yeah, I pawned the George Edward a spell back," Doc explained, his eyes bleak. "And my rifle. I'm down to three dollars and change in my pocket. I was figuring maybe I'd ride up to a sanitarium in Glenwood Springs over to Colorado way and throw myself on the charity of the good Catholic sisters that help run the place."

"Doc," Fletcher said, "I don't have much, but if it's money—"

"Hell no, Buck, it isn't about money. It's about dying. All my life, I haven't set myself to learn how to live, but how to die. The way I see it, I have two choices. I can ride to Glenwood and lie in a bed until there's nothing left of me but eyes and a cough. I'll die in an odor of sanctity, surrounded by holy nuns, and the whole time I'll be a-looking at my sock feet sticking up out of the bottom of the bed, wondering why in blue blazes I let this happen to me."

Doc's fevered gaze burned like fire. "Or I can die in one moment of hell-firing glory, my guns spitting lead until they finally down me. There would only be a little pain . . . then blessed nothing at all."

The little gambler looked at Fletcher with searching eyes. "If you were me, Buck, which death would you choose?"

"Doc, when you come right down to it, each man dies alone. I can't help you find the death you want."

"The hell you can't!" Doc grinned. "I've been around you for only a few minutes and already you got me into a shooting scrape. Trouble just naturally follows you, Buck. It surely does."

"Let it go, Doc," Fletcher said. "Don't push this any more."

"I'm pushing it. I got one adventure left in me, and you're it." Doc's sunken, hot eyes sought Fletcher's. "I'm not asking you, Buck. Hell man, I'm on my bended knees, begging you."

Doc Holliday had the Southern gentleman's quick, head-high pride and Fletcher knew that for him to unbend this far took a tremendous effort. When all was said and done, he owed Doc his life and had thought to pay that debt at some future time. But the dawning realization came to him that Doc had no future, only the present. The time was now.

"I'd be honored if you'd ride along with me, Doc," he said, surprised at how smoothly the lie spilled from his lips. "But when I tell you what you'll be getting into, I think maybe you'll change your mind."

The relief on Doc's face was obvious, but he drew what

was left of his pride around himself like a tattered cloak, salvaging what he could. "And just as well. Your draw has slowed considerable, Buck. You'll need me by your side."

Fletcher let that alone, allowing the man his dignity.

"Heard you mention Bosco Tracy," Doc said. "I've bumped into him a time or two, but we never had cross words." He shrugged his thin shoulders. "If we'd had, he wouldn't be around any longer to trouble you."

"Tracy is one of them. The other is Port Austin."

Doc whistled between his teeth. "Port Austin! Jesus, Buck, you've got a tiger by the tail. Port is a man to step around. He isn't completely sane, you know."

"There are others. All three of the Tracy boys and a couple of hard cases I don't know."

As the bodies of the Taylors were carried from the saloon—heavy men, not easily moved—Fletcher spared them but a single glance. He'd given them an out, but these had been angry men and angry men always think they can do more than they can. They had refused to take what he'd offered and had paid the price.

Returning his attention to Doc, Fletcher quickly told him about the theft of Star Dancer and the mysterious Arizona gambler who might have masterminded the whole deal.

"I plan to press Bosco and his boys real close," Fletcher concluded. "And this little detour has already cost me too much time."

"How far ahead of us are they?" Doc asked.

"Two days. Maybe three."

"We'll catch up with them, Buck," Doc said. "Depend on it."

Fletcher said nothing. He doubted very much that Doc could last any more than a couple of days on the trail, if that. Sick as he was, Arizona might as well be on the moon.

Hall stepped beside them. "You boys head on out now,"

he said. He looked at Doc, a grudging sympathy in his eyes. "Hell, man, you look terrible. You need to be in a hospital."

"Hell, Sheriff, I'm fit as a fiddle, and if things were any better with me, I'd have to hire someone to help me enjoy it."

The lawman shook his head. "Doc, you're dreaming. Now, get your pony and ride."

He turned to Fletcher. "I'll keep my word, I mean about informing the sheriffs down the line. I don't know if it will help you get your horse back, but I guess the more people who know, the better."

Fletcher touched his hat and uttered his thanks, acknowledging that the man was doing the best he could.

Then, as he and Doc stepped toward the door of the saloon, the bartender surprised Fletcher again. "Here," he said, "I got grub back here if you boys want to eat before you go." He looked at Fletcher. "I got hard-boiled eggs and some cheese. You like cheese?"

Fletcher shook his head, the dead men weighing on him. "Thanks," he said, "but I've lost my appetite."

"And I never did find mine," Doc said.

The bartender nodded, his grin wide. "Well, thanks for livening the place up. For a minute there it was like I was back in the good old days."

Fletcher walked with Doc to his hotel room and the little man stuffed what little he owned into a carpetbag. He said his horse was at a livery stable behind one of the other saloons, and the animal turned out to be a small, mouse-colored mustang with a hammerhead and a mean eye. A cloud of flies buzzed around the little horse and every now and again it lazily flicked its tail to drive them away.

Doc caught the sour expression on Fletcher's face and said: "You don't have to worry none about this little feller,

Buck. Every time you turn around, he'll have his nose up the ass of that big buckskin of yours."

Fletcher shrugged. "I never thought much of Texas mustangs and I don't see anything in this one to make me change my mind."

Doc opened his mouth to object, but Fletcher headed him off. "Before we leave, I've got some unfinished business to attend to over to the bank."

"You mean Hank Laughlin? Don't you bother yourself none about him, Buck. I'll just ride on over there and put a quick bullet into that big belly of his, then catch you up on the trail." Doc shrugged, his eyes glittering. "Drill his pimply kid too if you want."

Fletcher smiled. "Thanks for the offer, Doc, but this is something I have to do for myself."

Doc shrugged, looking small and shrunken and old. "Suit yourself, but it would be no trouble. No trouble at all."

There was no sign of the banker when Fletcher and Doc rode up to the bank. But Loughlin's son still had the calico kitten tied to the boardwalk, and now he was tormenting the tiny animal with a pointed stick.

Fletcher swung out of the saddle, and without a word opened his knife and cut the kitten free. He then untied the tight noose from around the animal's neck.

"Here," the kid said, his eyes ugly, "that's mine."

Holding the kitten close to his chest, Fletcher looked at the boy, anger building in him. "Anybody who would abuse a helpless animal doesn't amount to much," he said, his voice flat and hard.

The boy looked into Fletcher's eyes, saw something he didn't like, and backed off a step. "I'm going to tell my pa on you," he whined, fingers picking at an angry red sore on his cheek.

Fletcher ignored the boy and swung into the saddle.

"You plan on taking that kittlin' with us?" Doc asked.

Fletcher nodded. "I'm sure as hell not going to leave him here."

Doc shook his head. "I always figured you for a strange one, Buck. Now, in your old age, I swear you're getting stranger."

"Maybe so, Doc." Fletcher smiled. "Now, let's ride."

The kitten snuggled close to Fletcher's chest and with an animal's wonderful ability to quickly forget hard times, began to purr.

Watching this, Doc said: "You're a one to pick up all kinds of waifs and strays, aren't you Buck?"

"That I am, Doc." Fletcher smiled again. "That I am."

And he wondered if the irony of that statement was lost on Doctor John Henry Holliday.

Six

Fletcher and Doc forded the Cheyenne at Sam Lee's Crossing in the full heat of the afternoon sun.

Lee, a big man in a stained undershirt and plug hat, recalled taking five men leading a thoroughbred horse across a couple of days before.

"They was all hard cases, I could tell that right off," Lee said. "In my line of work, you get a nose for such things."

"Say where they were headed?" Doc asked.

Lee shook his head. "No. Another thing I've learned is not to ask too many damn fool questions."

"Live longer that way," Doc acknowledged.

After leaving the Cheyenne behind them, Fletcher and Doc headed south, riding well into the night, trying to close the distance.

It was the beginning of six long weeks in the saddle, weeks in which Fletcher and Doc stayed on the trail of Tracy and his outlaws every minute of every waking day, pressing them hard, hoping to give them no rest.

But not once did they catch sight of the gunmen.

They crossed into Nebraska, forded the Platte and rode into Colorado. Hall had been as good as his word and the news of Buck Fletcher's vengeance ride had spread far and wide.

Settlers in sod cabins, the men somber and bearded, the women often thin and worn, offered them whatever food they could spare and wished them well. Punchers spread out across the flat grasslands on spring roundup shared their coffee, bacon and beans, and offered them fanciful tales of seeing masked night riders trailing a fabulous golden stallion by the light of a waxing moon.

Wolfers, as savage and untamed as the animals they hunted, waved as they rode by and called out after them, speaking a wild language that was all their own, a language Fletcher and Doc could not understand.

And through it all, Doc held up well.

Fearfully thin, his frail body was often racked by blood-splashed coughing spells that left him exhausted, and fever burned hot and red on his sunken cheeks. Yet every morning before sunup he was in the saddle, uncomplaining. He ate little and at first drank not at all.

"Drinking a quart of whiskey a day helped me live," he once told Fletcher as they camped under cottonwoods on Jumping Fish Creek south of the Platte. "Now I plan on dying, I don't need the stuff anymore."

But he did.

Jug whiskey came cheap on the frontier and could be bought at any dugout trading post. Using Fletcher's dwindling supply of money, Doc later stocked up and, for a while at least, the raw whiskey seemed to help him. He coughed less and his appetite improved.

Doc knew, as did Fletcher, that this was a passing phase. Death still sat patiently on Doc's shoulder, biding its time, waiting for the moment when it would take him by the ear and drag him into eternity.

Thanks to Hall and his telegraph, Bosco and the others

must have come to the realization they were marked men. Wary now, they kept away from the towns and, more importantly, the railroad depots where hard, belted men loading a fine horse onto a train would be seen, remarked upon and remembered.

All this was a relief to Fletcher. If Bosco Tracy had made the decision to ride the boxcars south, he knew he might never have caught the outlaw before he disposed of Star Dancer. Fletcher had no doubt that he could eventually track down the thoroughbred, but by then it might be too late to enter John Slaughter's horse race and all hope for Ginny would truly be gone.

After the weeks of following Tracy, riding under a blazing sun and often by the thin light of slender moons, the trail suddenly went cold—and, bitterly, Fletcher was forced to the stark realization that the outlaw could have given him the slip. Bosco and the others might have turned west into the Rockies somewhere north of where he and Doc now were. If he didn't pick up a trail soon, there would be nothing for it but to double back and somehow make up the lost time.

It was the middle of May and, if Tracy was to deliver the horse by the Fourth of July, it stood to reason that he might already be making his way across the Divide.

Fletcher and Doc wasted two days trying to pick up Tracy's trail. No one they talked to had seen a party of riders leading a horse, and a sergeant in command of a patrol of the Sixth Cavalry coming up from the south said he'd seen nary hide nor hair of another human being for the past week.

At noon, after a third morning of futile searching, Fletcher and Doc stopped at a small creek running off the Arkansas a hundred hard miles south of Pueblo to rest the horses and boil coffee. It was then that Doc voiced the thoughts that Fletcher had so far been keeping to himself.

"You in the mood for an opinion, Buck?" he asked.

Fletcher nodded, watching the calico kitten pounce on a bug in the grass near his feet. "You were never much of a one to keep yours a secret, Doc."

"So be it." Doc squirmed on the hard, sun-baked ground, grimaced, reached under his bony hips, yanked out a rock, glared at it, then tossed it away. "I think Bosco and Port and the rest of those boys are already in the mountains and maybe halfway to the Arizona Territory. They out-coyoted us, Buck."

"I was figuring that same thing," Fletcher said, his mouth a hard, straight line under his ragged mustache. "I've been trying to think like Bosco Tracy, and if I was him, that's what I'd have done."

"We going after them?"

"If that's how the cards have fallen, then the answer is yes."

Doc smiled. "The Rockies are right pretty this time of the year. I guess this will be the last time I'll ever see them." He took the pot from the coals and poured an inch of coffee into his cup, filling up the rest with whiskey from his jug. His head was bent, his eyes hidden, but when he looked up again, he was still smiling. "So, now you've thought it through, what do you reckon ol' Bosco is up to?"

Fletcher shrugged. "He's smart. He left us a trail heading due south, then slipped without a howdy-do into the mountains. I think he headed into the Sangre De Christos at a point less than fifty miles north of here, near a place called Falling Rock Gorge."

"Why there? Why not further north, say toward Pike's Peak?"

Fletcher shook his head. "We were still hot on Bosco's

trail when we rode past Pike's Peak. He couldn't have headed into the mountains without us picking up his sign. Doc, some old trapper, his name escapes me, blazed a route across the Divide that starts at Falling Rock Gorge, and it was later used by Mormons heading for Utah. I've heard it's an easy crossing if the snow holds off and you can find water. If I was Tracy, right now I'd be heading through the pass at the base of Blanca Peak, planning to ride due west for Papago Wells and then Durango. Another eighty or so miles further west and I'd turn south. Now I'd be in the Arizona Territory and have a clear shot for Slaughter's ranch down in Cochise County."

Fletcher's smile was thin. "Well, more or less. There's still almost four hundred miles of rough, broken country standing in Tracy's way. And us."

"You really think that's what Bosco is doing?" Doc asked. "I'm hearing a lot of maybe in your voice, like you aren't all that sure."

"I'm sure. In fact I'm betting on it. Tracy is running out of time and that's the most direct and easy route. He wanted us to believe he planned to head south, into the desert country, but I'm not buying it. Tracy is smart enough to shy clear of desert and besides, he'd have to turn west eventually and he'd still have the mountains to cross."

Fletcher rolled a smoke then tested the temperature of his coffee. "No, we'll head for Falling Rock Gorge. Al Sieber told me an army scout by the name of Mickey Free once took some heavily loaded army supply wagons across the mountains at Blanca Peak, so it can't be real difficult."

Doc's pale face screwed up in thought. "Heard those names. Never met either man though."

"Sieber is all right. But I'd say you didn't miss much with Free. Sieber said Mickey Free is half Mexican, half Irish and whole son of a bitch."

Fletcher finished his coffee, tossed his half-smoked cigarette into the fire and rose to his feet. He scooped up the kitten, and his voice gentle, half-apologetic, said: "Time to ride, Doc."

Doc looked exhausted. His white hair hung over his forehead and his eyes were sunk deep in his head, lost in dark shadows. He was still three years shy of his fortieth birthday, but he seemed ancient and frail, a man destroyed by a terrible illness who grew old before he grew up.

But there was hidden steel in Holliday. A coughing fit earlier in the morning had left him weak and drained, yet he finished the last of his coffee and whiskey and rose unsteadily to his feet.

"Ready when you are, Buck," he said. Doc swayed from sickness and fatigue, lips chalk white in a face that showed the unearthly luminosity of approaching death. When Fletcher looked at him, he saw a desperate plea in Doc's eyes, begging for silence, not comment.

Like Fletcher himself, Doc Holliday had ridden with the best of them and the worst. Now, betrayed by his own diseased body, his death so very close, he was asking for understanding, for Fletcher to remember what he'd once been and not to judge him on what he had become.

For his part, Fletcher pretended not to notice Doc's sorry condition. He quickly dropped his eyes to the kitten in his arms, letting the man stagger to his horse like nothing was amiss.

But Doc, understanding how Fletcher felt, could not let it go.

"Hard to believe, isn't it, Buck?"

Fletcher looked up. "What's that?"

Doc glanced down at his suit hanging saggy and stained on his wasted body. "That this was once a man."

Fletcher opened his mouth to speak but was spared the

need to reply. A buckboard suddenly rattled into view along the bend of the creek, the man up on the driver's seat hoorawing along a couple of matched Morgans at a spanking trot.

When the driver caught sight of Fletcher and Doc, he slowed to a walk and then to a ragged halt, the bits of the horses jangling as the Morgans tossed their heads, unhappy at this unexpected interruption.

Quickly Fletcher took in the driver, wagon and the big man sprawled in the back, surrounded by sacks of flour, sides of bacon and a roll of baling wire.

The driver's black hair was cut short under his hat, but there was no mistaking the hard planes of his face and his wiry, muscular body. He was Apache, maybe Jicarilla judging by the hammered silver plaques sewn onto the front of his vest, and his black eyes were wary and suspicious.

Before Fletcher could speak, the Apache thumbed over his shoulder to the man in the bed of the wagon. "This is my boss. He's dead."

Fletcher glanced at the dead man. He had two bullet holes in his chest, and both had clipped the edge of the Bull Durham tag hanging from his shirt pocket.

Whoever had gunned this man had been good. Very good.

"Where are you taking him?" Fletcher asked, his curiosity roused.

"He was my boss, a big rancher and very important." The Apache shrugged. "Now, *le estoy tomando el hogar para enterrado.*"

Doc, irritated, stepped beside Fletcher and asked: "What did he say? I never could understand that Indian jabbering."

"It's Spanish," Fletcher said. "The Apache here says he's taking the dead man home to be buried."

The Jicarilla spoke again. "*El era valiente, pero absurdo.*"

Before Doc could ask, Fletcher said: "He says his boss was brave, but foolish."

Doc, who was always interested in such things, looked up at the Apache and asked: "Who gunned him?"

"A pistolero who calls himself Long Tom Nelson," the Apache said. "*El es rapido con un arma pero un mal hombre.*"

"Nelson is fast with a gun, but a bad man," Fletcher supplied.

Doc nodded. "I've met plenty of those."

The Apache, who seemed eager to let it all spill out, said: "The boss played cards with Nelson and by and by accused him of cheating." He nodded to the dead man. "They argued and this one went for his gun but Nelson drew very fast and shot him."

Shaking his head, the Apache continued: "My boss knew Long Tom Nelson rode with the terrible bandit Bosco Tracy. But still he went for his gun. That was very foolish and in the end it killed him."

"Where did this happen?" Fletcher asked, suddenly alert.

"That way," the Apache said, nodding toward his back trail. "Five, six miles. A town called Green Ridge. We always went to the general store there for the ranch supplies."

In the Apache way, the hand suddenly decided he was all talked out. He slapped the team into motion with the ribbons and drove off without another word.

Fletcher watched the wagon until it was out of sight, his brow furrowed in thought.

"Forget it, Buck," Doc said, knowing what the big man was thinking. "We don't have time. You can always ride back this way after you've won the race and plug this Long Tom Nelson feller at your leisure."

Fletcher was torn. Nelson might have been one of the men who had murdered Tiny McCue, and he owed it to the little puncher to track down his killers.

But if he went after Nelson, Bosco Tracy and the others would have even more of a head start and he and Doc might never catch up.

It was a puzzlesome thing and not easily settled.

"Listen, Buck," Doc said, pressing his case, "after you get your horse back and win Slaughter's race, you're going to be all tensed up. Leave Nelson where he is and you can ride back this way and gun him. Hell, killing him will help you relax. Make you feel better."

Fletcher shook his head like he'd finally come to a decision. "I can't step away from this, Doc. Tiny McCue rode for the brand, my brand, and I reckon I owe him this much."

"What about Bosco and the others?"

"Bosco will have to wait. We'll just have to make up the time."

Doc shrugged. "You're a stubborn man, Buck, and I won't try to change your mind. But I think you're making a big mistake."

Fletcher nodded. "Maybe so, but like I said, Tiny McCue rode for the FS Connected. Wherever he is, he's expecting me to go after his killers where and when I find them."

"He was a puncher," Doc said, a half smile on his lips. "I know where he is."

Seven

For the most part, prairie towns began as a collection of shacks, usually built around a creek or some other supply of fresh water. The cabins were located by chance and grew without planning; tough, ugly towns, precariously perched on the edge of nowhere.

Green Ridge was no exception.

The flat-topped bluff that gave the town its name rose right behind the main street in a series of steep, rocky steps that leveled out at a height of more than three hundred feet. At one time the ridge might have been green with pine, but the trees were long gone, used as raw material to build the cabins, general store and the town's solitary saloon.

When Fletcher and Doc rode in, dust hung heavy in the air, kicked up by a stage hauled by a six-mule hitch that stood outside the Ridge Hotel and Eating House.

The passengers would not overnight at the hotel, since this was just a stop on the stage route to Cheyenne, but would bolt down a quick meal before resuming the hot, jolting misery of their journey.

The hotel was the center of the commercial district, flanked on one side by the Horseshoe Saloon, on the other by the general store. There was a small bank, and beyond that a livery stable. Shacks were clustered at one end of town where the creek ran and a lone cottonwood shaded a cemetery laid out toward the ridge.

Green Ridge was hot, dusty and unwelcoming, but it was remote and quiet, the ideal spot for a man on the scout to hole up for a spell before moving on when talk about his scrapes with the law had died away.

No doubt, Fletcher thought as he looked around him, this is what would attract an outlaw like Long Tom Nelson to this place.

Doc kneed his mustang alongside Fletcher. "Saloon?"

Fletcher shook his head. "Let's talk to the sheriff first."

"Sheriff? In this burg?" Doc made a face. "What kind of sheriff would they have here?"

"It's a town, isn't it?" Fletcher asked. "If it's a town then it must have a sheriff."

An idler sprawled outside the general store let up on his whittling long enough to direct them to the edge of town. "Sheriff Lute Baker lives there," he said, jabbing his pointed stick toward a small timber shack with a tarpaper roof. "It's early yet. Good time to catch him sober."

Fletcher and Doc reined up outside the shack and Fletcher yelled: "Hello the house!"

No answer.

Doc tried it again and this time there was a thud from inside, like a man's feet hitting the floor.

"What the hell do you want?" a whiskey-roughened voice asked.

"We have business with the law," Doc said.

"Then hold on to your horses and be damned to ye for waking a man up at this time of the morning."

In fact it was almost two in the afternoon, the sun blazing white-hot from a sky the color of faded denim. There was no breeze and over by the cemetery the leaves of the cottonwood were still and silent. The dry, unmoving air smelled of dust and powdered horse dung, and the roof of the shack gave off the dark odor of warm tar.

After a few minutes the door of the shack opened and a man stepped outside. He was big in the belly, his puffy face unshaven, and a star was pinned to the front of his long johns, the only clothing he wore except for the battered, shapeless hat on his head, the scuffed, mule-eared boots on his feet and the gunbelt hanging low and loose under his huge gut.

"What can I do for you boys?" Sheriff Baker asked, his voice surly as he scratched under his beard and made a painful acquaintance with his hangover.

Fletcher leaned over the saddle horn. "We want you to arrest a man, Sheriff, and hold him for the U.S. marshal."

"Arrest a man, eh?" Baker asked. "And who might that man be?"

"He's one of the men who murdered my hired hand and stole a horse of mine," Fletcher said. "His name is Tom Nelson. He rides with Bosco Tracy and Port Austin and them and I'm pretty sure you'll find him over to the saloon."

Baker's face blanched gray. "You mean Long Tom Nelson?"

"That's him," said Doc.

Baker's voice was unsteady. "He killed a man for breakfast this morning. He and some rancher had been gambling all night and the rancher accused Tom of cheating. He didn't live long after that."

"We heard it from the dead man's hired hand," Fletcher said. He studied the lawman, his eyes hardening. "Now get over to the saloon and arrest Nelson."

The sheriff shook his head, so vigorously it looked like it would roll right off his shoulders. "No sir, not me. Long Tom is an outlaw and a gunfighter and he's lightning-fast with that Colt of his. Besides, like you already said, he's friends to Bosco Tracy. I want no part of him—or Tracy either come to that."

Doc, looking old and tired and mean, turned to Fletcher and said: "God, I hate lawmen." He swung his cold eyes to Baker. "You heard what the man said, Sheriff. Get on over there and arrest Tom Nelson for murder and horse theft."

His face suddenly cunning, Baker ignored Doc, his black eyes slanted to Fletcher. "Where was your hand killed an' your horse stole?"

"Up in the Dakota Territory, the Two-Bit Creek country," Fletcher said. "Why?"

"Why? Because that's way out of my jurisdiction. I'm the sheriff here and my authority only starts at one end of town and ends at t'other. I got no authority to go arresting a man for a murder committed somewhere else."

"Baker," Doc said, his voice velvet-soft and conversational, "I'm setting here seriously thinking about putting a bullet in you."

"If you're so tough, go and arrest Nelson your ownself," Baker snapped. He swung on his heel and barged back into his shack. The door banged shut and Fletcher heard the angry slam of a bolt.

Doc turned in the saddle. "Now what?"

Fletcher's face was grim. "Well, we tried the law. Now we do it ourselves."

"Nelson might not take too kindly to being arrested, Buck," Doc said. "Men like him never do."

"Maybe so, but we'll give him his chance."

"And if he doesn't take it?"

"Then I'll kill him," Fletcher said. There was no give in him. Baker had failed him and now he had it to do.

Doc rubbed his hands together gleefully. "Now you're talking, Buck. This is my kind of game."

Fletcher swung out of the saddle at the Horseshoe Saloon and tied his horse at the rail. Doc did the same, then stepped beside Fletcher as the big gunfighter scooped up the kitten from its accustomed riding place on his blanket roll behind the cantle of his saddle.

Holding the kitten in his left hand, close to his chest, Fletcher swung open the saloon doors and walked inside, Doc close behind him.

The saloon was a low, narrow room, windowless, with a rough pine bar running down one side. There was a scattering of tables and chairs and, even at this early hour of the day, the oil lamps were lit against the gloom.

Fletcher glanced quickly around.

A couple of old-timers sat at a table, playing dominoes for matchsticks, and a tall man in a light brown frock coat and frilled white shirt sat at the end of the room, his back to the wall, idly riffling a deck of cards through his fingers, his guarded eyes half closed but seeing everything.

Fletcher knew this could only be Long Tom Nelson. The man looked seriously out of place, a long way from the bustling trail towns where he and others like him preyed on the drovers who gambled, drank the throat-scorching whiskey and spent their chiming silver dollars on painted girls with hard, calculating eyes.

The bartender, a small, bearded man in a shabby black coat and collarless shirt, wiped the pine counter in front of Fletcher and Doc with a dirty cloth and asked: "What will it be, gents?"

"Rye," Doc said. "Your best bottle." He nodded to Fletcher. "He's paying."

The bartender placed a bottle and two glasses in front of them and when Fletcher poured himself a drink and tasted the rye, he found it mellow and smooth, a couple of steps above the usual run of frontier whiskey.

"Nice-looking kitten you got there, mister," the bartender said. "What do you call him?"

Fletcher shrugged. "I don't call him anything. A cat don't much care what you call it."

"He's called Wyatt," Doc said quickly, wiping his mustache with the back of his hand. "After a dear, gentle friend of mine."

"Hi, Wyatt," the bartender said, tickling the kitten under its chin. He looked at Fletcher. "I've got some milk. Will he drink milk?"

"Don't know. Mostly he eats what we eat and drinks what we drink and that's bacon, salt pork and coffee. And maybe the odd bug or two. He's right partial to bugs."

The bartender stepped away and returned with a brimming saucer of milk. He laid it on the bar and Fletcher put the kitten next to it. The little calico immediately began to lap up the milk and the bartender beamed. "He likes it."

"I guess he does," Fletcher said, "though I never much took to the stuff myself."

"Hey, you!"

Fletcher turned to the sound of the man's voice. Nelson hadn't stirred from his chair but he'd laid down his cards and was looking at him with glittering, snakelike eyes.

"I wondered when you were going to open your mouth," Fletcher said.

"Yeah, well wonder no longer because I'm opening it now. Get your damned cat out of here. Cats don't belong in a saloon and they make me sneeze."

"You're Long Tom Nelson, aren't you?" Fletcher asked.

"Mister, I don't plan on having a conversation with you. Pick up your cat and beat it or I'll shoot the damn thing right off the bar."

And Nelson drew.

Fletcher was taken completely by surprise. He'd expected there might be gunplay, but not at that moment, and not directed at the kitten.

Nelson's gun was coming up fast, swinging toward the calico. Fletcher pulled the short-barreled Colt in his cross-draw holster and Nelson, seeing this, reacted. His gun swung on Fletcher and roared, flaring orange. Fletcher felt the bullet hit high on his left shoulder and he triggered his own gun.

His bullet hit Nelson square in the chest and the man staggered backward. The gunsmoke got to Doc's shredded lungs and he began to cough. He stepped away from the fight, taking no part in it, his Colt still in the leather.

Nelson steadied himself and fired again, holding his revolver in both hands. But the concussion of the guns in the close confines of the room had blown out most of the oil lamps and the air was thick with powder smoke, making it hard to see.

The outlaw missed.

Fletcher fired, stepped out of the smoke into the clear and fired again. Nelson slammed against the wall and slid to the floor, his gun thudding to the ground beside him.

The outlaw's eyes were wide open, his head cocked to one side, but he was beyond seeing anything. He was dead.

"Damn it, damn it all to hell," Fletcher swore as he punched the empty shells out of his Colt and reloaded.

"Hell, mister, no need to get upset. You won." The bartender had stepped away from the bar and was looking down at Nelson's body, warily, like it might suddenly rise up and bite him. "You got two bullets into this man."

Fletcher shook his head. "He didn't know me. He didn't know what he was dying for."

"Main thing is, he's dead," Doc said between coughs. "The result's the same."

"He thought he was dying for a cat," Fletcher said. "He

didn't know I was evening the score for Tiny McCue." He shook his head again, unbelieving. "He thought he was dying for a calico kitten."

Doc's cough suddenly got worse; terrible, racking roars that rattled in his chest and sent bright red blood splashing over his lips and chin. Doc put his handkerchief to his mouth and collapsed, shuddering, into a chair.

Fletcher took a step toward him, but Doc held up a warning hand. "Stay away, Buck," he gasped. "I'll be all right. Just let me be."

The coughing lasted for several minutes and when it was over, Doc leaned over the table and put his head on his outstretched right arm, drained, his face the color of death.

Fletcher stepped to the table. "Doc, you can't go on like this. You have to ride for that sanitarium you told me about."

Doc shook his head. "Buck, don't you tell me what I can't do. Hell man, the chase has just begun and the worst is still to come." He looked up at Fletcher, his hot, fevered eyes blazing. "Show me your hand."

Fletcher didn't move, and Doc snapped: "Damn it, Buck, show me your hand!"

This time Fletcher stretched out his left hand and Doc took it in both of his, examining it carefully. It was a big hand, calloused and work-roughened, scarred by rope burns, the fingers thick and strong.

Doc shook his head. "This is a damn sodbuster's hand."

"I'm a rancher, Doc." Fletcher smiled, taking no offense.

"Rancher, farmer, it doesn't make no never mind." Doc's eyes sought Fletcher's. "I can tell you what it's not, at least not any longer."

"What's that?"

"It's not a gunfighter's hand."

Fletcher opened his mouth to speak, but Doc stopped him. "You're slow, Buck. You drew and handled your Colt like a plowboy. Nelson got his shot away before you even had your gun level. He missed, but only because you were real lucky."

"He didn't miss," Fletcher said, and now Doc looked down at the big man's hand again, seeing the blood trickle from under the sleeve of his shirt, drops dripping red on the table.

Doc's face showed his alarm. "Buck, Nelson got a bullet into you and he was the least of them. Once, years ago, you showed me something, so maybe, just maybe, you can still shade Bosco Tracy. But right now you're no match for Port Austin." Wearily Doc rose to his feet. "But I am."

He stepped closer to Fletcher. "Now, let me take a look at that shoulder."

After spending a few moments inspecting the wound, Doc nodded in his best professional manner and said: "The bullet is deep, all the way into the thick muscles of your shoulder. I'm going to have to cut it out of there."

"Then do it fast, Doc," Fletcher said. "We got to be riding."

"We?"

"You just done told me you're the only who can handle Port Austin."

Doc's smile was thin. "Yeah, and I told you true."

At Doc's direction, Fletcher sat on a chair, watching intently as Doc removed a slim-bladed knife from the sheath he kept attached to his suspenders and doused it in the dregs of the whiskey in his glass.

"Yeah, I know, Buck." He smiled. "Terrible waste of good whiskey, isn't it?"

"Not if it cleans that blade," Fletcher said, his voice wary. "You didn't stick anybody with it?"

"Not recently," Doc answered.

The little bartender had left; now he returned with Sheriff Baker, whose black eyes searched the saloon and took in with a single knowing glance what had happened.

"No need for unpleasantness here," he said, after he'd studied Nelson's body. "I've been told it was a fair fight and the dead man drawed first."

"He wasn't dead when he drawed, Sheriff," Doc said dryly, his knife poised near Fletcher's shoulder. "That came later."

Fletcher nodded in Nelson's direction. "What was he doing here? How come he split from Bosco Tracy and the rest of them?"

"A woman," Baker said. "He came riding into town and said he'd left Bosco Tracy and three others to visit with a woman he'd met right here in this saloon a year ago past. Her name is Lizzie and she's only about as good as she needs to be."

"By any chance, did Nelson say Tracy was leading a horse?" Fletcher asked.

"Sure he did. Nelson held nothing back. When a man says he rides with Bosco Tracy, well, that's kind of like a suit of armor. It protects him from harm. Nelson said he planned to join up with the Tracy boys in the Arizona Territory after a spell. He said they'd bought the horse from a rancher up in the North Platte country and were taking him down Cochise County way to enter him in a big-money race."

"Did you ask him if they had a bill of sale for the horse?" Fletcher asked, his face hardening.

Baker shook his head. "No, no sir, I never did. So long as Nelson behaved himself in town, which he did up until he killed that rancher this morning, how he and the others got the horse was none of my damn business."

"Yeeeouch!"

Fletcher yelled as Doc's knife, directed by an unsteady hand, dug deep into his shoulder.

"Hurt, don't it?" Doc smiled.

The knife dug deeper.

Fletcher gritted his teeth against the pain and, seeing this, Baker called out over his shoulder to the bartender: "Ephraim, whiskey for this man."

Ephraim hurried over with a brimming glass of rye and Fletcher downed it in a single gulp.

"Told you the bullet was in deep," Doc said, his face stiff and intent. "But I'm getting close."

"Doc," Fletcher gritted, "I swear, were you this rough with your patients when you were a dentist?"

"Nah," Doc said, working the tip of the knife around in Fletcher's wound. "I only hurt people I like." He concentrated on what he was doing then suddenly beamed. "Got it, by God!"

Triumphantly, Doc held up the bloody lead slug in his fingers and Fletcher felt the room spin around him.

"Ephraim!" Baker said. "More whiskey."

Fletcher held up a hand. "No, no more whiskey. I have to be able to ride out of here."

"Ephraim," Baker said again, his horrified eyes on Fletcher's bloody shoulder, "more whiskey, but make it for me."

"And me," Doc said.

The saloon doors burst open and a blond young woman ran into the room. Her tough, shrewd eyes sought and found Baker. "Sheriff, I just heard. Can it be true? Is my dear Tom gone?"

His arms wide open, Baker stepped toward the woman. "Now, now, Lizzie. It was a fair fight. Tom drew on this gentleman here and got gunned. That's all there was to it."

Lizzie spared Fletcher a fleeting, spiteful glance, wailed

and threw herself on Nelson's body. "Tom, Tom, come back to me," she sobbed.

The woman called Lizzie hugged the dead man close for a few moments, then, dry-eyed, turned to Baker, her voice hard and matter-of-fact. "Tom willed me everything, Sheriff. He always said that if he went first, I could have all his worldly possessions."

Without waiting for a reply, Lizzie expertly wrenched the silver-plated Colt from Nelson's stiffening hand, examined it critically, then placed it carefully on the table. She plucked the diamond stickpin from his cravat, slid the gold pinkie ring from his finger then, one by one, went through his pockets. When she finished she had a watch and pile of coins and notes in her hand that she quickly counted.

"Eighty-eight dollars and fifteen cents," she said, disgust edging her voice. "I always said Tom Nelson was a cheap tinhorn."

Lizzie looked hard at Baker with flinty gray eyes. "His horse and saddle are mine, Lute. And his clothes and the Winchester and spare revolver up in his room."

The sheriff, wanting no part of this woman, nodded. "As you wish, Lizzie."

Doc, who seemed quite overcome, raised a hand that still held his bloody knife and with the back of his wrist wiped away tears. "Damn it all," he said, "but she reminds me of my own sweet Kate."

Eight

Fletcher and Doc rode out of Green Ridge an hour later and camped that night in the shadow of Blanca Peak, the great, craggy mountain rising almost a mile above their heads.

The smoke from their fire drifted straight toward the stars and the air smelled of aspen groves and wildflowers and pine.

They had now entered the strong spine of the nation, wild and lonesome country, the haunt of beaver, wolf and bear, the grassy slopes of the peaks home to deer and elk and the majestic moose.

Around them, the animals had left no mark, nor had humans. Only the beaver had changed the land, building lodges of sticks that created dams and diverted the courses of the creeks and streams.

Fletcher's shoulder hurt bad where Doc had mangled it, and he did not refuse when Doc handed him coffee heavily spiked with whiskey.

Out in the darkness the coyotes were already calling back and forth and an owl glided over their heads on silent wings like a whispering ghost.

Doc, his pale, thin face colored by the firelight, watched

as Fletcher rolled a smoke, waited until he lit it with a brand from the fire, then said: "Think maybe ol' Bosco and the others will be laying for us somewhere up here?"

Fletcher nodded. "I'd say you can depend on it. He knows we're after him, so it would only make sense for him to cover his back trail. As a precaution if nothing else."

The kitten jumped onto Fletcher's lap and curled up, asleep in moments.

"Who will the bushwhacker be?" Doc asked. "Port Austin maybe?"

Fletcher nodded. "Maybe." He thought it through for a while, then added: "Maybe Bosco's brothers. Luke and Earl Tracy are no bargain, or so I've heard."

Doc smiled. "They're salty all right. I been told they're maybe as good as Bosco himself with a gun."

This last comment sparked something in Fletcher. He lifted the little cat off his lap and gently laid it, still asleep, by the fire. He rose, wincing as the pain in his shoulder hit him, then stepped away from the light.

He drew, fast, from the crossdraw holster, leathered the Colt and drew again.

His eyes glittering in the firelight, Doc watched, sipping his whiskey, saying nothing.

Fletcher drew a couple of dozen times, then did the same thing with the gun on his right hip, each time aiming off into the darkness, at shadows only he could see.

Now he pulled both guns, pretended to fire the Colt in his right hand dry, then attempted a border shift, the guns spinning past each other, firelight flashing scarlet on their barrels.

Fletcher caught a Colt in his left hand, but he missed the second gun with his right. The revolver arced past him and thudded onto the grass.

Without saying a word, Fletcher picked up the Colt, holstered it and stepped back to the fire.

A few long minutes passed before Doc said anything, and when he did speak his voice was soft, carefully measured, trying to step lightly. "You showed me nothing there, Buck," he said. "Your draw is slow and you missed the shift."

Fletcher looked at Doc with unhappy eyes. "What are you telling me, Doc? You think I don't know that?"

"What the hell happened to you, man?" Doc's eyes were blazing, abandoning his attempt to spare Fletcher's feelings. "I've seen some fast draws in my time, but when I saw you kill that two-bit gunman Clem Hasty in the T.S. Horn Saloon in Abilene in '75, you really showed me a thing or two. I turned to them who were with me and said, 'That boy don't have to take second place even to Ben Thompson or young Wes Hardin.' That's what I said, all right."

"I got married," Fletcher said, "had a child, settled down to ranching. I put my guns away."

Doc shook his head. "You won't near cut it against Port Austin and maybe not Bosco Tracy either."

"I'll try, Doc. I'll surely try."

"Then you'll die trying."

Doc, realizing Fletcher was stung, now decided to mend fences. "Just as well I'm with you, Buck. You take ol' Bosco and leave Port Austin to me."

Despite himself, Fletcher smiled: "Think you can shade him, Doc?"

"Hell no, I can't shade him. But I'll have the edge on him."

"How come?"

"Because when we get into it and the shooting starts, Port will want to live and I'll want to die. A man who isn't scared of dying can take a lot of lead and still shoot back." Doc's eyes burned red in the firelight. "Like I said, you leave ol' Port to me. I'll settle his hash but good."

Fletcher threw the butt of his cigarette into the fire. "You're not even a little bit scared of dying, Doc?"

Doc shrugged. "Death is nothing. It's easy. It's like taking off your old coat and putting on a new one. When a man dies, he doesn't go from light to darkness, but from light to light. This is something I believe."

"Good way to think," Fletcher allowed.

"I don't think, Buck. I know." Doc poured himself another drink from his jug. "I've seen Death and he doesn't scare me none. Over the years, he's come at me a lot of different ways, wearing a lot of different faces, saying different things. But every time I've seen him, he was never dressed all in black, but in the purest dazzling white. That's on account of how he was not there to drag me off into the darkness, but to lead me into the light."

"Damn it, Doc, you sound like a prayer-meeting preacher," Fletcher said. "And you're spooking the hell out of me."

Doc laughed, a good, wholesome sound unexpectedly bursting from his ravaged body. "Well, now you know how come I've managed to live with him all these years."

"Who?"

"Death."

Fletcher slapped his thigh. "That's it, Doc, I've heard enough. No more of this talk of death and ha'ants and such. I'm turning in."

"Pleasant dreams, Buck Fletcher," Doc said, grinning.

The pale lemon sky was tinted with bands of red when Fletcher rolled out of his blankets next morning. He put on his hat, kneeled by the fire and added a few more sticks, then put the coffee on to boil. They'd need more wood.

He stomped into his boots and buckled his gunbelt around his hips, then walked toward the line of aspen at the foot of the mountain. There should be plenty of dry firewood around the roots of the trees; enough, anyway, to boil the coffee and fry up some salt pork.

Fletcher reached the trees and stopped. Something was troubling him, something he felt but could not define. He was responding to an animal instinct as ancient as man himself and suddenly he was alert and wary, all traces of sleep leaving him.

He drew his gun and stepped into the aspen.

Nutcrackers and jays fluttered in the branches above him as he stopped to listen. Apart from the rustle of the birds, he heard nothing.

Fletcher shook his head, allowing himself to relax. He holstered his Colt, smiling at his own foolishness. Doc, with all his talk of death and dying, had him boogered and now he was acting like the old lady who saw a man's shadow on her garden path.

He began to do what he'd come here to do in the first place, gather up some wood. Fletcher's searching eyes looked down around his feet—and he saw the prints.

Someone had stood here last night, watching the camp.

Kneeling, Fletcher looked closer. Whoever it was had stood here with almost unbelievable patience, because once planted, he had not moved his feet a single time.

And he had worn moccasins.

Casting around the area for other clues, Fletcher found nothing. He could not even find the spot where the man had tethered his horse, and surely he had one. How else had he gotten all the way up here?

And how long had he stood here, perfectly still, studying the camp?

If Fletcher had been spooked before, he was more spooked now.

The man could only be connected with Bosco Tracy. But

why didn't he shoot Fletcher and Doc while he had the chance?

Fletcher had plenty of questions and no answers.

When he walked back to the camp, a small bundle of wood in his arms, Doc was up and moving around. He looked even worse than usual this morning. His breath was coming in short, agonized gasps and there were huge, black circles under his eyes.

Doc's shoulders were bent, like those of a very old man, and the thick blue veins in his hands stood out in stark contrast to his white skin.

Fletcher dropped the wood onto the fire, then nodded back toward the aspen. "Saw something in there."

Doc's reply was sour. "You still spooked from last night?"

Fletcher let that go. "Moccasin prints." He moved the coffeepot closer to the flames. "Somebody stood there and watched us."

"An Indian?" Doc asked, suddenly interested.

"Don't know." Fletcher shrugged.

"The coffee is still to bile. Let's step over there and take a look."

Doc, in his undershirt and pants, his suspenders hanging loose over his skinny hips, studied the prints for several minutes, rubbing his chin. "Small, aren't they?" he asked.

In fact, Fletcher hadn't noticed just how small the prints were. Now he saw that they were too short and narrow to be those of a full-grown man.

"A small Indian, maybe?" he offered.

"Could be," Doc said. He looked around at the surrounding trees. "Maybe a woman."

"What would a woman be doing by herself up here?"

Doc shrugged. "I don't know."

Fletcher stood for a while thinking it through, then said: "Well, let's have coffee and a bite to eat and then saddle up."

He glanced up at the towering height of Blanca Peak, the pines on its slope giving way to spruce where, in a few months, the winter snow would lie thick. Normally Fletcher loved the mountains for their timeless beauty and hallowed solitude but now he felt uneasy, as though there was somebody, or something, hidden, watching him.

"You feel it, too, huh?" Doc asked.

It was in Fletcher's mind to say he felt nothing, but it would be a lie and serve no purpose. "Yeah. It's kinda spooky around here, like I'm being watched."

Doc smiled. "We are being watched, Buck. I just hope to hell it isn't over the sights of a Winchester."

The two men ate a hasty breakfast and then saddled up. They had camped for the night on a long, steep bench, parts of it covered by ponderosa pine and Douglas fir, the mountains rising sheer on either side. Their route would follow the bench higher, along the aspen line, then through a narrow, rocky gorge, with stunted, twisted spruce growing from its sides. At this point they'd be at least five thousand feet high, but beyond that, Fletcher expected a gradual downward slope onto the grass and flowering meadows of the San Luis Valley. They would then follow the course of the Rio Grande, keeping to the north of the river, and head directly for the distant San Juan peaks.

This was rough, forbidding country, a white, freezing hell in winter and often not much better in summer. But now, in spring, with the sun already shining warm and the balmy smell of the pines in the air, the going was relatively easy. Fletcher and Doc followed the bench upward, the higher altitude making Doc wheeze deep in his chest as his ragged, abscessed lungs battled for every breath of the thinning air.

Doc rode slumped and weary in the saddle, a red-stained handkerchief constantly held to his lips. Glancing at his companion out of the corner of his eye, Fletcher knew the man must die very soon. Only his indomitable will and stubborn courage had kept him alive this long.

His mind went back to the cabin on the Two-Bit and Ginny. How long before she looked and acted just like Doc, desperately trying to breathe with destroyed lungs, the blood bright on her mouth, the shadow of death pale on her face?

Fletcher swallowed hard. He must recover his horse and somehow, he didn't quite know how, win John Slaughter's race.

Even if he got his horse back, was Star Dancer up to the task? Was Slaughter's American stud as fast as everyone said it was?

Shaking his head, Fletcher rode on. For now, those were questions without answers. Only time would answer them—for good or ill.

Doc's voice, low and urgent, broke into his thoughts. "Buck, on your left. Something moving in the aspens."

Fletcher followed Doc's pointing finger and studied the trees. There! Something had just moved, setting the jays to fluttering among the branches. Sliding his Winchester from the boot, Fletcher kneed his horse toward the aspen line, his eyes wary.

"Dust a few shots in there," Doc suggested. "Maybe you can nail whoever it is."

Fletcher shook his head. "Doc, I can't go shooting at something until I see what it is I'm shooting at."

"I always did, and then I'd go see what I'd hit later." Doc shrugged. "Man lives longer that way."

Reining up the buckskin about twenty yards from the trees, Fletcher threw his rifle to his shoulder and yelled over the sights. "You in there! Come out with your hands high or I'll start throwing lead."

No answer.

A few tense moments ticked by and Fletcher, dry-mouthed, felt sweat trickle down his back. His horse tossed his head, irritated by a cloud of swarming flies, and Fletcher heard Doc gasp as he tried to suppress a cough.

But it was Doc who ended it.

He drew his Colt and thumbed three fast shots into the trees, sending leaves and twigs tumbling to the ground, squawking birds scattering into the air in fright like tattered scraps of paper tossed by a wind.

Annoyed, Fletcher turned in the saddle. "Doc, I—"

"Don't shoot, mister. Please don't shoot no more."

It was a voice from the trees—a girl's voice.

Doc, never one to let sentiment stand in the way of gun business, rose in his stirrups. "You in there, come on out," he said. "Step real easy now or by God I'll drop you where you stand."

The branches of the aspen rustled, then a small, thin figure stepped out into the open.

The girl looked to be about twelve, but was small for her age. She wore the ragged remnants of a flowered, cotton dress and her feet were wrapped in deerskin, tied at the top with rawhide laces. Her brown eyes were huge in a pale, peaked face and greasy brown hair hung lank over her shoulders.

Doc, still holding his Colt on the girl, turned to Fletcher and said out of the corner of his mouth: "Homely little thing, ain't she, Buck?"

Fletcher, unwilling to say it, just bit his lip and nodded.

"Hell, I'd say that little gal fell out of an ugly tree and hit every damn branch on the way down."

"Let it go, Doc," Fletcher sighed. "And stop pointing your gun at her. She's only a child."

Doc shrugged. "I could plug her for you. Maybe save us a lot of trouble later."

But when Fletcher looked hard at him, Doc was grinning and already holstering his Colt.

"What's your name, girl?" Fletcher asked.

"Mary. Mary Bracken." The girl pointed up the bench, toward the gorge. "My pa's up there. He's hurt real bad."

"How bad?" Doc asked.

"His leg is broke."

"How long have you been up here?" Fletcher asked.

The girl shrugged her skinny shoulders. "A long time. We spent the winter here."

Doc's jaw dropped. "You survived a winter in these mountains? How the hell did you do that?"

"Pa says the good Lord watched out for us."

Doc shook his head. "Hell, child, even God his ownself couldn't last a winter up here."

Mary's young face was earnest. "But we did."

"You watched us for a long time last night, didn't you?" Fletcher asked.

"I smelled your coffee and bacon. I stood in the trees so I could smell them."

"You should have come over and said howdy," Doc said. "You could have had some."

"I was afraid. There were other men passed this way before you. I watched them too, but I thought they were bad men and they scared me."

"These men," Fletcher said, leaning forward in the saddle, "did they have a horse with them, a big bay horse?"

The girl shrugged. "They all had horses. I didn't notice what color they were."

"How many men?"

"Three, I think. No, there were four." The girl made a face. "They were drinking whiskey, then two of them started to fight."

"With guns?" Doc asked, his face eager.

Mary shook her head. "No, it was a fistfight. Then one of the men, I think his name was Earl, got knocked down and it was over. I heard him say, 'Don't hit me no more, Bosco.' "

Fletcher slid his rifle back into the boot. "Where's your pa, Mary? We can take a look at his leg."

Doc's eyes slid to Fletcher. "Hell, Buck, we don't owe this kid and her pa anything. Time's a-wasting. We got to be riding."

"I have one about her age at home, Doc," Fletcher said. "I just can't ride away and leave her. You heard what she said; her pa's leg is broke."

Doc shook his head. "You know, Buck, back in the old, wild days I pegged you for a sinner, but you had me fooled. Here you were a saint all the time."

Fletcher laughed. It felt good and it helped ease the tension in him. "Mary, where's your pa?" he asked finally.

The girl pointed toward the gorge. "Up that way."

"You lead us and we'll follow," Fletcher said.

He turned his horse and Mary saw the calico kitten for the first time.

"Oh," she gasped, "can I hold him?"

"He doesn't take real kindly to being held, but I guess you can try," Fletcher said. He reached behind him, caught up the kitten and handed him to Mary.

She hugged the little animal close, and Fletcher heard the kitten purr. "I guess he likes you," he said.

"What does he eat?"

It was a child's question but Fletcher answered it seriously. "Oh, salt pork, milk if he can get it. Oh yeah, and bugs. He eats a lot of bugs."

"What's his name?"

"Wyatt."

"That's a funny name."

Fletcher nodded toward Doc. "He's named after a friend of his. Another saint by all accounts."

Doc looked pious. "Wyatt was true blue."

"Lead on, Mary," Fletcher said. As the girl walked away from him, holding the kitten close, he turned to Doc. "True blue, huh?"

"As ever was," said Doc.

The girl walked on with a long, effortless stride, Fletcher and Doc riding close behind.

She led them toward the gorge, then suddenly turned to the north, stepping into a narrow, high-walled canyon. Gradually the canyon opened out and then curved around, encircling a flat, grassy basin about ten acres in extent. A stream of clear water bubbled along a narrow creekbed that cut diagonally across the basin and then disappeared under a small opening in the wall on the other side.

A few spruce grew in the clearing and the grass was dotted here and there by daisies and bright blue forget-me-nots. It was a sheltered spot that might be free of snow most of the year, but Fletcher could see no cabin or any other sign of habitation.

As if reading his thoughts, Mary stopped and pointed to the canyon wall opposite. "Over there," she said. "Do you see the cave?"

Even after the girl pointed it out to him, Fletcher could scarcely make out the cave opening. It was small, no more than three feet high and the same across, and brush covered most of the entrance.

"Pa's in there," the girl said.

Fletcher and Doc stepped from the saddle outside the cave and, dropping to all fours, followed the girl inside.

It was dark in the cave—and the sickening stench of rotting meat hit them like a gigantic fist.

Nine

"What the hell?" Doc said, standing at Fletcher's elbow. "I can't see a damn thing in here. And what's that god-awful stink?"

"Mary?" Fletcher asked, taking a step forward, his eyes desperately trying to probe the gloom.

He heard the girl giggle somewhere off in the darkness.

"Mary? Is that you?"

Fletcher reached into the pocket of his shirt, found a match and thumbed it into flame.

In that split second as the match flared, he saw a wild, shaggy face come at him, the bloodshot eyes wild. But he didn't see the tree branch that crashed into his head and sent him reeling, senseless, to the floor of the cave. Nor did he realize that Doc was falling beside him.

Fletcher woke to pain.

When he tried to rise, his head exploded into a million stars, each of them a separate, searing, white-hot point of agony.

Groaning, he laid back, his eyes staring up into nothing but darkness. Slowly he became aware of someone standing over him and the man's gagging, feral smell, like something long dead and buried.

"Is he coming to?" a voice asked from the gloom.

"Yeah, paw, but he ain't goin' nowheres. I tied him up good."

"How 'bout the old one?"

"He's still out, if'n he ain't dead already."

"Him first then, Clem. Though he's right scrawny and there ain't much meat on them skinny old bones."

Fletcher heard the men laugh and the one who had been standing over him stepped away, but then came back. The man's boot swung at Fletcher's head and thudded into his temple. Pain spiked into Fletcher savagely and he had to bite his lip to stop from screaming.

Then, mercifully, the darkness took him again.

When Fletcher woke, he had been propped up against a wall of the cave, with Doc, his head lolling on his chest, beside him.

Fletcher's wrists were tied behind his back, the ropes knotted so tight his hands were swollen and painful, and his head throbbed unmercifully. They had taken his guns and the folding knife from his pocket.

A fire had now been lit in the middle of the cave and in the flickering orange glow he saw Mary sitting around the flames with two men and another creature with long, matted hair that could have been a woman.

Carefully keeping his eyes half-shut for fear of being seen to be conscious again, Fletcher studied the men. They were both huge, overgrown with hair, the older one's beard shot through with gray. Both were clothed in breeches and capes crudely sewn together from half-dressed deerskins and they seemed more animal than human.

The stench of rotting meat was almost unbearable and

Fletcher had to swallow hard to fight down rising waves of nausea.

Without turning his head, he looked around the cave. Bones and scraps of meat littered the floor and a half-eaten deer carcass, already crawling with maggots, hung from a hook driven into the far wall.

To one side of the carcass was a narrow shelf, a natural break in the rock, and on this sat five grinning human skulls, each one cleaned and polished, the foreheads adorned with crudely painted totem animals.

Fletcher had heard of cannibalism, but this was the first time he'd ever met it face to face and it chilled him to the bone.

The Tonkawa Indians of southwestern Texas ritually ate the flesh of their sworn enemies the Comanches, often boiling the human flesh together with horsemeat to make a grisly stew.

Years before, he had ridden through the Donner Pass in the Sierra Nevada, a scene of terrible tragedy in the severe winter of 1846–7 when a party of eighty-two settlers from Illinois became snowbound there. The starving people built crude shelters of logs, rocks and hides and ate twigs, mice, their animals and their shoes. Finally, driven by their aching hunger, they ate their own dead. Only forty-seven of them survived.

But the settlers had been forced to cannibalism by starvation. The people in this cave, as wild and savage as wolves, ate human flesh from choice, probably waylaying travelers or luring them into a trap as Mary had done to him and Doc.

Fletcher reckoned the Brackens—if that was their real name—had passed on Bosco Tracy and the others because there were four of them, too many to handle easily.

Bitterly, he realized that they had taken Doc for an old, frail man and had figured the two of them as easy prey.

Fletcher's eyes found the calico kitten in the gloom. The little cat nosed toward Mary, but the girl snarled and backhanded him away from her, sending him tumbling across the cave floor.

The crone at the fire—she looked like an old woman but was probably no more than thirty—cackled and pointed at the kitten, who had fled to a dark corner of the cave, his eyes blinking scared and uncomprehending in the gloom.

Rising to her feet, the woman cut off a chunk of the rotting deer and returned to the fire. She skewered the dripping meat on a stick and thrust it into the flames.

"Buck."

Fletcher turned to Doc, surprised. He had thought him unconscious or dead and his urgent whisper shocked him.

"No, damn it, don't look at me," Doc whispered again.

Fletcher turned away and Doc murmured. "Buck, we've borrowed a whole heap of trouble."

Nodding slightly, scarcely moving his pounding head, Fletcher acknowledged the obvious.

"Buck, those damned animals didn't find my knife."

Doc's knife was in a sheath attached to his suspenders, covered by his coat, an easy thing to overlook.

Knowing his deep, baritone voice carried far, Fletcher dared not attempt to whisper. He nodded again, his eyes on the people around the fire.

"Listen," Doc said, his voice soft and urgent, "I'm going to turn my back toward you, real slow. Do you think you can untie my hands?"

Again Fletcher gave an imperceptible bob of his head. His wounded shoulder hurt and he felt dizzy and sick, but it was something that had to be done if they had any hope of getting out of here alive.

Slowly, moving with agonizing slowness, Doc inched his back along the rock, with each tiny move turning his shoulders slightly in Fletcher's direction. Over at the fire the men lit pipes, then the older of the two began to sharpen a Green River knife on a stone at his feet. He said something, pointing with his knife over his shoulder to where Fletcher and Doc lay, and the younger man laughed.

Fletcher read the signs. Soon they'd begin slaughtering.

Doc too sensed the urgency. He moved along the rock a little faster turning his back at a more acute angle toward Fletcher.

There! Fletcher felt Doc's fingers brush his own. Doc moved a bit closer and Fletcher found the rope around his wrist.

The knot was very tight and Fletcher's fingers were swollen and clumsy from his own bonds. But ten years of heavy ranch labor had made them strong, his fingernails short but hard and tough.

Slowly, wincing as pain shot through his fingers and wrist, Fletcher worked on the knot. It was not easy and he stopped often to allow some circulation to return to his hands.

Long minutes ticked by, Doc impatiently whispering for him to "quit stalling and hurry the hell up."

Over by the fire, the older man tested the knife with his thumb and nodded his satisfaction.

The killing would be soon.

With strength born of desperation, Fletcher's fingers teased the knot. Finally he felt it loosen a little and was able to work free one end of the rope. Just a bit more . . .

The older man rose and, holding his knife low, stepped toward Fletcher and Doc. He had an old Dragoon Colt strapped around his waist and his eyes glittered red in the firelight.

Fletcher's fingers worked frantically. There, the knot was loose.

For a few moments, Doc didn't move. Then, slowly, his right hand inched toward the sharp, double-edged knife in his suspenders. He found the blade and quickly shoved it behind his back.

The older Bracken stepped close to Doc, towering over him, a grin playing on his slack mouth, showing black, rotten teeth. The man said something that sounded more animal growl than human speech, and bent over Doc.

He grabbed Doc by the hair and forced his head back, exposing his throat. He held the knife in his right hand, arm across his chest, ready for a vicious backward slash designed to take off the little gunfighter's head.

Doc moved.

His knife flashed. He held the blade with a cutting edge upward and the honed steel buried itself deep in the elder Bracken's belly. Doc then sliced up, gutting the man like a hog.

Bracken screamed, the shrill cry of a wounded animal. He took a step backward, looking down at himself, shocked and unbelieving as his guts spilled out, purple and glistening, over the top of his skin breeches. The man staggered, screaming in pain and terror, then crashed heavily to the floor of the cave.

Quickly, Doc turned and slashed the rope free from Fletcher's wrists. By the fire, the younger man was climbing to his feet. He grabbed a Winchester, levered a round into the chamber, and stepped fast toward Fletcher and Doc, the rifle held waist-high and ready.

Then Fletcher caught a lucky break.

When the elder Bracken dropped, he'd fallen on his back, then rolled on his left side, the walnut handle of his big Dragoon sticking up out of the holster. Fletcher dived, grabbed the gun in both hands and rested his elbows on the fallen cannibal. He fired at the younger man and saw him jerk in mid-stride and stop right where he was. Fletcher fired again. Another hit. The man roared and took a single step backward, his rifle coming up fast.

From somewhere above Fletcher's head, the towering mass of rock that formed the wall of the canyon groaned and a shower of tiny pebbles and dust pattered from the cave roof over his hat and shoulders.

The younger Bracken's eyes sought Fletcher in the gloom. He fired, cranked the rifle and fired again.

Fletcher rose to one knee. He hammered two fast shots at the man, both taking effect, and Bracken dropped his gun and fell backward, his head crashing into the fire, sending up a shower of sparks.

The cave roof groaned again. Louder and more ominous this time.

The shower of falling rocks grew heavier and a deep, menacing rumble filled the cave.

Worried now, Fletcher glanced up quickly. The roof of the cave was not solid rock as he'd first supposed, but an accumulation of stony debris that had fallen into a narrow gorge from the top of the canyon walls thousands of years before. More and more, mostly huge granite boulders, had built up over the centuries until the gorge had completely filled, looking no different than the canyon wall itself.

But somehow, the massive rocks had not fallen all the way to the bottom of the gorge but had jammed together and formed the arched roof of the cave. The concussion of the gunshots had dislodged some of the smaller, supporting rocks and the rumble could be a grim warning that the whole roof was about to fall.

Fletcher felt the ground under his feet shake, and bigger

rocks began to crash to the cave floor, some of them the size of anvils.

Doc was standing in the middle of the cave, mesmerized by what he was seeing, looking up at the roof as though unable to move. Mary and the older woman had pulled the younger Bracken from the fire and were bent over his scorched head, wailing softly as they rocked back and forth.

It seems even animals will mourn their dead, Fletcher thought briefly, no pity in him. He reached down and quickly searched through the elder Bracken's pockets and found what he was looking for—his beautiful Sheffield knife. He slipped the folder into his own pocket and straightened up.

Now to get his guns.

He stepped to the fire, ignoring the wailing, screeching women and found his Colts and gunbelts. Doc's revolver was close by and he grabbed that too. The ground trembled and the terrible rumbling above Fletcher's head turned into a deafening roar. It seemed that the whole canyon was about to crumble in on itself and fall on top of them.

"Doc!" he yelled.

But the little man stood as though rooted to the spot, his eyes on the rapidly disintegrating roof.

Fletcher ran to Doc, grabbed him by the arm and dragged him toward the cave entrance. He was aware of the kitten, ears back, tail straight out behind him, dashing between his feet, running hell-bent for safety.

Doc pulled away from Fletcher's hand, blinked once or twice like a man coming out of a trance, and now, finally realizing the terrible danger, he too ran for the entrance.

Fletcher dived through the opening, rolled, then sprang to his feet and dragged Doc after him.

It was not a moment too soon.

With a tremendous, crashing roar, the roof of the cave

fell, a cloud of thick, choking, yellow dust pouring out of the entrance.

Fletcher stumbled away from the dust, pulling Doc after him. He ran into the middle of the clearing, then looked back. What he saw stunned him.

The cave entrance was completely sealed by huge boulders, the dust cloud drifting upward, a thick yellow shroud climbing slowly toward the top of the canyon wall.

No one could have lived through that, Fletcher thought, the sudden, shocking violence of the collapse leaving him shaken and unbelieving.

Mary Bracken and the rest of her cannibal clan would never again waylay and devour innocent wayfarers. They were entombed inside their cave forever.

Doc, who was still holding his bloody knife, bent over and cleaned the blade on the grass. When he straightened his eyes were once more focused and aware, and he was smiling.

"Jesus, Buck," he said, looking back at the cave, "I got to hand it to you. When you're around a man never has the chance to get bored."

Ten

Fletcher caught up the horses where the Brackens had stashed them under a rock overhang near the cave and led them back to Doc, who was standing watching the kitten, a slight smile playing around his white lips. The calico made a half-hearted spring at a grasshopper and missed.

"That damn cat is all stalk and no pounce," Doc said, shaking his head. "And if it's true that a cat has nine lives, he's using his up mighty quick."

"So are we," Fletcher said.

He picked up the kitten, placed him on his blanket roll then swung into the saddle. "Let's ride, Doc," he said, his tone bitter. "We've wasted enough time here already."

He and Doc rode out of the clearing and back into the narrow canyon without a single backward glance toward the cave.

The Brackens, including Mary, had dealt themselves a hand in a deadly game and they had lost. That's all there was to it. A wise man once said that you can't do evil to other people without doing it to yourself—and in the end the Brackens' evil had killed them.

Fletcher and Doc did not consider the Brackens' deaths something to unnecessarily occupy their thoughts, not when long miles stretched ahead of them, most of it across the wildest country on earth. And both knew that at the end of their journey there lay a meeting with Bosco Tracy and Port Austin, two of the deadliest gunmen who ever lived.

All in all, Fletcher considered as they left the canyon and headed back up the bench, they had plenty to think about, none of it a comfort to a man.

Over the next two weeks, traveling across the backbone of the nation, Fletcher and Doc rode through the San Juan peaks at Wolf Creek Pass and headed west under the great shadow cast by Hesperus Mountain.

They traveled through lush valleys where the grass grew as high as their stirrups, pine-covered mountains around them, their slopes shaped by wind, rain and time into fantastic towers and parapets, rising skyward thousands of feet like the fortresses of giants.

Fletcher used his gun only when they needed meat, and they camped by streams that ran cold and swift and clear from the mountains, broiling antelope steak over fires of sage and mesquite.

As the days passed, Doc said he felt a lot stronger thanks to fresh air, sleep and regular food, away from his accustomed saloons with their unhealthy dankness, smoke and constant clamor.

Leaving the tallest peaks of the Rockies behind them, they crossed the San Juan River at Silent Pete Elliot's trading post, just twenty-five miles north of the Arizona border, and stopped briefly in a dusty, one-street cow town optimistically named High Hopes to stock up on supplies.

Doc, leaning heavily on his cane, decided to have a stroll around town to take in the sights while Fletcher was dickering in the general store.

But Doc was a man born to trouble.

Outside the Crystal Palace Saloon he ran into half a dozen drunk and rowdy cowboys from one of the surrounding ranches, primed with forty-rod and ready for any mischief.

The young punchers, mistaking Doc for an elderly, kid-glove dandy out West for his health, decided to hooraw him, demanding that he set up drinks for one and all and threatening the direst penalties if he didn't.

At first Doc took it in the spirit of good fun and, after being carried into the saloon on the punchers' shoulders, he dipped into his meager funds and bought a round of drinks. But when the laughing cowboys grew even rowdier, pushing and shoving, slapping the back of Doc's head, loudly demanding more whiskey, his patience, always a fragile thing, snapped.

Doc skinned his Colt and cut loose with a few shots that precipitated a hasty stampede for the door, one of the punchers trailing a bloody leg. He then finished his drink in slightly ruffled but dignified silence.

"It seems," said a stern and unsmiling Fletcher when Doc told him about the scrape, "that I can't leave you alone for two minutes without you getting into all kinds of trouble."

"Buck," replied Doc, unrepentant, "you were always a master of understatement."

On the first day of June Fletcher and Doc rode into the Arizona Territory.

They splashed across Walker Creek, the sawtooth ridge of the Carrizo Mountains showing to the east, bathed in the rosy light of the red-streaked morning sky. Ahead of them lay four hundred hard miles to John Slaughter's ranch in Cochise County and a six-gun showdown from which Fletcher had no real confidence he would emerge the victor. He had never in his life taken a backward step for any man, but now he remembered Port Austin—and the slick, deadly gunman was a load to handle.

He and Doc camped that night near Defiance Plateau, on the southern bank of a sandy, willow-lined creek running between two enormous, spear-shaped rock formations that jutted upward a hundred feet above the flat.

Of Bosco Tracy they had seen no sign. It was as though the outlaw had vanished off the face of the earth. Yet, after their brush with the Brackens, Fletcher knew he and Doc had made good time.

Tracy was ahead of them, sure, but he couldn't be that far ahead.

"Unless he's riding the boxcars," Doc said, when Fletcher brought up the subject. "Plenty of rail depots around here."

Fletcher nodded. "That's always a possibility."

If Tracy wanted to unload the horse fast and hightail it down to Old Mexico to spend the money, it would make sense for him to take the Southern Pacific. The word about the murder of Tiny McCue and the theft of Star Dancer would not have reached all the way to the Arizona Territory. As far as the law was concerned, Bosco Tracy would just be another traveling rancher with a horse for sale.

"Maybe," said Doc, pouring coffee into his cup, "we should take to the rails our ownselves."

"I've been studying on it," Fletcher said, rolling a smoke. "Maybe tomorrow I'll think it through and decide then."

From across the campfire, Doc's eyes searched Fletcher's face. "You don't really think Bosco took the Southern Pacific, do you?"

"No I don't. There's still plenty of time between now and the Fourth of July, so why spend his own ill-gotten money on a train ride?" Fletcher smiled. "Besides, you already told me I don't scare him none, so I reckon he's in no rush."

Doc absorbed this, then said: "I saw dust on our back trail just before sundown. What do you make of that?"

Fletcher shrugged. "Lot of riders come this way, heading for the Mogollon Rim and the Tonto Basin country. Plenty of ranches down there now the Apaches are gone."

This answer seemed to satisfy Doc. He put his jug of whiskey to his ear, shook it speculatively, then poured a hefty shot into his coffee.

But he wasn't about to let the dust cloud go.

"Seems to me, we should take turns standing guard tonight," he said. "Let's just say I feel a mite uneasy."

Fletcher was tired but felt pleasantly relaxed. He had eaten well on broiled antelope steak and now the heat of the fire was making him drowsy. "Whatever you say, Doc, so long as you stand the first watch."

"Hell, Buck, I was planning on it." Doc smiled.

Despite Doc's fears the night passed without incident.

When Fletcher stood his watch, the coyotes were calling out in the darkness and the moon rode high in the sky, creating deep, slanting shadows among the mysterious ravines and arroyos of the plateau.

As the night gave way to morning, Fletcher watched the shadows wash out one by one from the canyons, and the coyotes ceased calling. The fish in the creek splashed as they jumped at mayflies, sending out circles of ever-widening ripples across the untroubled surface of the water, setting the leaves that had fallen from the surrounding willows to bobbing.

He built up the fire and put coffee on to boil, then woke Doc who, as usual, grumbled about the early hour and Fletcher's damned cheerfulness.

In fact, Fletcher was far from cheerful. The hunt for his stolen horse was beginning to weigh heavy on him. Time was running out and they seemed no closer to Bosco Tracy.

The fact that he still had to face the guns of Port Austin continued to nag at him like a bad toothache. Doc had claimed that fight for himself, but Fletcher knew the little gambler, for all his speed from the holster, was no match for the outlaw.

When the time came and the chips were down it was something he must do himself.

But was he good enough?

Fletcher poured coffee into his cup then rolled his first cigarette of the day, his face stiff and grim.

Maybe ten years ago he had been a match for Austin. But now . . .

He let the question trail off in his mind. One way or another, he would discover the answer soon.

Doc returned from the creek, his suspenders around his hips, drying his wet, snow-white hair with a scrap of towel.

He stepped up to the fire and poured himself coffee, his faded blue eyes all at once searching over Fletcher's shoulder to the grassy valley that lay beyond the camp.

"Riders coming," he said, jerking his chin toward the flat, his tone calm and conversational. "Three of them."

Fletcher sprang to his feet, drawing as he turned.

But this was not Bosco Tracy and his men.

Two Mexican vaqueros rode on either side of a woman astride a white mare. Her hands were bound behind her back and her mouth was gagged with a bandanna.

The Mexicans had seen the camp, and now they rode toward Fletcher, reining up about twenty yards from where he stood to prove their lack of bad intent.

One of the vaqueros, a slender, good-looking man in a tight jacket, the bottoms of his pants split at the sides to show off his expensive riding boots, rode a few steps forward.

"*Buena manana, caballeros, oliamos su café.*"

Tense and wary, Fletcher holstered his gun and nodded toward the coffeepot on the fire. "We have plenty. Help yourself."

The Mexican nodded, his teeth flashing white as he smiled. "*Gracias.*"

The other rider dismounted and then helped the girl from the back of her horse. Immediately her beautiful black eyes sought those of Fletcher, the urgent, clamoring plea in them evident even to Doc who stood close by.

The vaquero caught the exchange and the sudden hardening of Fletcher's mouth under his ragged mustache and said: "My name is Ramon. I and this other"—he nodded toward the second vaquero—"are returning this lady to her husband." He shrugged. "We have been on her trail for many days."

"Who is she?" Doc asked, looking uncomfortable and unhappy as he assessed the woman.

"Her name is Donna Adelina Pilar Cantrell. She is the wife of my patron, the rich and powerful rancher Don Carlos Raimundo Vicente Cantrell." Ramon stepped to his saddlebags, found a couple of tin cups and kneeled by the fire. He poured coffee into both, using only his left hand, his right staying close to the Colt on his hip.

"The land of Donna Adelina's father borders that of my patron in Sonora. He gave the *senora* to Don Carlos to make—how do you say it?—an alliance. Donna Adelina is young. One day she will inherit both lands and be a very rich woman."

When Ramon stood he motioned with a nod of his head to his companion. "*Desatela, Paco.*"

The vaquero did as he was told and untied the woman, finally removed the gag from her mouth.

Seeing her now as she stood proud and defiant, her dark eyes flashing hatred as she rubbed her chaffed wrists and glared at Ramon and Paco, Fletcher was stunned by the girl's spectacular beauty.

She was no older than nineteen or twenty, black hair falling in glossy waves to her waist, her breasts swelling firm and voluptuous under a white shirt. Her full, soft lips were pouting, now that she knew both Doc and Fletcher were watching her closely, and her long legs with their shapely thighs were outlined against the canvas of her split riding skirt.

Donna Adelina, Fletcher decided, was all woman, with the kind of beauty that could bring the dogs out from under the porch and keep a man sleepless o' nights.

Ramon handed the girl a cup of coffee. She smiled sweetly, dropped a little curtsey—then threw the boiling-hot coffee in his face.

"You pig!" she screamed. "I will take nothing from you!"

The vaquero threw his hands to his face and stumbled backward. When he removed his hands his face was bright red, blisters already showing on his cheeks and forehead.

Furious, Ramon walked up to the girl and drew back his right arm, ready to backhand her across the face. As the man's hand swung, Fletcher moved in quickly and grabbed his forearm, his grip like steel.

Ramon gasped and tried to pull his arm away, but Fletcher held it tighter. "Taking this gal back to her husband is your concern, not mine," he said, his voice low and hard. "But striking a woman is something I will not tolerate."

Paco's hand dropped to his gun, but stayed there, frozen, when he found himself looking into the muzzle of Doc's Colt.

"Don't even bat an eyelid, Pancho, or I'll drop you where you stand," Doc said, his smile eager and ice-cold, thumb on the eared-back hammer of his gun.

Adelina glanced at Fletcher then nodded to Ramon.

"Don't concern yourself with him, *senor,*" she said. "Hank Riker will kill him for what he's done to me."

Ramon jerked his arm from Fletcher's grasp, his fingers straying to his blistered face. "If I'd struck you in my anger, Don Carlos would have killed me," he said. "But I would have died at the hands of a better man than that cheap tin-horn gambler you claim you love."

"I do love him, Ramon," Adelina snapped. "Riker is young, he's alive. I won't go back to that old man you call my husband. I will never again close my eyes and shudder when I feel his hands crawling like blue spiders over my breasts and belly, his breath cold on my face, smelling of the grave."

She turned to Fletcher. "Will you help me *senor*? I don't want to go back to the hacienda of Don Carlos Cantrell. I care nothing for him or his lands."

"Where is this Cantrell feller's spread?" Doc asked, deflecting the woman's question.

"His land borders that of the rancher John Slaughter and, like him, he has range running south into Mexico and all the way to Sonora. My father's ranch is there too, but it is less than a quarter the size of that of Don Carlos."

"Well," said Doc, holstering his gun, speaking to Ramon, "you boys best shove the gag back in this little gal's mouth and take her back down there, pronto."

"No!" Adelina cried. She ran into Fletcher's arms. "Don't let them take me."

Fletcher was suddenly interested. It was a long shot, maybe an impossible coincidence even in this sparsely populated land, but he gambled for it anyway. "Adelina," he said, keeping his voice level like he was only half-interested, "this man Riker, does he ever race horses?"

If the girl was surprised by the question, she didn't let it show. "Hank Riker is a card player, one of the very best."

She frowned for a few moments, then her lovely face cleared. "Wait, he did tell me he'd bought a horse. Yes, now I remember, he said it was a fast thoroughbred and he planned to enter it in John Slaughter's horse race everyone is talking about."

Adelina laid her fingers on the back of Fletcher's wrist. "You were young once. You understand how it is with lovers. Hank told me to run away from the hacienda of Don Carlos and wait for him at the ranch of a friend of his near Roof Butte. Hank has many friends. He said we'd soon be rich and that we'd ride on the train to Denver and live in style." She rounded on Ramon. "But then this pig caught me before I could reach Roof Butte, to take me back."

Ice in his belly, Fletcher gently pushed the girl away from him and asked: "You say Hank Riker has many friends. Is one of them a man called Bosco Tracy?"

Surprised this time, Adelina shook her head. "I've never heard of him."

"How about Port Austin?"

"Him neither. Who are these men?"

The girl was telling the truth, that much was obvious from the genuinely puzzled expression on her face.

"They're outlaws," Fletcher said. "And killers."

Adelina smiled. "Hank Riker would never know men like that."

Doc, who had been listening intently to this exchange, nodded to Fletcher.

"Buck, a word in your shell-like ear if you please."

The little gambler walked over to the fire and Fletcher joined him. "Before you say anything, Doc, I'm pretty certain this Hank Riker could be the man who hired Tracy and the others to steal my horse. It just seems to add up. If we keep the girl with his, she'll lead us right to him."

Doc shook his head. "Buck, there are a lot of thoroughbred horses and a lot of gamblers. You heard her; she said she'd never heard of Bosco Tracy or Port Austin and I think she was telling the truth."

"That proves nothing. If Riker was dealing with a known outlaw and killer like Bosco Tracy, he'd try to keep it quiet."

The eyes that searched Fletcher's face were haunted, almost scared. "Buck, I tell you this, a black-eyed woman riding a ghost horse is nothing but bad luck. I'm begging you to stay away from her. Let the two greasers take her home before something terrible happens."

Doc had the Southerner's superstitious dread of black-eyed women, since they were said to possess the gift of second sight and to have consort with witches and to dance naked with demons in dappled ha'ants among the deep woods.

He was equally fearful of white horses, and a Georgia gentleman of his generation would rather walk barefoot on red-hot coals than ride one.

The superstition dated to the War Between the States, when many a young Rebel cavalier rode gallantly off to battle astride a white horse. Instead of being hard to see in battlefields shrouded with gray powder smoke, ghost horses stood out stark against the background—with fatal results to their riders.

Now a black-eyed woman riding such a horse had ridden into his camp and, for Doc, this could only be a dreadful premonition of disaster.

Fletcher understood how Doc felt, knowing from his own war experience the jinx of ghost horses and the high incidence of casualties among the showy but vulnerable white-horse troops of the U.S. Cavalry.

But witch or no, Adelina could lead him to the man who might be responsible for the theft of his thoroughbred and Tiny McCue's death. It was too good a chance to pass up, especially now when it seemed every hand he'd been dealt, one way or another, had turned out to be a loser.

It could be that Hank Riker was not the man he was looking for, but he wasn't willing to walk away from the possibility that he was indeed the mysterious gambler.

Doc sensed the determination in Fletcher and let it go. "So be it, Buck," he said. "But that woman will bring us powerful bad luck and there's an end to it."

Fletcher nodded, his face grim and unsmiling. "I reckon I'll just have to take my chances, Doc."

He turned and walked away, stepping close to Ramon, who was glaring at Adelina with naked hatred. The young vaquero's face was a mess, the blistered skin already peeling away in strips, and his eyes were red and inflamed.

"We've decided to keep the girl with us," Fletcher said, his voice level and matter-of-fact. "You should ride on now and find a doctor who'll give you a salve for those burns."

Ramon shook his head. "My patron wants Donna Adelina back. I will take her with us, I think."

Adelina laid her hand on Fletcher's arm, her frightened eyes slanting to the vaquero. "Look at him. He wants to kill me so bad he can taste it. I would never make it to the hacienda alive."

"She stays with us, Ramon," Fletcher said, his tone flat and final. "Now ride."

The vaquero's hand was close to his gun and Fletcher knew he was thinking about it. But while Ramon thought, Paco, who had killed men in the past, acted.

He drew, his Colt coming up fast and smooth from the holster.

Doc's bullet hit the cylinder of Paco's gun as it came level, then gouged along the top of the frame and tore off the man's thumb. The heavy lead slug bounced off the Colt's hammer and crashed into Paco's chest, high in the right side.

The vaquero dropped his revolver like it was a red-hot iron and slumped to his knees, a gasp whispering through grimacing lips that were suddenly chalk white.

Ramon moved his hand away from his gun and stepped back, signaling that he was out of it.

Walking over to Paco, Doc looked down at the wounded man, the muzzle of the Colt in his hand curling gray smoke.

"My friend, you are hurt bad," he said.

Paco nodded. "*Senor, soy ya muerto.*"

Doc turned to Fletcher. "What did he say?"

"He says he's already dead."

"Your time is short," Doc said, his hand on Paco's shoulder. "Best you ride for Sonora and be buried by your kinfolk."

Paco's eyes rolled in his head and he pitched forward onto his face.

"Well, I'll be damned," Doc said. "I was talking with a dead man."

Ramon's dark eyes hardened. "That man has comrades," he said. "There are others out searching for Donna Adelina and they will come after her. Soon," he warned, anger edging his voice, "you two will join Paco, though your deaths will not be so quick, I think."

"Mister," Doc said, "get on your pony and ride and take that"—he motioned with his gun to Paco—"with you."

The vaquero nodded. "You seem old, and the old are wise, yet you are hard and without feelings."

"Lost those a long time ago," Doc replied.

With Fletcher's help, Ramon draped the dead man across his horse, then gathered up the reins and swung into the saddle.

He touched the brim of his sombrero and said: "*El adios, pero yo estara detros.*"

Then he swung his horse around and, leading Paco's mount, cantered away.

"Damn it, Buck, I don't understand a word of that foreign gibberish," Doc said. "What did he say?"

"He said he'd be back," Fletcher answered. "And I got no reason to doubt him."

Eleven

Fletcher, Doc and Adelina rode due south. The trail they followed seemed to be seldom traveled, rolling timber country mostly, but when they topped the rises that lay in their path, they could see, across a hundred miles of blue distance, red, upflung mountain ranges and mesas outlined against the sky.

As the day began to shade into evening, the landscape changed and they rode into arid, semidesert country, the cactus around them ablaze with blossoms, from the vivid scarlet of ocotillo to the pale, smoke gray of the palo christi.

To the southwest lay the colossal red-and-yellow rampart of the Mogollon Rim, its lower slopes covered in cedar, sweeping downward to the green valleys and timbered hills of the Tonto Basin. This they would bypass, staying to the easier, eastward trail along the course of Black Creek.

Doc sat uneasily in the saddle of his little mustang, the presence of the black-eyed woman on the ghost horse preying on his mind.

His eyes constantly searched their back trail, and he dropped behind now and then to scout hills they'd crossed or forests of checker-barked junipers they'd just ridden through, his hand never far from his gun.

At a bend of the creek near a narrow, rocky canyon carved out of a flat-topped mesa, Doc caught up with Fletcher again.

"I don't like it, Buck," he said, "I don't like it one bit."

Fletcher grinned. "Doc, don't tell me you're still spooked by the white horse."

Doc shook his head, his face bleak. "It isn't that. Well, it isn't only that. I have a feeling is all, a feeling we're riding into a heap of trouble."

Reining up his horse, Fletcher rose in the stirrups and studied the canyon. It was green with willow and cottonwood and seemed cool, shady and inviting, a good place to camp for the night.

Beside him, Adelina looked all in, tired shadows smeared blue under her eyes, and that made up his mind.

"We'll camp here for the night," he said. "In the canyon." Still grinning he turned to Doc. "How does that set with you?"

The little man shrugged. "When I have this feeling nagging at me one place is as good as any other."

Fletcher swung out of the saddle and led his horse into the canyon, the others following. The walls of the gorge enclosed a flat, grassy space about fifty yards wide, dotted here and there by small boulders and struggling patches of cactus. A narrow stream ran through the middle of the canyon and, judging by the distant sound of falling water, was fed by runoff from one of the sheer rock walls.

The waterfall was much deeper inside the canyon and Fletcher made a mental note to explore it later.

He and Doc staked the horses on a good patch of grass growing near the cottonwoods, then built a fire for coffee.

Day had now shaded into night, and the sky was bright with stars, the waning moon touching the trees and grass around the camp with silver.

The calico kitten was curled up under Fletcher's thigh, showing no inclination to embark on a nocturnal hunt, and he decided the little animal was as tired as the rest of them.

Adelina found soap and a towel in her saddlebags and told Fletcher she was going back in the canyon to bathe.

Watching her leave with unhappy eyes, Doc poured whiskey into his coffee and slowly shook his head.

"What's on your mind, Doc?" Fletcher asked, feeding the calico kitten scraps of bacon.

"Nothing much."

"Something's eating at you. Spill it."

"Think about it, Buck. If you was an ordinary woman, would you go back in that canyon in the dark by your own-self?"

"If I needed privacy I would. Yeah, I guess I would."

"No you wouldn't. Only a black-eyed woman would do that, the kind of woman who isn't afraid of ha'ants and demons and such."

"Doc," Fletcher said, smiling as he built a smoke, "Adelina wanted to bathe, that's all. You didn't expect her to do it here did you, with two men gawking at her?"

Doc put the back of his hand to his mouth and coughed, long and hard. When he took the hand away again, Fletcher saw it was stained with blood.

"Buck," he gasped, splashing more whiskey into his cup, "you go back there and make certain she isn't putting all kinds of heathen hexes on us and talking that Mex gib-berish."

Fletcher laughed. "Doc, she's bathing. Maybe she's . . . she's as nekkid as a jaybird."

"Go," Doc gasped again, his finger pointing into the darkness of the canyon beyond the firelight. "Go, Buck, go."

"Hell, if it makes you feel better I'll make sure she's not talking to no boogerman."

Fletcher rose to his feet, set the kitten down and stepped away from the fire, lighting his cigarette as he did so. Doc's voice stopped him.

"Buck, you like that little gal, don't you?"

Fletcher turned. "I guess. She's kinda nice and she smells good and she's right pretty. She reminds me a lot of Savannah."

"Have you thought about something?"

"What's that?"

"That you plan to kill the man she loves."

Fletcher let that go, no answer springing immediately to his mind. He had not thought about Hank Riker in those terms, but now Doc had said it, he had to face up to that reality. If Riker was indeed the mysterious gambler, he would kill him to even the score for the murder of Tiny McCue and for robbing Ginny of the only chance she had to get well again.

What that would do to Adelina he could not guess, but it was something he'd face when the time came. There was no point in worrying over it right now. His mind made up, Fletcher walked into the darkness of the canyon, toward the sound of the falling water.

After thirty yards or so, the canyon narrowed, the walls so close they almost brushed Fletcher's shoulders, but then they opened up again into an enclosed area of about a hundred acres that was almost rectangular in shape. Sage grew here and there in the sandy soil alongside coarse tufts of spiked scrub grass. Along the bottom of the cliffs struggled a few spruce and stunted cedar, almost hidden by the long shadows cast by the canyon walls.

As he walked into the clearing, Fletcher saw that a steady shower of crystal-clear water cascaded from high up the wall to his right.

The water was not falling from the top of the canyon, but

midway up the wall, seemingly the runoff of an underground stream that flowed deep inside the mesa.

The showering water splashed into a natural rock basin at the foot of the wall, where it formed a pool about thigh-high to a pretty woman. Fletcher knew this as a certainty, because a pretty woman was standing in it.

Adelina stood under the waterfall, letting it splash over her naked body, her wet hair falling over her shoulders like a cape. The bright moon was slyly peeping over the canyon wall, bathing the girl in silvery light, casting deep shadows under her pink-tipped breasts and between her thighs.

Fletcher's jaw dropped to his chest. He stood transfixed, stunned by Adelina's unearthly beauty so that all at once he found it hard to breathe.

The girl turned this way and that under the fall of the water, first firm breasts then swelling hips shimmering into view, and Fletcher was rooted to the spot, unable to move.

He had to get away from here!

Like a man waking from a deep sleep, he shook his head and took a single, stumbling step backward. Too late, he felt his spur catch on a fallen log behind him and he crashed heavily onto his back with a thud that could be heard all around the canyon.

Fletcher lay stunned for a moment, and when he looked up, Adelina was standing over him, holding her inadequate scrap of towel in front of her.

"Were you spying on me, Mr. Fletcher?" she asked.

"I . . . I . . . was worried about you," Fletcher said, the lie sounding unconvincing even to himself. But gamely he tried to salvage what he could of it. "It's . . . it's so dark back here."

The girl shook her head. "No it isn't. The moon lights up everything. But, then, you already know that."

Fletcher rose unsteadily to his feet. Adelina was very close to him—and she was smiling.

"Did you like what you saw?" she asked.

Unable to speak, Fletcher nodded, his jaws locked in place.

The girl's head was tilted back, looking at him, her full, red lips parted so that Fletcher saw the white gleam of her teeth. Her pink tongue ran along her top lip and her dark eyes were bright with promise.

"I'm a woman who needs a man, Buck," she whispered. "And I need a man right now."

She dropped the towel, her body like an ivory statue in the moonlight, and put her arms around Fletcher's neck, her hungry mouth open, seeking his own. Fletcher pulled her close, his hands traveling over her smooth body, still wet from the water. Their lips met and he was melting into her, becoming one with her.

Adelina tore her mouth from his and took a little step back from him. "The buckles of your gunbelts are hurting me."

Quickly, Fletcher unbuckled his belts and dropped them at his feet. He reached out for the girl again and she came to him, her mouth once again open, inviting.

The sweet woman smell of her was making Fletcher's head swim. Doc was right, he thought, this black-eyed woman was a witch and she had cast her spell on him. But what a delightful spell!

Adelina slowly sank to the grass, pulling Fletcher with her, her mouth still on his, hungry, seeking. Demanding.

Fletcher drifted, sensing, feeling, without thought. Then it came to him . . . in the past, how many times had he and Savannah . . .

Savannah!

Fletcher rolled off Adelina and rose to his feet, blinking,

trying to get his eyes back in focus as he attempted to throw a loop on his conflicting emotions.

"*Cual es la materia*?" the girl asked. She was still on the ground, her legs slightly apart, and her face was puzzled.

Fletcher shook his head. "Nothing is the matter. It's just that I suddenly remembered I was married." He smiled. "Sometimes with a man like me, it takes time to pound a memory like that into his thick head."

Adelina smiled. "When a loaf of bread is already cut, who will miss a slice?"

"No one I guess," Fletcher said. "Unless you happen to choke on it."

The girl rose to her feet, then bent and picked up her towel. "Earlier today I thought perhaps you were more man than even Hank Riker, but I was wrong. You had your chance, Mr. Fletcher. There won't be another."

Adelina stuck her nose in the air, spun on her heel and walked back to the basin where her clothes were piled. Angrily, using a lot of quick movements, she began to dress.

Fletcher watched her for a few moments, then bowed his head and sighed. To himself he said: "Easy come, easy go."

He picked up his gunbelts and walked back to the fire, where Doc looked at him, a question writ large and eager on his face.

"Don't ask, Doc," Fletcher said. "Just don't ask."

"Ah, so she turned you down, huh?" Doc said.

"Something like that," Fletcher replied.

"Did you catch her doing one of them witch hexes?"

Fletcher smiled. "Adelina casts a spell all right, Doc, but not the kind you mean."

The attack came just after daybreak.

A bullet slammed into the fire, scattering burning twigs and sparks, sending the coffeepot flying. Doc and Fletcher scrambling for cover, Doc dragging Adelina with him behind the shelter of a small boulder.

"See anything out there?" Doc asked.

Fletcher shook his head. "Not a damn thing."

"You in the canyon!"

"Who are you and what do you want?" Fletcher yelled.

"My name is Don Carlos Raimundo Vicente Cantrell. I want my wife."

Doc turned to where Fletcher stood behind a flat shelf of rock jutting out from the side of the canyon wall. "Now do you believe me when I said a black-eyed woman riding a ghost horse was bad luck?"

"I won't go to him," Adelina said, her beautiful face pale. "I'll kill myself first."

Fletcher thought this through for a few moments, then yelled: "Don Carlos, your woman says she wants to stay with us."

"Send her out. There's no need for Adelina to die."

Fletcher glanced at the girl and she shook her head at him. "I won't go. Tell him that. Tell him I won't live in that prison he calls a home where every single day of my life is a living hell."

To the girl, Fletcher said: "That's way too much to tell." To her husband he yelled: "It's no good, Don Carlos. She doesn't want to go with you."

"*Entonces usted todo dado!*"

"What's that mean?" Doc asked.

"It means," said Fletcher, his face grim, "that as far as he's concerned, we're both dead men."

Beyond the canyon lay a hundred yards of open ground that rose gradually to a craggy hill topped with jumbled volcanic boulders, piñon and a few stunted spruce.

Fletcher now saw men moving among the boulders,

vaqueros mostly, but he spotted at least three Apache scouts and that could mean big trouble.

An old man with a mane of white hair seemed to be the one issuing the orders and Adelina confirmed with an unhappy nod to Fletcher that this was indeed Don Carlos.

There seemed to be at least two dozen men up there in the rocks, and maybe more. Fletcher weighed the odds and decided he and Doc would be lucky to leave this box canyon alive.

The morning wore on until the sun was right overhead and it became unbearably hot, the canyon itself, enclosed by the high mesa walls, slowly becoming a furnace.

Standing at the shelf with his rifle at the ready, Fletcher smelled the stale, rank odor of his own sweat. A panting lizard stopped on the shelf, raising one foot, then another, the rock too hot to let them stay put for any length of time.

Now and again a rifle crashed up among the rocks and a bullet whined into the canyon. But Fletcher knew Don Carlos's men were shooting blind, hoping a lucky ricochet would catch either him or Doc.

Adelina went to the stream and filled their canteens, and Fletcher took off his hat and poured half of his over his head. The water cooled him for a time, but he still felt sticky and grubby, his back itching under his shirt where sweat trickled.

When the sun disappeared behind the western wall of the canyon, it got a little cooler and the willows and cottonwoods cast long shadows on the grass. Out among the rocks, Fletcher saw Don Carlos rise to his feet, shout and wave his sombrero.

They were coming!

"Doc!" Fletcher yelled.

The warning was not needed. Doc was already on his feet, leaning over the rock, his Colt ready in his hand.

Out of the corner of his eye, Fletcher saw the kitten bolt for the safety of the trees, his instinct warning him that there was danger here.

The horsemen boiled from behind the rise, at least twenty of them, and they were coming fast.

Fletcher threw his Winchester to his shoulder and fired at one of the leading riders. The man threw up his arms and toppled out of the saddle. He cranked his rifle and fired again. And again. Both misses. Fletcher grunted, angry at himself for his sloppy shooting.

Doc's Colt was hammering, shot after shot. As far as Fletcher could see he hit no one, but his steady fire made the oncoming riders halt their charge, reining up in a thick cloud of dust as they took to their rifles.

Bullets split the air around Fletcher, whining off rocks and the canyon walls only to buzz away like angry bees. He sighted on the chest of one of the Apaches, forcing his muscles to relax so his rifle would not quiver, and pulled the trigger. The Indian yelped and doubled over in the saddle, his gun falling from his hands.

Doc had reloaded his revolver and had stepped away from his sheltering rock, moving further back into the canyon.

"They're charging again!" he yelled.

The horsemen were coming on at a gallop again, and from somewhere behind him Fletcher heard Adelina give a startled cry of fear.

There was no stopping Don Carlos's riders. Fletcher backed away, following Doc, who had the girl by the arm, pushing her toward the spot where the walls of the canyon narrowed.

A rider charged into the canyon, his Colt blazing. His face still red and blistered, his eyes crazy, Ramon ignored Fletcher, leveling his gun at Adelina. He fired and Fletcher saw the girl stumble and fall. Ramon thumbed back the hammer to fire again and Fletcher shot him. The .44-.40 bullet lifted the vaquero right out of the saddle and Ramon crashed to the ground, puffs of dust drifting upward around his body.

Fletcher had no time to watch Ramon fall. A man with a huge black beard was almost on top of him, his revolver blasting. Fletcher levered his Winchester, but the bearded rider's horse slammed into him, sending the rifle spinning out of his hands.

Fletcher thudded solidly against the canyon wall and fell to his right. He rolled, drawing from his crossdraw holster as he came up on one knee and slammed three shots into the bearded man, who was sending his own bullets Fletcher's way.

Hit hard, the rider yanked on the reins, frantically trying to turn his horse away from Fletcher's accurate fire. But his frightened mount went down, its back legs collapsing, then rolled heavily on top of him. The man screamed once as his ornate silver saddle horn crushed his chest, then lay still.

Fletcher looked around for another target. He heard Doc's Colt roar and saw another rider go down.

Then, as suddenly as it had begun, it was all over.

Four of Don Carlos's men lay dead, their bodies half-hidden by the thick cloud of dust that drifted over the battlefield, and the rest had fled.

Up among the rocks Don Carlos was beside himself. He screamed at his men, calling them cowards and old women, as he slapped at them with his sombrero.

Fletcher watched as one of the Apaches angrily began to talk back, gesticulating with his rifle toward the canyon. Without another word the old man drew his gun and fired at point-blank range into the Indian's chest. The Apache dropped, a dead man when he hit the ground.

They'll be back, Fletcher thought grimly, and next time they won't dare fail.

Twelve

The attack came just minutes later. But this time it was only one man, the surviving Apache. He rode a paint pony and led the horses of two of the dead, charging toward the canyon at a fast gallop.

"What the hell . . ." Fletcher muttered.

Then he realized what was happening.

"Doc!" he yelled. "Kill those damn horses!"

It was too late.

Yipping his war cry, the Apache rode across the mouth of the canyon, making no attempt to fire at Doc and Fletcher. When the riderless mounts were close to the canyon entrance, the Indian turned in the saddle and shot both of them.

One of the horses went down, screaming, blood from a wound in its neck spurting in a wide fan of scarlet. The other staggered into the canyon and collapsed, its eyes rolling, a shattered leg kicking wildly until Fletcher put a merciful bullet into its brain.

"That crazy Indian, why did he do that?" Doc asked.

Beside him, Adelina held her bloody left arm where Ramon's bullet had hit. The girl was deathly pale and she was biting her lip, obviously trying her best not to cry out.

Fletcher went to the girl and led her to a flat-topped rock

where he had her sit. Then he looked over the top of the girl's head at Doc. "Do you know what will happen to those horses and the dead men when the sun hits them tomorrow?"

Doc's pale face went ashen gray. "My God, we won't be able to stand the stench."

"Uh-huh. That's what Don Carlos is counting on. I don't think he'll risk another charge, not when he can force us to surrender. And that way, there's no danger Adelina will be hit by a stray bullet."

"Does he care?" Doc asked. "That Ramon feller tried to kill her."

"Ramon wasn't acting on his patron's orders. He had a score to settle. I kinda think that despite everything Don Carlos wants his beautiful young wife alive."

Fletcher looked down at the girl. "Now, let me take a look at that arm."

Ramon's bullet had passed through the fleshy part of Adelina's upper arm without hitting bone, but the entrance and exit wounds were ugly and inflamed, and Fletcher knew the girl must be in considerable pain.

He stripped inner bark from one of the willows growing along the creek and gathered some dry sage leaves, grinding them together in his palm. He wet down the resulting mixture with a little water and used it as a poultice for Adelina's wounds.

"The willow bark will help with the pain and the sage will prevent an infection," he said. "At least, that's what the Indians say."

Despite the pain she was in, the girl's reply was cool. "Thank you Mr. Fletcher," she said. "You are very thoughtful."

Fletcher bound up Adelina's arm with one of the seemingly inexhaustible supply of clean handkerchiefs that Doc, out of dire necessity, kept stuffed in his blanket roll.

When he finished he thought Adelina looked pale and tired, but her dark eyes when she glanced at him were hard and unforgiving.

"Hell," thought Fletcher wearily, "hath no fury . . ."

He picked up his rifle and studied the hill. Nothing was moving up there. It seemed Don Carlos was indeed content to wait and let time and sun do what his charge had failed to accomplish.

Fletcher's fingers went to his shirt pocket for the makings but froze halfway as a weird, blood-curdling scream shattered the brooding silence of the canyon. The echoes bellowed from wall to wall, and after they died away, Fletcher, Doc and Adelina looked at each other in stunned disbelief.

Fletcher's buckskin's head was high, his ears pricked forward in alarm, muscles quivering, and Adelina's white mare was up on her toes, dancing in place as she whinnied softly at something she could smell and sense but not see.

Only Doc's fly-buzzed mustang, its ugly, hammerhead hanging low as it drowsed in the heat, seemed unaffected by the scream.

"What in the holy hell was that?" Doc asked, eyes wide, his hand straying to the Colt in his shoulder holster.

At first Fletcher could not reply, then it dawned on him that in this country only a wild mustang stallion could have given a cry like that.

The scream had come from the other end of the canyon, where Adelina had bathed under the waterfall. The horse must have made his way down from the top of the mesa for water and something, perhaps the smell of blood, had frightened him.

But if it was a wild horse, how had he gotten down from the top of the mesa? And if there were a trail down, did that mean he could get back up again without leaving from the front of the canyon?

Fletcher felt hope flare in him. Could there be a way out of this trap they'd found themselves in? And if that's how things panned out, was there another way down to the flat from the cap rock of the mesa?

If the only way down was at the back of this canyon, then Don Carlos could leave a couple of riflemen to pick them off at their leisure as they tried to return.

In that case, would they be trading one trap for another?

Fletcher had plenty of questions but no answers.

Then he'd take it one step at a time.

Leaving Doc's question unanswered, Fletcher threw the little man his rifle and said: "I'm going back there to take a look-see."

Doc's eyes slanted to Adelina, suspicious and accusing. He gave an almost imperceptible nod toward the woman and said: "I didn't care for the sound of that scream. It could be the place is ha'anted, Buck. Be careful."

Fletcher nodded. "You just keep an eye on the hill, Doc. I don't think it's going to happen, but you never know; they may try to rush us again."

He spared a single glance for Adelina, who was sitting on the grass stroking the kitten. She looked up at him with the thinly veiled hostility of a woman scorned, and walked back to where the canyon narrowed.

Once back in the clearing, he studied the ground carefully. He'd been right about the horse, but there had been more than one. He hadn't noticed them in the darkness the night before, but the tracks of unshod hooves were everywhere, most of them around the water tank where the soft ground was churned into mud.

The walls of the canyon on either side of him soared six hundred feet high, sheer precipices of rock carved out of the mesa by ancient floods, the waning afternoon sunlight sparkling in the rushing water that cascaded from the cliff to his right. Only the wall facing him, rising in a series of eroded steps and benches to the red sandstone cap rock offered any hope of a way to the top.

This wall was different from the other two, little of it solid stone. It was composed of long shelves of horizontal rock and black shale. Here and there were patches of terra-cotta, rifts of red, copper deposits and beds of yellow, white and orange parti-colored clay.

Fletcher walked to the base of the wall and studied it closely. Around him bees hummed in the clusters of yellow flowers that grew close to the wall and the sound of the water splashing into the tank was a constant, pleasing backdrop of sound.

He discovered that the steps of the benches were less steep than they seemed from a distance, and were in fact a series of gradual, undulating rises to the top of the mesa. But parts of the ascent were steep, especially toward the cap rock, stretches of the shelves climbing at an angle of almost forty-five degrees.

The benches themselves were narrow, no more than four feet wide in places, covered in coarse sand, pebbles and gravel mixed with glittering scales of mica, bits of quartz and breaks of agate and carnelian.

Judging by the hoof prints, the wild horses used this trail down the canyon wall regularly. But mustangs were as surefooted and nimble as mountain goats and, dangerous as it was, must make the trip daily, lured here by the pool of fresh water in the rock tank.

Just how dangerous the path up the benches was came home to Fletcher with a jolt when he saw the bleached bones of several horses half-hidden in the grass at the base of the wall.

The animals had fallen from the wall and died here—something that could easily happen to his own horse and maybe, Fletcher realized unhappily, to himself.

He took off his hat and wiped sweat from his brow with his forearm, gazing up at the wall.

There was no other choice. They would have to chance it. To wait in the canyon was certain death. At least the trail to the top of the mesa would give them a chance, even if it was a slender one.

Fletcher walked back to the others and quickly told them his plan.

"We have to do it now, before it gets dark," he said. "It's a climb to make in the daylight."

"If any of Don Carlos's men happen to come this way, we'll be pinned against that cliff like sitting ducks," Doc said.

"That's a chance we'll have to take," Fletcher said, slightly rattled at the little man for stating what was painfully obvious. "I don't like it any more than you do, Doc."

But in the end Doc was fatalistic, echoing Fletcher's own thought that if they stayed in the canyon they would die under the guns of Don Carlos and his men or starve to death. Adelina bit her lip and remained silent, knowing that any protest she might make would be pointless.

But when Doc saw the wall they were to climb, he was appalled.

"My God, Buck, that's five hundred feet straight up," he said, scanning the cliff, his mustang's reins in a white-knuckled hand.

"I reckon closer to six hundred," Fletcher said. He looked at Doc and then Adelina with somber eyes. "Five or six, it doesn't make no never mind—it's still a long ways to fall."

Adelina surprised him. "I'm willing to take the chance,"

she said. "Even if I die, it's better than a life with my husband."

"Hell, lady, you're young enough to outlast him," Doc said, his dislike for Adelina evident in the tone of his voice. "Go back to him now and maybe none of us will have to climb this damn cliff."

The woman shook her head. "Never! Every moment with him is a moment I die inside. Yes, I might outlast Don Carlos, but by then I'll be an old woman, not in body, but in soul." She gave Fletcher a sidelong glance. "That is why I love Hank Riker. He is a *mucho hombre* and he will keep me forever young."

Fletcher let that go. He had almost yielded to temptation in Adelina's arms and his conscience still nagged at him, but mercifully as a friend and not as a judge.

"Doc," he said, "we got to get going." He smiled, wanting to take some of the sting out of what he was about to say. "Do you think you could lead the way with that sheep you call a horse?"

"Don't you worry none about this little feller," Doc said, suddenly on his dignity, rubbing the mustang's knobby forehead. "He'll make it up there. Just you look to that big buckskin of yours."

Doc turned away, muttering something about lumbering buckskins with damn feet the size of damn dinner plates, and Fletcher, despite the knot of fear in his stomach, smiled.

"Lead the way, Doc," he said. "Adelina will follow, then me."

Fletcher turned away, then stopped. "Wait," he said. He scooped up the calico and handed him to Doc. "Let him ride on your blanket roll. I think he may be safer with you if your horse is as good as you say he is."

"He's as good as I say," Doc said, placing the purring

kitten behind his saddle. "I just wish your buckskin was half as good."

Doc led his horse to the foot of the first shelf, then stopped. He turned to Fletcher. "What happens if we get up there and find no other way down?"

Fletcher's mouth was a hard, grim line under his sweeping mustache. "Then, Dr. Holliday," he said, "we'll be dancing with the devil and Don Carlos will be playing his tune."

Thirteen

Doc led his mustang up the slope of the first shelf, the little horse kicking loose showers of sand and gravel as it found its footing.

Fletcher waited until Doc had cleared the first bench and started to climb the second before nodding to Adelina that she should start her ascent. The white mare was less willing to make the climb than Doc's mustang, and balked at the narrowness of the path and the loose surface under her hooves.

Despite her wounded arm, Adelina hauled on the reins and slowly, reluctantly, the mare began to climb.

Fletcher watched Doc as he rose higher up the wall. He was now almost halfway to the top, moving steadily, his mountain-bred mustang taking the dizzying climb in stride.

Every now and then a shower of pebbles and sand fell to the floor of the canyon, and in places Doc seemed to be stepping warily along rock shelves no wider than his own narrow shoulders.

Swallowing hard, Fletcher stepped onto the first level and began to climb, dragging the reluctant buckskin behind him.

Above him the blue bowl of the sky was slowly fading to

a pale lilac, and down on the canyon floor the shadows were stretching longer and the bees were finding their way home.

Climbing higher, Fletcher reached the second bench, then the third. He was now almost three hundred feet above the flat and there was no turning back. The only way was forward . . . and higher.

Here the bench was very narrow, no more than four feet wide, and the buckskin stepped warily, eyes rolling white in his head, the saddle bumping and scraping against the rough sandstone wall.

A long way below, the canyon floor was full of shadows cast by the looming cliffs and the thinning air smelled of dust and sage and the raw-iron tang of the tumbling waterfall.

In happier circumstance, as the day died around him, Fletcher might have enjoyed the peace and tranquility of the canyon, but now, climbing higher along a bench that grew noticeably narrower with every step, his only thoughts were of survival. That, and with the grim possibility that Don Carlos and his men might enter the canyon at any time and blast them off the wall like they would tumble tin ducks in a Dodge City shooting gallery.

Adelina's mare was acting up even worse than before, sending down showers of rocks and debris that pattered off Fletcher's hat and shoulders. At one point the mare reared wildly and it was all the girl could do to stop the horse from trying to turn around—certain disaster on that scant ledge.

Fletcher's buckskin caught the mare's panic, and he too reared, not liking the steep trail ahead and the narrowness of the shelf.

Fighting the horse, Fletcher pulled on the reins, forcing the buckskin to climb higher. Ahead of him, the white mare was almost totally out of control, rearing constantly, her hooves pounding the ledge, a series of heavy thuds that dislodged an avalanche of small rocks and gravel.

Moments later, to Fletcher's unbelieving horror, the constant battering dislodged a big chunk of the bench, just behind the mare's pounding rear hooves. A bite-shaped section of the shelf, about three feet long, fell away and crashed four hundred feet to the canyon floor. The bite reduced the width of the bench at that point to a little over a foot—too narrow for the buckskin to pass.

There was no going back, no turning around. Fletcher realized with sickening certainty he would have to jump for it and so would the horse.

He glanced down at the terrifying chasm below, yawning endlessly just beyond the scuffed toes of his boots, and wave after wave of nausea hit him. He took off his hat and pressed the back of his head against the wall, fighting to breathe.

Fletcher had always loved the mountains, the rugged sweep of the bald, towering peaks, their lower slopes green with spruce and juniper, and always the unexpected, broad valleys with their hidden creeks and lakes and long, silent distances.

But this was very different. To be perched on a narrow rock ledge hundreds of feet up with no room to turn was a new experience and one he did not relish.

Slowly, as his churning stomach returned to normal and his head ceased to swim, Fletcher glanced up to where Adelina was still climbing, her mare, now that she'd caused all the damage she could, apparently settled down.

Doc was already on top of the mesa, standing with his mustang on the cap rock. The little horse stood, as it always did, hipshot, head hanging, his tail swishing this way and that, as though the climb up a sheer, six-hundred-foot wall had been no big thing.

Bitterly, Fletcher bet himself that the same flies had followed the mustang from the canyon floor and were already buzzing around his ugly sledgehammer of a head.

Doc waved his hat and yelled something Fletcher could not hear. He raised a hand in reply and steadied himself for the jump he had to make.

The buckskin, sensing Fletcher's tenseness, acted up again, pulling hard on the reins as he tried to back away, a spurting rash of rocks rattling downward from his prancing hooves.

Desperately, Fletcher fought the horse, speaking to him in a low, calming whisper. Gradually, reassured by the human voice, the buckskin quietened down, though his eyes were still rolling white, wild and frightened in his head.

Fletcher knew the time to make the jump was now—and he hoped he could coax the buckskin to follow.

The part of the ledge where he stood was about four feet wide. Then came the bite-shaped gap and, beyond, the ledge widened slightly to a width of five feet, though it wasn't level but had a slight downward cant toward the canyon floor.

Holding the reins in his hand, Fletcher took one last look at the darkening depths beneath him and jumped.

His boots hit the far ledge and skidded from under him on the loose gravel. He fell heavily on his back, bounced, and rolled to his right, plunging over the side of the ledge.

The reins saved him.

Momentum swung Fletcher hard to his left. Desperately he held the leather with one hand, the horrifying plunge to the bottom of the canyon opening up under him like a great, gaping mouth.

At first he thought he was going to pull the buckskin over with him. Even the big horse's great strength was severely tested by a two-hundred-pound burden suddenly hanging on his head.

The horse backed up on the ledge, gravel bursting from under his hooves as he fought for traction on the slippery surface. The buckskin's head came up, his eyes rolling, and Fletcher was slammed hard against the wall.

Fletcher fought for a toehold, his boots skidding against loose rock and shale. He glanced downward at the canyon bottom, now deep in shadow, knowing that if the reins slipped out of his frantically clutching left hand the fall would break every single bone in his body.

Scared now, he tried again to find a foothold. His boots scrambled, skidded, scrambled again, dislodging rock and shale that plummeted into the dark abyss.

The buckskin was tossing his head, backing along the ledge, trying to get rid of this heavy burden that threatened to pull him over the edge.

As the horse backed up, lifting his head, Fletcher felt himself being dragged upward and his right hand shot out, his fingers just managing to grip the bench. He clung on for dear life, then let go of the reins, his left hand coming up quickly to grasp the edge.

He hung there for a few moments, gathering his strength. From somewhere he heard Doc yell and he thought he heard Adelina scream.

Slowly, painfully, he dragged himself up, all his weight on his strong, rancher's fingers. He shoved his right leg over the bench then hauled himself up, rolling over onto his back. For a few moments Fletcher lay there, his breath coming in short, agonizing gasps. There was a sharp pain in his chest on the left side and he figured he'd broken a rib in the fall over the edge, and maybe two.

He struggled to his feet and took up the buckskin's reins. The horse snorted in alarm and tried to back away from him, but Fletcher held on, wrapping the leather around his fist.

He still had to make the jump.

This time, could he make it without tumbling over the ledge?

Fletcher set his chin, his face grim under the shadow of his hat. The shortest answer to that question was to do it and the less thinking about it he did, the better.

He jumped.

This time his feet slammed solidly onto the ledge and held. He turned and pulled on the reins, urging the buckskin forward. The big horse balked, wanting nothing to do with the gap in the rock bench opening up in front of him.

Fletcher yelled words of encouragement to the horse, but the animal stubbornly refused to move from the spot, his front legs stiff, knees locked and rigid.

"Come on, boy," Fletcher said, yanking on the reins. "It's only a little jump."

The horse rolled his eyes and whinnied. But he stayed where he was.

Up on the cap rock, Doc yelled something. Fletcher turned and saw him draw his Colt. Doc lay belly-down on the rock, his arms straight out in front of him, carefully sighting the gun with both hands.

He was going to shoot the horse!

"No!" Fletcher shouted. He waved his arm frantically. "No, Doc!"

Doc fired.

The bullet hit the canyon wall just behind the horse, thudding venomously into the sandstone, kicking out a shower of small rocks and dirt.

The buckskin was startled, but didn't move.

"Damn it, Doc!" Fletcher yelled. "You'll bring Don Carlos down on us!"

Doc ignored Fletcher's warning and fired again.

The bullet burned across the buckskin's rump and the horse screamed in fear and surprise. He jumped forward, sailing effortlessly over the bite in the rock, almost knocking Fletcher over when he landed. The buckskin took the slope to the next bench almost at a canter, Fletcher scrambling as best he could in front of him.

The horse didn't even hesitate for a moment when he reached the steep incline up to the top of the mesa. He gathered speed and galloped up the slope, dragging Fletcher with him.

Finally the scrambling buckskin reached the level cap rock of the mesa and slowed to a stop, reassured by the calm presence of Doc's mustang and the nearness of the white mare.

Fletcher patted the horse's neck, calming him down further. He looked at the wound on the buckskin's rump. Doc's bullet had burned a four-inch notch across the horse's sleek hide, but had done no permanent damage.

Doc was grinning as he punched out the spent shells from his revolver and reloaded.

"Damn it all, Buck," he said, "if that wasn't the best damn pistol shot I ever made."

"I thought you were trying to kill him," Fletcher said. "Or did you miss?"

Doc holstered his Colt. "Miss hell! I wanted to burn him was all. Hit him right where I aimed. Got him moving just fine though, didn't I?"

Fletcher shook his head. "Doc, I don't know whether to hug you or shoot you. I'm going to have to study on that for a spell."

Doc laughed, a joyous peal that dropped the hard years off him and revealed for a fleeting instant the young man he still was. "Hear that," he said, turning to Adelina. "That's all the thanks I get for saving his damn-fool neck."

And to Fletcher: "By the by, Buck, when you were hanging onto the reins of your horse, a-chewing on your own heart, I wasn't about to let you fall and end up all smashed up and horrible at the bottom of the canyon."

"How were you going to save me?" Fletcher asked, intrigued.

"Hell, I couldn't save you. All I was going to do was put a bullet in your head. Call it a Christian act of mercy."

"Your deep concern touches me, Doc," Fletcher said, his face straight. "It truly does."

Doc touched the brim of his hat. "Anytime, Buck. Anytime."

Fletcher looked around him, at the cap rock of the mesa stretching away into the gathering darkness, studded here and there with white and black sage and spikes of struggling yellow grass.

From where he and the others stood, they were not visible to Don Carlos and his men on the hill. And if the besiegers had heard the shots, which they probably did, they might think Fletcher or Doc had been shooting at a deer. Still, it was time to move. Come daybreak, Fletcher hoped to be clear of the mesa and on his way south again.

That was, if they could find a way down—no easy thing in daylight and harder still in the dark.

Fletcher took the calico kitten from Doc and put him on his accustomed place on his saddle roll, wincing as he stretched up with his left arm.

"What's wrong with you?" Doc asked, his eyes suddenly concerned.

"I think a couple of my ribs are broke," Fletcher replied.

"You better let me take a look," Doc said.

Fletcher shook his head at him. "Later. We don't have time right now." Gathering up the reins of the buckskin, Fletcher led him forward, stepping out across the cap rock, and Doc and Adelina followed.

Thousands of years of wind, sand and rain had done their

work to smooth out the top of the mesa, though here and there they had to step around great upthrust slabs of black shale and red sandstone piled one on top of the other, the result of violent convulsions of the earth's crust in ancient times when the rock they walked was still molten.

A cold, white moon rose high in the cloudless sky, illuminating the way ahead. Up here on the mesa, the air was clear and cool, smelling of sage and greasewood, slightly musty, as though Fletcher and the others were making their way through the dusty corridors of time.

No one talked and the only sounds were the slight thud of their footfalls, the chiming of Fletcher's jinglebob spurs and the jangle of a bit when a horse tossed its head.

The darkness drew around them like a cloak, and out in the broken hill country six hundred feet below, coyotes lifted their heads to bay at the moon, their smooth, spring coats flecked by the yellow petals of the evening primroses that grew everywhere on the slopes and valleys.

After half an hour, Fletcher threw up a hand, stopping Doc and Adelina in their tracks. "Listen," he said, his voice urgent.

Out from the darkness came a muffled drumming, the sound of many running hooves.

"It's the wild horses," Adelina said.

"And just ahead of us," Doc added.

Fletcher tilted his head, listening. Judging by the sound, the horses were running away from them, toward the other end of the mesa.

He swung awkwardly into the saddle, favoring his hurting ribs, and handed the kitten to Doc. "I'm going after them," he said. "Doc, you and Adelina follow."

"Buck, you can't ride across this mesa in the dark," Doc objected. "You'll break your damn-fool neck."

"I'm going to press the mustangs close," Fletcher replied.

"If there's a way down, they'll show it to me as they escape."

Doc opened his mouth to object, but Fletcher was already gone, spurring the buckskin in pursuit of the herd.

The big horse's hooves hammered hollow on the cap rock, his neck stretched as Fletcher urged him into a fast gallop. Ahead of him, Fletcher could see only moon-streaked darkness and once, off to his left, he caught the flash of the green-fire eyes of an animal.

He had no clear idea where the mesa ended.

At this speed he could ride right over the edge before he knew what was happening and that would be a disaster.

But it was a chance he had to take.

The buckskin was running flat out now, charging straight ahead, his pounding hooves clattering out the ringing racket of a kettledrum on the rock. Fletcher knew that a single pothole or an unexpected fold in the cap rock could mean death or serious injury for both him and the horse, but he gave no thought to slowing down. He must reach the mustangs before they disappeared. With the dreaded man-smell so close, if there were a way down to the flat they would surely take it.

Then he saw them.

The wild horse herd, around thirty animals, was milling together in the distance, kicking up thick clouds of red dust. They must be very close to the end of the mesa, hopefully seeking a way down to the sage flats.

Fletcher slowed the buckskin to a lope, then a walk. A steeldust stallion with a white mane and tail detached itself from the herd and trotted a few yards toward him, snorting, angrily tossing his head.

As Fletcher watched, the rest of the herd gathered together and, half-hidden by dust and darkness, disappeared over the edge of the mesa. Then the steeldust gave one last defiant snort and stamp of its hoof and he too was gone. The dust, shot through by the silver sheen of the moon, hung in the air for a few moments, then slowly sifted back to the cap rock.

The herd was gone, as though it had never existed, like spirit horses created by a trick of moonlight and darkness.

Fletcher swung out of the saddle, walked the buckskin to the edge of the mesa and looked down.

His eyes had grown accustomed to the darkness, but even so, it took a few minutes before he could make out what lay below.

A steep talus slope, shaped like an inverted V, stretched away from him into the gloom. Over the years the runoff of rainwater from the top of the mesa had carved a deep ravine into the mesa wall, filling it up with an accumulation of sand, gravel and loose rock.

It would be a perilous descent, Fletcher decided, especially in the dark, but where the mustangs had gone, he and the others must follow.

When Doc and Adelina joined him, he pointed out the way down.

The girl, who looked all-in, grimaced. "Is there no other way?" she asked.

Fletcher shook his head at her. "Not unless you want to go back the way we came."

There could be no argument on that point, and Adelina bowed to the inevitable.

"How do we do it?" she asked.

"Easy," Fletcher smiled, pretending a confidence he was far from feeling. "We ride down."

Doc peered down into the slope and shook his head. "Well, Buck," he said, "I said this would be my last adventure and that's just as well. I don't think my poor nerves could stand another. You may not believe this, but I'm a sensitive soul."

Fletcher's smile was bleak, remembering Bosco Tracy and Port Austin. "The adventure isn't over yet, Doc."

"Not by a long shot," Doc agreed, doing his own remembering.

He scooped the calico kitten from his saddle roll and handed him to Fletcher. "Here, take this. I'm tired of playing wet nurse to your damn cat." Doc gathered up the reins of his mustang and climbed wearily into the saddle. "Well," he said, "here goes nothing."

And he rode over the edge of the mesa.

Fourteen

Fletcher watched as Doc took the talus slope, a new respect for the little man's mustang growing in him.

It was the ugliest horse Fletcher had ever seen, its blunt head always surrounded by flies, and he doubted if it went eight hundred pounds, but it was all heart and its wiry stamina seemed to have no bottom.

Until Doc and the horse were swallowed by the darkness, he watched in the uncertain moonlight as the mustang stood on its legs when it could, slid down the slope on its rump when it couldn't, Doc clinging to its back like a leech.

After a few minutes Doc hallooed from the bottom of the slope. "I'm down," he yelled, his voice distant and faint.

Fletcher turned to Adelina. "You next. Just take it slow and easy and you'll make it."

The girl stepped into the saddle and sat her horse, looking down at Fletcher.

"You're wrong, you know," she said.

"About what?"

"About what you think of Hank Riker. He didn't steal your horse."

"Who told you about that?" Fletcher asked, his eyes hard.

"Doc. While you were back exploring the wall of the canyon."

"Doc talks too much."

Adelina shook her head at him. "I know Hank Riker. He's a good man and he'd never be a party to murder and horse theft."

Fletcher thought that through, then said: "Well, if that's the case, he's got nothing to fear from me."

"Just don't make any mistakes, that's all," Adelina said.

"If Riker turns out to be the man, then he's the one who made the mistake," Fletcher said.

"You just won't let it go, will you?" Adelina flared.

"Not until I know the identity of the gambler who ordered Bosco Tracy and Port Austin to kill my hired hand and steal my horse. Like I told you, Adelina, if it wasn't Riker he's got nothing to fear."

"Fear? You? Listen Mr. Fletcher, Hank Riker can take care of himself." And with that, the girl slapped her horse with the reins and rode over the mesa rim.

Fletcher stepped to the edge and watched Adelina go until she too was covered up by the darkness. Then he swung into the saddle and followed her. It seemed that the buckskin was trying to make amends for his behavior on the canyon bench, because he took the talus slope well, sliding most of the way on his rump, but making no attempt to unseat his rider.

The buckskin took the last third of the slope on his feet, picking his way across the loose debris as if he'd done this a hundred times.

When Fletcher arrived at the bottom, Doc and Adelina were waiting for him.

"Now what?" Doc asked, smiling, but looking tired and old.

"We ride south and put some miles between us and Don Carlos."

"I need something to eat and a few hours sleep, Mr. Fletcher," Adelina said, her eyes blazing.

"Later," Fletcher said, no give in him, "when we've opened up the distance between us and"—he spaced his words deliberately—"your husband."

If Adelina was stung, she didn't let it show. She turned on her heel, walked to her horse and swung into the saddle. "Ready when you are, Mr. Fletcher," she said.

Fletcher nodded. "Right. Then let's ride."

They rode across the sage flats for the next three hours, Fletcher often fading behind to scout their back trail, but there was no sign of any pursuit. Just before daybreak, they camped at the bend of a creek within sight of the peaks of the White Mountains. Since Doc was completely exhausted and could take no part in making camp, Fletcher boiled coffee and broiled a few slices of their dwindling supply of bacon.

Doc did summon up the energy to check on Fletcher's ribs, proving that, despite all the long, rakehell years behind him, he still had not lost the medical man's habit of shaking his head every so often, muttering "Tut-tut-tut" under his breath from pursed lips.

"Well," Doc said, after his examination, "they're not broken. Bruised real bad, but not broken." He gave Fletcher a bleak smile. "And the bullet wound in your shoulder has healed real well. Nothing like clean mountain air to help a man get well again."

"Doc," Fletcher said, "as a dentist, you make a fine physician."

The little gambler shrugged. "I was also a pretty good dentist."

After Fletcher and the others had eaten, they rolled up in

their blankets, lying under a dark sky that flashed from horizon to horizon with heat lightning, and slept for a few hours before taking to the trail again.

Over the next few days they traveled steadily south. Leaving Rose Peak behind them, they crossed the Gila, a river that took its rise among the Mogollon peaks of New Mexico, and rode into wild and broken country, the cactus-, piñon- and greasewood-covered foothills of the Penoncillo Mountains.

The three riders forded the San Simon and then headed west, toward the Chiricahua Mountains and Fort Bowie, the northernmost limit of Cochise County, Texas John Slaughter's stomping grounds.

Fort Bowie, a dusty, sun-baked huddle of adobe buildings and log-and-mud-plaster jacales set among towering, cone-shaped hills was no longer a military post. After Geronimo's surrender a year before, the Second Cavalry had packed up and left for its new home in Colorado.

The Butterfield stage station lay close to the old sutler's store, now a saloon, and the officers' quarters served as a makeshift hotel. The headquarters building still stood, as did the blacksmith's shop and the stables.

But little of Fort Bowie spoke of military glory. It was a sad, seedy, down-at-heel settlement, squalid and dismal, panting away what was left of its life under the scorching sun.

When Fletcher, Doc and Adelina rode into the fort the place was crowded with silver miners, shaggy prospectors, punchers from the surrounding ranches, a few bearded settlers and their worn wives in for supplies, the usual collection of frontier drifters and a scattering of lean, careful-eyed horsemen who sat light in the saddle, looking straight ahead of them but seeing everything.

The fort lay at the center of what had once been the stronghold of the great Apache war chief Cochise. And it was from here, in the Chiricahuas, that he had made his war on the white man. For ten years, no one with a pale skin entered the Mules, the Whetstones, the Dragoons or the Chiricahuas without gambling with his life. Many did, and many died, all too often screaming.

Against all the odds, Cochise passed away a wrinkled old man, full of sleep, and two firebrands, Geronimo and young Victorio, took his place. And a new cycle of burning and butchering began.

But, that late June of 1887, the Chiricahua Apaches were long gone, banished to Alabama and Florida, enduring a harsh captivity that would finally break them in body and spirit.

Fletcher learned that Bosco Tracy and his riders had stopped in Fort Bowie for supplies just four days before and, while there, Port Austin had killed another man, a fast Mexican pistolero of reputation said to be "*un mal hombre verdadero.*"

According to the old-timer who ran the general store, Austin had outdrawn and killed the man with a single bullet through the heart.

"He is," opined the storekeeper, a man inclined to be talkative, "the fastest ranny with a gun I ever did see. I kept store in El Paso one time and back in '82 I seen Dallas Stoudenmire work his Colts, and mister, he wasn't a patch on Port Austin."

The words brought little comfort to Fletcher and even Doc seemed worried; Stoudenmire's flashing speed and shooting skill had already passed into six-gun legend.

While Adelina found a room and a bathtub at the hotel, Fletcher and Doc did some detective work around the fort. They gradually pieced together that Bosco Tracy, making no attempt to keep his identity secret, had said he was heading for Tombstone to deliver a racehorse to a man he claimed had already bought and paid for him.

"I know Tombstone well," Doc said, as he and Fletcher drank rye at the saloon. "Back in the old days, I was in a street fight there; me and Wyatt Earp and his brothers Morg and Virgil."

"Wyatt Earp?" Fletcher asked. "Is that the man you named the cat for?"

"The very same." Doc tested his whiskey, made a face and nodded. "Nice feller Wyatt, and right handy with a gun. Didn't drink though, but I was never one to hold that against him."

Fletcher built a smoke, taking his time, thinking things through. He thumbed a match into flame, lit his cigarette and said: "Seems to me, if Hank Riker is in Tombstone, we got the thing nailed."

Doc shrugged his scrawny shoulders. "Lot of gamblers in Tombstone. There's nothing to say Riker is our man."

Fletcher allowed Doc his doubts, then said: "We'll mosey on down that way and talk to the gent. If he's in the clear, we'll go elsewhere."

Adelina, looking fresh and pretty, joined them at their table. Doc offered her whiskey from his bottle, but she shook her head and refused. "I just came here to thank you both for saving me from Don Carlos," she said, her voice cool and measured, totally devoid of warmth. "But from now on I plan to ride alone."

"To Tombstone?" Fletcher asked. He kept the question casual, as though it had just sprung, half-formed into his head.

"Why, yes," the girl said, surprised. "How did you know?"

"Ol' Buck here figures that's where Hank Riker is," Doc said quickly, answering for Fletcher.

Adelina thought for a few moments, then said: "Hank is in Tombstone and he'll be there until after the big horse race. As you know, he was supposed to meet me after that at Roof Butte, but that's now impossible."

"So if Mohammad can't go to the mountain . . ." Fletcher began.

"Exactly," Adelina said. "I will join Hank in Tombstone."

"You can ride with us, Adelina," Fletcher said. "We're going the same way."

Anger flared in the girl. "You still think Hank was behind the theft of your horse and the killing of your hired man, don't you?"

"It's a possibility," Fletcher said, refusing to be baited.

"You're wrong," Adelina said. "I know Hank Riker and he'd never be a party to something like that."

"Then he has nothing to fear," Fletcher said.

"You've said that before, Mr. Fletcher. And I've told you this before—Hank doesn't scare easy."

Fletcher smiled. "Good, because neither do I."

In the end, Adelina agreed to ride south with Fletcher and Doc, her good sense telling her that Don Carlos and his gunmen could still be on her trail.

They rode out of Fort Bowie at daybreak the next day, under a mint green sky, streaked with narrow bands of lilac and red.

Ahead of them lay a hundred miles of wide, lonely country, a hard land of little rain where strange, wind-carved sandstone buttes marched to their south and west, to lose themselves in the blue haze of the distant peaks of the Chiricahua Mountains.

Fifteen

Tombstone, then in the tenth year of its life, was still brawling and boisterous, clinging to the dream of one day amounting to something. Perched high up on the desolate eastern slope of the San Pedro Valley, the population had shrunk somewhat after water flooded some of its mines, but the town still boasted that it was home to ten thousand souls, fifteen saloons, eight restaurants and five major hotels.

As Fletcher, Doc and Adelina rode in along Allen Street, just as the brassy sun was setting behind the mountains, the wide thoroughfare was clogged with mule-drawn wagons, mounted punchers, miners in plaid shirts and heavy boots, pigtailed Chinese laborers from Hop Town to the west of the city center, bold-eyed, painted whores with names like Shoo-fly, Diamond Annie, Margarita and Gold Dollar; and, here and there, members of the respectable element of the town, the merchants and their wives, the women dressed in the height of fashion in big-bustled gowns of watered silk brought all the way from Denver and Cheyenne.

This noisy tidal wave of humanity parading along Allen kicked up clouds of red dust that clung to boots and the bottoms of women's gowns, and Fletcher, momentarily forgetting his troubles in all this excitement, rode through it and around it and loved its every last sight and sound.

Tinpanny pianos tinkled from saloons filled with roaring men and laughing women as Fletcher and Adelina followed Doc into Toughnut Street. They rode to the Dexter Livery and Stables, a long, low-roofed timber barn with a pole corral built along one side, a waterwheel slowly revolving and creaking behind it.

Doc swung out of the saddle and led his mustang inside, and Fletcher and Adelina followed.

A thin-faced man in a collarless shirt and baggy black pants stepped out of the office, one empty sleeve of the shirt pinned to his shoulder.

"Name's Miles Anderson. Two bits for each horse," the man said. "And I'll throw them a bait o' corn."

"They could use it," Fletcher allowed. "Been eating scrub grass and cactus of late." He glanced at Anderson's empty sleeve. "The war?" he asked.

The man nodded. "Antietam."

"Tough fight," Fletcher said. "I was there."

"On what side?"

Fletcher smiled. "The winning side."

"Figured you for some kind of damn Yankee," Anderson said without rancor.

"It was a long time ago," Fletcher said, taking no offense.

Anderson nodded. "That it was, and now it all don't matter a hill of beans, do it?"

As the man put up the horses and tossed them some hay and corn, Fletcher glanced around the stable. There was no sign of Star Dancer, nor, it turned out, had Anderson seen or heard of such a horse.

"Of course, he could be in one of the other liveries around town," he offered.

"How many stables are there?" Fletcher asked.

Anderson rattled them off—the Tombstone Livery and Feed, Dunbar's Corral, Pioneer Livery, West End Corral, OK Livery and Corral, Lexington Livery and the Arizona Corral.

"If the horse you're looking for is in Tombstone, he'll for sure be in one of those places," Anderson said.

It was Adelina who spoke next. "Do you know if Hank Riker is still in town?" she asked.

Anderson looked blank. "What line of work is he in?"

"He's a gambler."

"Lot of gamblers in town," Anderson said, his mouth pinched and sour. "I don't know any of them by name, nor do I care to."

After they'd stepped outside the stable, Doc turned to Fletcher and asked: "Now what? I guess you want to check every livery in town."

Fletcher nodded. "You guessed it right."

"Then count me out, gentlemen," Adelina said. "I'm finding myself a hotel with a soft bed. I'm tired of sleeping on rocks and rattlesnakes."

The girl left them then, though Fletcher was reluctant to let her out of his sight, hoping she would be the bait that would draw in Hank Riker.

But the search for Star Dancer had to come first.

Anderson agreed to take care of the calico kitten until Fletcher returned. Over the next hour, battling to make progress along clogged boardwalks jostling with people, he and Doc visited livery stables from one end of Tombstone to the other but found no trace of Star Dancer.

Only the OK Corral remained, Doc superstitiously leaving it to last. "It isn't that I regret gunning those cowboys, every last one of them a damn rustler and a Democrat to boot," he told Fletcher, "but when a man believes in ghosts and ha'ants like I do, well, the place do make his skin crawl and that's a natural fact."

The corral lay in the northwest section of the business district, bounded by Freemont Street to the north, Allen Street to the south and Third and Fourth Streets to the west and east.

Fletcher and Doc walked across several vacant, bottle-strewn lots and stepped into the center of this square, most of it taken up by the stables, sheds and blacksmith's shop of the OK Corral, flanked by an assay office and the small studio of a photographer named Camillus S. Fly.

Doc nodded to a narrow, empty lot near the corral. "That's where the street fight happened," he said. "Seems a long time ago now."

Fletcher, wise in the ways of gunfights, cast a critical eye over the lot. "How many men?" he asked.

"At the start, I recollect there were nine of us, but a couple skedaddled right quick when the fight commenced."

"Close shooting," Fletcher said.

"It was," Doc allowed. "Way too close for aimed work. It was pretty much just point and shoot until the gunsmoke got real thick—then we were firing at shadows."

Fletcher smiled. "You came out of it all right, Doc."

Doc nodded, his white face lined and old. "Yeah, I was real unlucky that day."

In the gathering darkness, oil lamps nailed to the wall on each side of the stable door cast flickering pools of orange-and-yellow light on the weathered boards. A creaking tin rooster, cut from a hardtack box, stood on an iron pole at the V of the roof and pointed its beak in the direction of the wind.

It was, noted Fletcher idly, from the south and it smelled of sage and juniper and the sharp, ozone tang of distant heat lightning that flashed stark and dazzlingly bright over the peaks of the Dragoon Mountains.

A man stepped into the doorway of the barn, his figure a bulky silhouette against the glow of the lamps that burned inside.

"What can I do for you fellers?" he asked. "If'n you've come to rent a hoss, I ain't got none." He took a step closer to Fletcher and Doc. "Got a mule, if'n you like mules."

Now that the man was closer, Fletcher saw him to be big in the belly, wearing brown canvas pants and suspenders of the same material pulled up over the shoulders of a stained and dirty red undershirt.

"I'm looking for a horse all right, but not to rent," Fletcher said, his voice level, prepared to be friendly. "Big bay thoroughbred that was stole from me."

The man's eyes suddenly became wary, his gaze flickering from Fletcher to Doc and back again.

"I don't have a horse like that in here," he said quickly. Too quickly.

"Mind if we look?" Doc asked.

The man peered at Doc closely, trying to penetrate the gloom. "Doc? Doc Holliday, is that you?"

"As ever was."

"Hell, man, I didn't recognize you under all that white hair." He shook his head and with admirable, if dangerous, honesty, added: "You look like hell, like you already got one boot in a pine box."

"I'm fit as a fiddle, Clem," Doc said. "See, I remember you too. You still get stinking drunk and puke all over yourself?"

"Sometimes." The man called Clem nodded, taking no offense. "Got it down now to Saturday nights mostly."

"We want to take a look inside, Clem," Fletcher said, still trying to be reasonable.

"Hell, over my dead body."

Doc's Colt suddenly appeared in his hand, the muzzle an inch from Clem's nose. "Mister, that can be arranged."

Clem was not an overly smart man, but he wasn't stupid either. He knew you didn't argue or try to reason with a man like Doc Holliday and he proved it now. He stepped aside and waved a hand into the interior of the barn. "Be my guest."

There were a dozen horses in the barn at the OK Corral—but Star Dancer wasn't one of them.

"Tole you so," Clem said as Fletcher stepped outside again, disappointment weighing heavy on him.

Fletcher nodded unhappily, then glanced over to the cramped alley where Doc had won his street fight—and saw big trouble walking purposely toward him. There were two of them, both tall men wearing black, low-crowned hats and fashionable frock coats that reached to their knees. Clean white linen showed under the V's of their lapels, and each wore a neatly bowed string tie.

"My God," Doc gasped in stunned disbelief, following Fletcher's eyes. "It's Wyatt and Morg."

The men stepped closer, both clearing the skirts of the frock coats from the guns at their hips, and Doc grinned.

"Hell," he said, his voice a strange mix of relief and chagrin, "for a moment there I took you boys for the Earps."

"Who the hell are the Earps?" the taller of the two asked. Then, without waiting for a reply, he said: "My name is Luke Tracy and this here is my brother Earl." He stood easy, young and confident, his legs apart, thumbs tucked into his gunbelt on each side of the buckle. "I hear you've been all over town looking for a horse."

Fletcher, knowing what was to come, nodded. "That would be my horse. It was stolen from my ranch on the Two-Bit up in the Dakota Territory."

"Real shame," Luke Tracy said. "I'd call it a crying shame, wouldn't you, Earl?"

Earl laughed. "That's what I'd call it, all right."

"Well," Doc said, trying to give Fletcher an out, "it's been real nice talking to you boys. Now, will you give us the road?"

"Not so fast," Luke said. "I want to know if your friend there is accusing us of horse theft."

"That," Fletcher said, "and the murder of my hired hand."

"Say it again," Luke demanded, his handsome face pretending an outrage he didn't feel, mouth twisting into a mean smile under his sweeping blond mustache. Luke was said to have killed four men in stand-up gunfights, and it was plain to Fletcher that the man was eager to make it five.

"You heard me the first time," Fletcher said. "I'm accusing you and your brothers and a man named Port Austin of murdering my hired hand and stealing my horse. If you deny it," Fletcher added, putting a match to the fuse he knew was ready to be lit, "you're a damned liar."

"Hard words," Luke said. And he went for his gun.

He was fast, very fast. And his brother was even faster.

Fletcher drew, realizing as he did that he was a heartbeat behind both men. As Doc's gun blasted beside him, he threw himself flat, his Colt coming up to eye level in both hands.

Taken by surprise at Fletcher's sudden move, Luke fired but his bullet split the air above Fletcher's prone body. Fletcher fired and saw the man jerk, then take a step back. But Luke fired again, kicking up a startled exclamation point of dust just in front of Fletcher's face. Fletcher, spitting out dirt, fired back and again Luke was hit.

Doc was firing steadily and Earl had also been hit hard, but was still in the fight.

Transferring his aim from the waif-thin Doc, Earl hammered two quick shots at Fletcher, who had now risen to one knee. Both missed. Fletcher emptied his gun into Earl, threw it into his left hand and drew the long-barreled Colt from the holster on his right hip.

But Earl was down on both knees, coughing up blood all over his shirtfront, out of the battle.

Luke still stood, swaying from his wounds, but getting in his work, firing at Doc. Doc stepped quickly from his own curling gray gunsmoke and shot at Luke. Once. Twice. The man staggered a few steps then fell on his back, a cloud of red dust kicking up around him.

Earl dragged himself to the fallen man, whispered, "Luke . . . Luke . . ." and collapsed over his brother's lifeless body.

The ringing hammer of the guns died away and an eerie silence descended over the OK Corral, thick gray gunsmoke, smelling rankly of sulfur, drifting away, borne on the southern breeze.

"By God," Doc whispered, shaking his head, "history repeats itself."

He reloaded his Colt then stepped to the bodies of the dead men. Doc quickly rifled their pockets and Fletcher saw him thumb through a small pile of gold coins in his hand, then shove them into the pocket of his frock coat. Doc took a nickel-plated watch from Earl's vest, regarded it critically, put it to his ear, then tossed it away in disgust. He had better luck with Luke's gold hunter and chain, and these he hung across his own narrow chest.

"Each of them had five new double eagles in their pocket and the whiskey smell is on them," Doc said when he returned to Fletcher, showing him the coins in his palm. "Their share of the money for your horse, you think?"

"Maybe so," Fletcher said. He looked at Doc, expecting

the usual criticism of his draw, but the little gambler had already said his piece and was silent on the subject.

Fletcher pointed to the dead men. "If Luke and Earl were in town, then so is Bosco."

"And Port Austin," Doc reminded him.

Fletcher nodded, his face grim. "Yeah, and Port Austin."

Looking around him, Fletcher saw no sign of Clem, but there was a clamor of many voices and the sound of pounding feet coming toward them.

"Let's fade," Doc said, taking Fletcher urgently by the arm. "We don't want to get tangled up with the damn law."

The two men stepped into the darkness beside the C. S. Fly studio, then made their way back to Allen Street. They had not been seen.

Fletcher and Doc were walking past Spangenburg's Gun Shop when they caught sight of Clem. The man was ill at ease, glancing nervously over his shoulder as he hurriedly crossed the street, now almost empty as people flocked to the scene of the gunfight and the two dead Tracy brothers.

Fletcher and Doc angled across the street and caught Clem on the opposite boardwalk. Fletcher grabbed the man by the front of his dirty vest and slammed him roughly against the wall of the New York Coffee Shop.

"You hurried off to warn somebody," Fletcher said, pounding the livery stable owner against the warped pine boards. "Who did you warn, Clem?"

"Nobody," the man gasped, his eyes wide with fear. "I didn't warn nobody."

"You're a liar, Clem," Fletcher snarled. He slammed the man against the wall, harder this time. "Who did you run off and tell that we'd killed the Tracy brothers? Damn it, who?"

"Nobody, and be damned to ye your ownself. I told nobody."

"Buck," Doc whispered his voice velvet-soft, "let Clement go. I'll handle this."

Fletcher slammed Clem against the wall one last time and stepped aside. Doc had his Colt drawn and it was pointing unwaveringly at the man's groin. "Clem," he began, conversationally, "I've killed one man tonight and now I'm going to shoot your balls clean off."

"No, Doc!" the man yelled, terror cracking his voice.

"You won't be much good to the whores after that, Clem," Doc said.

The man peered through the gloom and saw only ten different kinds of hell in Doc's eyes. He shrieked in fear then yelped: "It was Hank Riker. I told him you'd killed the Tracy boys and that you'd be coming after him. See, I knowed your horse had been stole and it was Riker who ordered it. A whore who slept with Port Austin tole me that. Port, he talks big to whores, wants them to think he's a real bad man."

"Where is Riker?" Fletcher asked.

"Gone. He just rode out of town, a woman up on the saddle behind him."

"Where's my horse?" Fletcher asked, his eyes hard and merciless.

Clem gulped and swallowed. "The horse ain't in Tombstone no more. Bosco left it at my stable like you figured, said he was selling it to Riker. But after Riker paid him, Bosco hoodwinked him. He took the money and the horse and hauled his freight. That was just yestidday."

"Was Port Austin with him?"

"Yeah, he rode out with Austin."

"Why were Luke and Earl still in town?" Doc asked.

"They wanted to spend their money on whiskey and whores an' catch up with Bosco later. They weren't scared of Riker's gun, and if the hoss was stole like you say, he couldn't very well go to the law."

"How much did Riker pay Bosco and the others?"

"A thousand dollars. Bosco took a double share and the other three split the rest." The man's eyes went frantically from Doc to Fletcher. "An' that's all I know, mister. Honest."

"Which way is Riker headed?"

"South. I think he plans to head down Sonora way with his woman."

Fletcher shook his head. "I don't understand why you would warn Riker, Clem, I really don't. Why would you do something like that?"

The man's eyes were very frightened. "Riker heard you was on what folks are calling a vengeance ride. He gave me ten dollars and said he'd give me another ten if I warned him if you ever showed up in Tombstone."

Doc raised the muzzle of his Colt until it was pointing right at Clem's huge belly. "Buck, you want me to put a bullet in him?" he asked.

The man yelped in terror, but Fletcher pushed Doc's gun away. "Let him be, Doc. We're going after Riker."

Disappointment was writ large on Doc's face. He holstered his Colt and said to Clem: "Well, old boy, maybe next time."

Ten minutes later, Fletcher and Doc rode out of Tombstone under a clear night sky full of stars, the kitten in his accustomed place behind Fletcher's saddle. A bright moon rode high over the distant ramparts of the Dragoons and the cool desert air smelled clean, heavy with the scent of sage.

Doc turned his head, his eyes on Fletcher, and opened his mouth to speak. But he turned away without saying a word, then glanced back again.

"Spit it out, Doc." Fletcher smiled, looking straight ahead. "Otherwise you'll choke on it."

Doc laughed and shook his head. "Damn it, Buck, I swear you can read minds."

"I can read yours well enough to know you're itching to say something."

"Just this—you did well back there at the OK Corral, Buck. Almost as good as you were in the good old days."

Fletcher thought that through for a few moments, then said: "The Tracy boys were overconfident, Doc. They'd killed many times before, but I figure they were up against men who knew of their reputation and were scared. When a man's scared, he'll hesitate for a split second before going for his gun, hoping to the very last that the whole thing will just blow away. That momentary hesitation is all the edge professional gunmen like Luke and Earl Tracy ever need."

Fletcher turned and looked at Doc. "We weren't afraid but they didn't realize that until it was too late."

"They didn't realize something else, either," Doc said.

"What's that?"

Doc smiled, lips thin under his mustache. "That I'm a killer. And so are you."

Fletcher was stung into silence.

Killer.

It was a description he'd once hoped lay far behind him, lost in a wild, rakehell past he could scarce remember.

But now it rode with him once again.

And the knowledge of it was like ice in his belly.

Sixteen

Hank Riker's trail lay clear across a shadowed land made bright by the moon.

Fletcher and Doc rode alert in the saddle, their eyes on what lay ahead and to either side of them. Around them shallow hills lifted cold and aloof, covered in sagebrush and cactus, and beyond these, rising out of the desert, loomed the shadows of eroded sandstone buttes, lofty spires of rock sculpted by wind and rain into fantastic shapes.

Riker's horse, carrying its double burden, left hoof prints that dug deep into the sand and Fletcher knew they must be gaining on the man fast. And when he and Doc caught up with him?

Fletcher's mouth was a tight, grim line. There was only one answer to that question—he would kill him.

But would the man's death be for Ginny and Tiny McCue? Would it be because Riker had masterminded the horse stealing and murder that had deprived his child of her one chance of life and had robbed Tiny of his?

Or would it be only for his personal, hell-bent sense of revenge?

Fletcher studied the trail ahead, his mind untroubled.

Hank Riker had done him and his a great injury—and now the man must face the consequences.

There was no right or wrong to the thing. He was carrying out the unspoken but well-understood law of the frontier. It was a law as primitive as it was ancient, demanding an eye for an eye, a tooth for a tooth.

It was the reckoning.

And there could be no going back from it.

Fletcher and Doc rode under the star-scattered canopy of the night, restless eyes constantly searching the trail ahead.

After an hour they found Adelina.

The girl was sitting by the trail on a carpetbag, the right side of her face badly bruised and swollen, and she was sobbing.

"What the hell happened to you?" Doc asked, with his usual lack of sympathy for the fairer sex in distress, a legacy of his turbulent days with the temperamental Big Nose Kate Haroney.

The girl ignored Doc, but rose to her feet and ran to Fletcher's stirrup. "Hank said I was slowing him down, Buck. He tried to push me off his horse and when I begged him not to leave me he . . . he . . ." Adelina's fingers strayed to her face. "He did this to me."

"How long have you been here?" Fletcher asked.

The girl shrugged. "Half an hour. Maybe longer." She looked up at Fletcher, her dark eyes desperate. "Take me back to Tombstone with you, Buck. I'll be your woman. I'll do anything you want. Just take me with you."

Fletcher shook his head. "Adelina, when you ride with the devil you can't kick when he burns you." He turned in the saddle and pointed to his back trail. "Tombstone is that way. You'll be there by daybreak."

"You're just going to leave me here?"

Fletcher nodded. "Yes I am. I'm going after Riker."

Adelina stepped back. "What kind of man are you?" she snapped, her face reddening.

"Right at this moment, a mighty tetchy one," Fletcher said. And he kneed his horse forward.

Behind him, Adelina stood, watching him go. Then she cupped her hands around her mouth and yelled: "*Usted bastardo,* Fletcher!"

Doc looked at Fletcher, smiling. "No need to translate, Buck," he said. "I think I caught the gist of that one."

Fletcher nodded. "Thought you might." He turned his head and glanced back at Adelina, then turned to Doc. "You know, something tells me that young lady can take care of herself. I doubt that she'll ever be forced back to the cold arms of her husband."

"Black-eyed woman like that," Doc said, "will always get her own way." He smiled. "At least most of the time."

They rode on south through the waning night . . . and came upon Hank Riker just before dawn.

The man's horse was lame, hobbling as it grazed on the sparse grass that grew along the bank of a dry creek. The creek was surrounded by a few ancient cottonwoods and it looked like water had not run there in a very long time.

Riker, an arrogant grin on his handsome face, watched Fletcher and Doc come, his thumbs tucked into the armholes of his flowered gambler's vest. "My horse gave up on me," he said. "That's what comes of taking a woman with you."

Fletcher sat his saddle, looking down at the gambler, his eyes hard and pitiless. The man was in his mid-twenties; handsome in a cheap, flashy way, his black hair carefully parted in the middle, a thin, pencil-line mustache adorning his top lip. He wore a pearl gray frock coat and black-and-white checkered pants and Fletcher saw the glint of a gunbelt buckle at his waist.

"You know why I'm here," Fletcher said. "Something lies between us and now it must be settled."

"I don't have your horse, as you can see," Riker said, relaxed and confident, showing no trace of fear. "Bosco Tracy and Port Austin took him."

"I know that," Fletcher said. "I also know it was you who hired those men to steal Star Dancer. They killed my hired hand in the doing of it."

Riker shrugged. "That was none of my work, Fletcher. I didn't order a killing."

"You gave the orders, Riker. You may have been in Tombstone when my man was killed, but it was your finger on the trigger just the same."

Riker's mouth twisted into a smirk. "You can't pin anything on me. Nothing you say will hold up in a court of law."

"You don't get it, do you Riker?" Doc asked. "Right here, this is the court, and me and Fletcher are judge, jury"—he hesitated for a single heartbeat, then added—"and executioner."

For the first time Riker looked worried. His gaze slid from Doc's cold eyes to Fletcher's, even colder, gleaming like gunmetal in the gloom. Fletcher watched as fear suddenly spiked at the man.

"Take me back to Tombstone," Riker said. "I'll face a judge and jury there."

Fletcher leaned forward in the saddle. "Let me tell you about somebody, Riker," he said, his voice soft but the words lancing through the darkness like bullets. "It's a story about a little girl, a sick little girl named Ginny, and I think you ought to hear it . . ."

Riker held up a dismissive hand, his mouth twisting into a scornful smile. "Spare me, please," he said.

But Fletcher pressed on. He told Riker about his daughter's illness and the clinic in Switzerland and how he needed to win John Slaughter's horse race to raise the needed ten thousand dollars. And when his story was over, he looked closely at the man, prepared not to judge the bottle, but its contents. He was hoping for Riker's salvation, trying to find even a hint of remorse or the tiniest suggestion of compassion.

He found neither.

"A touching story, I'm sure," Riker said. "But your kid means nothing to me." He looked up at Fletcher, some of his old arrogance returning. "Now, I demand you take me back to Tombstone and the duly appointed law. You can press your wild charges there."

"Buck, should I drill the son of a bitch now?" Doc asked, his face eager.

Riker's hands went to his gunbelt. He slowly unbuckled and let the belt with its holstered revolver fall to the ground. "I'm unarmed," he said. "If you shoot me now it will be cold-blooded murder."

Fletcher shook his head. "I'm not going to shoot you, Riker," he said. "Like Doc said, this is a court of law and we'll do the thing legally."

A triumphant smile lit Riker's face. "Well, what are we waiting for? Let's hit the trail."

As though he hadn't heard, Fletcher continued: "I'm going to hang you."

"You're whaaa . . ." Riker's face was stricken, terrified.

Even Doc, a man not easily shaken, jerked his head around, and looked at Fletcher with a bug-eyed mix of surprise and alarm.

Fletcher swung out of the saddle and took his cattleman's rope from the horn. His eyes cold, mouth a thin, hard line under his ragged mustache, he stepped toward the gambler.

Riker dived for his gun, but Fletcher saw it coming. He swung his right leg fast, his boot catching Riker under the chin. The man gasped and fell back, gagging, his hands clutching his throat.

"Doc," Fletcher said, his voice flat, "bring the condemned man's horse over here."

Doc swung out of the saddle, for once stunned into silence, and caught up Riker's horse.

"Under that tree," Fletcher said, nodding toward a gnarled, thick-limbed cottonwood.

Fletcher threw the rope over a hefty branch, then hauled Riker to his feet. He placed the loop around the gambler's neck, shoved the man's left foot into the stirrup and forced him to mount.

Quickly Fletcher tied the dangling end of the rope around the cottonwood's trunk and stepped back to Riker.

"Sentence has been passed on you for a murderer and horse thief. Have you anything to say?"

Riker reached deep and at last found his courage. "Damn you," he said. "You go to hell."

"Maybe, old fellow," said Doc, "a prayer to your Maker would serve you better."

But Riker ignored him. "This is a dog's way to die," he said.

"It's of your own doing," Fletcher said, no give and no pity in him. "You should have steered clear of the Two-Bit and left my horse alone."

The night was slowly shading into a hazy, cobalt blue twilight and high above the cottonwood the Morning Star was shimmering brightly. The land was hushed and there was no breeze, the bit of Fletcher's buskin jangling loud as the horse tossed his head and snorted. Over by a dying willow, the calico kitten was jumping high in the air, trying to catch flickering night flies.

"Is there anything else, Riker?" Fletcher asked.

"Go to hell."

"So be it," Fletcher said. He hit the rump of Riker's horse with his hat and, startled, the mount broke into a hobbling trot.

Riker swung, his legs kicking, as the creaking rope tightened around his neck.

It took him a long time to die.

After five minutes, his left leg gave one last convulsive jerk, then his body was still, slowly swinging back and forth under the tree limb in its sharp, gambler's finery.

Doc looked hard at Fletcher. "Jesus, Buck," he said, "you sure make a bad enemy."

Fletcher, unmoved, glanced up at the swinging man. "Riker paid the price," he said. "It was a reckoning."

He mounted his horse, took from his shirt pocket the tally book that every cattleman carried, found a stub of pencil and scribbled a few words on it. Fletcher ripped the page from the book and rode to Riker's body. He removed the gambler's diamond stickpin, shoved it through the scrap of paper and repinned it to the man's cravat.

He and Doc rode away from the cottonwood as the night brightened into dawn, and behind them the body of Hank Riker still swung, his tongue sticking out of his mouth, bloodshot, bulging eyes staring into nothingness.

The paper pinned to his cravat left a message for those who might ride this way, a message, being men of the West and wise to its ways, they would understand. It said simply:

HANK RIKER
UNREPENTANT
HORSE THIEF

Seventeen

Fletcher and Doc rode south toward John Slaughter's ranch in the San Bernardino Valley, entering a broad, verdant land bordered by the Santa Cruz River to the west and the Chiricahua Mountains to the east.

It was because of the mountains that Slaughter had made no attempt to expand further east, the ten-thousand-foot peaks representing a formidable barrier, a chain of terrifyingly rugged, abrupt ledges, cut-up and twisted pinnacles and crags, and unexpected, dizzying precipices.

Instead, he had staked the range to the south, well into Sonora.

Ahead of the two riders lay Slaughter's one hundred thousand acres of the San Bernardino and his upward of eighteen thousand longhorns. Five hundred people were said to live at his ranch, two hundred of them Chinese vegetable farmers, most of the rest the lean, desert-hardened punchers and vaqueros who looked after his cattle herds.

Within the land they rode, no plain or valley was so wide Fletcher and Doc could not see mountains to the east and west. And from every mountain slope they could look across valleys on either side and see more mountain peaks beyond.

To the east rose the Dragoons, then the table land of the

Sulphur Springs Valley and beyond that the Chiricahuas. To the west soared the Serrita Mountains, beyond those the Baboquivaris, and to their south, the nine-thousand-foot pinnacle of Mount Wrightson and then far-flung Santa Rita chain.

The rapid change of a mile in elevation from the valley floors to the tops of the high peaks made for a striking change in vegetation. Heat and drought-resistant plants grew on the flat, desert-black grama and fluff grass, creosote bush, mariola and tarbrush, giving way to thick stands of aspen, yellow pine and spruce on the mountain slopes.

In the canyon bottoms where there was flowing water much of the year, Fletcher saw sycamore, velvet ash, silverleaf oak, madrone, chokecherry and coyote willow. The drier arroyos were lined with desert willow, cottonwoods and hackberry.

Antelope grazed in the open valleys, mule deer in the foothills. Bajadas, desert bighorn, and whitetail deer took to the rocky slopes and peaks. Javelinas ate prickly pear, apparently without pain, and the Mexican gray wolf, or lobo, occasionally drifted north out of the Sierra Madre to hunt them.

It was a wild, untamed land, so vast and beautiful a man could look around him and find it hard to breathe, his heart beating like a hammer in his chest, eyes looking out on forever, awed into silence by the perfection of his God's creation.

All of it, the mountains, the valleys, the silent arroyos and majestic mesas had been brought into being when sedimentary limestone and sandstone deposited under ancient, Paleozoic seas were wrinkled by horizontal compression, exerted by tectonic plates floating on unimaginably vast lakes of red-hot magma.

Later, during a period that lasted seventy-five million

years, molten rock escaped through the weakened surface crust and was deposited along the sides of the folded limestone, creating mountains that glowed red-hot and were later cooled, hissing like angry dragons, by ancient rains.

It was in the shadow of these mountains, in an arroyo cool with black willow and cottonwood, that Fletcher and Doc camped for the night. Come first light they would saddle up and ride to Slaughter's ranch, just twenty miles to the south.

Fletcher prepared coffee and bacon, and not much of either. Despite being heavily salted and smoked, bacon, unless it was packed in brine, did not stand up well to the trail. Fletcher scraped off green mold with his English folding knife and sliced the meat thin, so it looked like he and Doc had more than there actually was.

After the men ate their meager fare, they eagerly sought their blankets. Later, as the night brightened into dawn, they saddled up and once again took to the trail.

Fletcher and Doc rode into John Slaughter's ranch and into turmoil.

A funeral procession was leaving from the front of Slaughter's sprawling house; Mexican women, as was their custom, shrieking their grief behind the wagon bearing the coffin, black lace mantillas covering their heads.

Fletcher guessed the little man leading the procession, dressed up in a dark blue, go-to-prayer-meeting suit, must be Slaughter himself; the woman beside him his equally legendary wife Viola.

Slaughter carried the corona, the funeral wreath that would be placed on the deceased's grave, and his face was grim, stiff and unmoving.

Fletcher reined up beside a vaquero who was watching the procession, and like the rider, doffed his hat as the wagon trundled and squeaked its way past, clouds of dust kicking up from the wheels.

"*Mi amigo, que es muerto?*" Fletcher asked the man.

The vaquero turned and studied Fletcher for a few moments, apparently trying to gauge the extent of his Spanish. Finally he seemed to make up his mind and said: "His name is Juan Garcia. He was shot yesterday."

"By whom?"

The vaquero's brown eyes hardened. "Pistolero. Hombre by the name of Port Austin."

Austin's name hit Fletcher like a fist. The gunman had been here and he'd killed again.

"But how . . ."

Fletcher's question went unanswered. The vaquero spurred his horse to the rear of the procession and joined another fifty or so riders who were following the coffin, some of their mounts draped to their hooves in black crepe.

One of the mourners, a lanky Anglo with pale gray eyes and a drooping salt-and-pepper mustache, detached himself from the rest and walked his horse over to Fletcher and Doc. "Are you here to see the boss about the hoss race?" he asked.

Fletcher nodded an affirmative and the man said: "Best you wait until after the buryin'. Maybe he'll talk to you then, maybe not."

The man glanced from Fletcher to Doc, taking in their lean, haggard appearance and ragged, trail-worn clothes. "You boys been riding the grub line?" he asked.

Fletcher nodded again. "I guess you could say that."

"Head on over to the cook house. They're preparing a funeral feast over there and they'll feed you."

"Thank you kindly, I appreciate it," Fletcher said.

The rider touched his hat brim. "See you around."

Fletcher watched as the puncher rode after the procession, then Doc came up beside him and said: "Well, let's eat, as the man said. This funeral is none of our affair and I'm hungry enough to force down a chicken, feathers, beak, cluck and all."

"The funeral is our affair," Fletcher said. "Didn't you hear what the vaquero told me?"

Doc shook his head. "I was too busy watching ol' John. Time hasn't mellowed him. He still looks as mean as hell with the hide off."

"The vaquero says the dead man was shot by Port Austin," Fletcher said.

Doc whistled through his teeth. "Well, that do put the cat among the pigeons, don't it?" he said. "John Slaughter isn't a man to let a matter like that lay."

Fletcher sat his saddle deep in thought for a few moments, then said: "You're right about one thing, Doc. We should eat while we have the chance. Tell you what, I'll have the chicken and you can make do with the cluck."

Slaughter's cookhouse was a huge barnlike building, built to seat and feed up to five hundred people at a time.

Fletcher and Doc reined up outside and tied their horses to a hitching post. A fat, sweating cook in a stained white apron saw them through the open doorway and yelled: "You boys are way too early. Ain't nothing ready yet."

Like the puncher had earlier, the cook took in the sorry, famished appearance of the two men and shook his head, his inborn Western hospitality getting the better of him. "By the look of you boys, I guess you won't last that long." He nodded to a doorway further down the building. "Go take a seat inside and I'll see what I can do."

Fletcher and Doc did as they were told and stepped into the cool interior of the dining room. The entire floor area was filled with tables and benches and, over by the far wall, coffee steamed in a huge copper urn, cups lying beside it.

Fletcher helped himself to coffee, as did Doc, and found it black, strong and bitter, the way he liked it.

The cook appeared a few minutes later, bearing a platter of thick steaks in one hand, in the other a plate piled high with tortillas. "This is the best I can do at short notice," the cook said. "Make the most of it."

"Looks just fine to me," said Doc.

The cook directed Fletcher and Doc to plates and silverware and soon both men were eating hungrily. Even Doc, his appetite always an uncertain thing, eagerly devoured a couple of steaks and a stack of tortillas.

After he sopped up the last of the gravy from his plate with a tortilla, Fletcher pushed back from the table, sighed his satisfaction, and built himself a smoke.

He had just lit the cigarette when a young puncher stepped into the dining room, his big-roweled Texas spurs chiming. "Mister Slaughter's compliments and he says he'll see you now." The puncher took in Fletcher's guns. "Maybe best you hang those on your saddle horn. The boss is a mite touchy about strangers wearing low-slung guns right now."

Fletcher stepped outside and unbuckled his gunbelts, hanging them on the saddle horn as the puncher had suggested. Doc's Colt, in its shoulder holster, was hidden by his coat and, not being of a trusting nature, he kept it right where it was.

Fletcher and Doc led their horses to the main house and tied them up outside. They followed the puncher into a room with its own door to the side of the main dwelling where Slaughter had his office.

The little rancher stood in the middle of the floor, buckling on his gunbelt. He was wearing boots with two-inch heels, but even in those, Fletcher doubted that Slaughter's height topped five-foot-four.

But his black eyes when he looked at Fletcher were fierce

and searching, and Fletcher realized that if you were not this man's friend, he was best left strictly alone. As sheriff of Cochise County, he'd brought peace to southeast Arizona by hanging, shooting and jailing more rustlers, horse thieves, bandits and bad men than any other Western lawman in history.

"What can I do for you boys?" Slaughter asked. Without waiting for an answer, he added: "If you wish to compete in my horse race, leave your five hundred dollars entry fee with my foreman." Slaughter picked up his Winchester and fed shells into the magazine. "He'll also want to see a bill of sale or some other legal proof of ownership for your horse."

"That's part of the reason why we're here," Fletcher said. "But there's something else."

Slaughter laid the barrel of his rifle on his shoulder. "You've got two minutes," he said, his voice brusque and flat. "I have a posse to lead."

Quickly, Fletcher told of the theft of Star Dancer and his long search for Bosco Tracy and Port Austin. He told how he and Doc had killed two of the Tracy boys in Tombstone then rode south after Bosco. He did not mention the hanging of Hank Riker, though Slaughter, of all people, would understand that necessity.

After Fletcher had finished speaking, Slaughter said: "Bosco Tracy and Port Austin were here. They said they wanted to enter a horse in the race. But when Juan Garcia, one of my vaqueros who was acting on my orders, asked them for a bill of sale for the horse, they failed to produce one.

"Juan said he would take the matter to me, but Austin called him a dirty, lying greaser and drew down on him. Juan was a good rider and a brave man, but he was no revolver fighter and no match for Port Austin. His gun did not clear the leather before Austin shot him."

"Where are Austin and Bosco Tracy now?" Fletcher asked.

"The last I heard, they were headed west toward the San Pedro. I'm going after them and I intend to bring them back here, give them a fair trial and hang them both."

Slaughter's dark eyes flashed a warning. "Names? And they'd better be the ones you were born with."

Fletcher introduced himself and Slaughter nodded. "Heard of you. A spell back, didn't you run with John Wesley Hardin and that wild Taylor crowd?"

"It was a long time ago," Fletcher said.

Slaughter nodded, but made no comment, though Fletcher could see his mind turning. He motioned to Doc. "And who are you, old timer?"

"Doctor John Henry Holliday, at your service," Doc said, giving an elegant little bow.

The little rancher's black eyes searched Doc's ravaged features, his face shocked and unbelieving. "Doc? Is it really you?"

"As ever was."

Slaughter shook his head. "Hell, man, I thought I'd strung you up years ago after that shooting scrape of yours in Tombstone."

"Your mercy," Doc said, a slight, mocking smile playing around his pale lips, "is legendary."

"Is that what they say?" Slaughter asked.

Doc shook his head. "Hell no, they don't."

The rancher roared and slapped his thigh. "Damn it, Doc, you could always make me laugh. I'm glad I didn't hang you."

"So," said Doc, "am I."

Slaughter sobered and looked at Fletcher. "I'm riding out now and you're welcome to tag along. Maybe we can get your horse back." He took in Fletcher from his scuffed, down-at-heel boots to the crown of his battered, sweat-stained hat and asked: "Do you have the five-hundred-dollar entry fee?"

Fletcher smiled and slapped the money belt under his shirt. "It's right here."

"Good," Slaughter said. "The race is four days from now, so we have to catch up with those outlaws fast." He glanced from Fletcher to Doc. "All right, let's ride."

Slaughter's posse consisted of thirty of his own hard-bitten riders and a couple of Ute Indian scouts. A chuck wagon would follow at its best speed, driven by a black cook named Herbert and his assistant, a small, thin Mexican boy called Pablo who looked to be about twelve years old.

Before the posse rode out, Viola Slaughter bustled out of the house, a long, yellow woolen scarf in her hands. She draped it around her husband's neck and said: "Now, when it gets cool at night, you stuff that into your shirt, John. It will keep your chest warm."

"I'll be sure to do that, my dear," Slaughter said, giving his wife a peck on the cheek. He swung into the saddle and waved his hand. "Let's go."

As the others rode out, Fletcher reached behind him and scooped up the calico kitten from behind his saddle. He kneed his horse over to Viola and said: "Ma'am, I'd appreciate it if you could keep my cat until I get back."

Viola smiled and stretched out her hands for the little animal. "Why, of course, I'd love to," she said. "What's his name?"

"Wyatt," Fletcher said.

"Is there anything I should know about him? His little likes and dislikes?"

Fletcher shrugged. "Only that he's right partial to milk and he eats bugs."

After Viola had taken the kitten into the house, Fletcher spurred after Doc and the others.

Deep inside him, he knew the showdown was coming soon and that men would die.

Would he be one of them?

Eighteen

Slaughter, mounted on a tall, Palouse gelding, led the posse due west, across the Sulphur Springs Valley toward the San Pedro River basin.

They rode until well into dark, then camped in the valley in a thick grove of willow and cottonwoods a few miles south of the mining boom town of Bisbee. Despite the tracking skills of the Utes, they had not picked up the trail of Bosco Tracy and Port Austin. It was as though the outlaws had vanished from the face of the earth.

"Hell, it's as though they've vanished from the face of the earth," Slaughter told Fletcher as they drank coffee around the fire. Herbert and his chuck wagon had caught up to them earlier and they had eaten well on fried antelope steak, potatoes and onions with a wedge of peach pie to follow, Slaughter then being old enough and rich enough that he no longer cared to rough it on the trail.

"Could be," said Fletcher, rolling a smoke from the contents of his slender tobacco pouch, "that they've headed north into Bisbee. From all I've heard, it's a lively town."

Slaughter shook his head. "They knew I'd come after them, so they're still heading west. I don't think they'll be making any detours, to Bisbee or anywhere else."

Fletcher thought, but did not voice, the idea forming in his head that, being the kind of men they were, Bosco and Austin probably valued John Slaughter's reputation as lightly as they did his own.

Aloud he said: "I'm almost out of tobacco. I think I'll head that way and stock up."

"I have plenty of cigars and a chaw if you need it," Slaughter said. "No need for a smoking man to go traipsing all that distance to Bisbee."

Fletcher smiled. "Thanks all the same, John, but I still reckon on going up there come first light."

Across the fire, Slaughter's black eyes glittered. "Despite what I said, you think those two killers are in Bisbee, don't you?"

Fletcher nodded. "It's possible."

"You're wasting your time. They're just ahead of us, I tell you, riding hell-bent for the San Pedro country."

"A man's entitled to his opinion, John."

Slaughter sighed and shrugged his thick shoulders. "Well, I'm not your keeper, so you do as you please. But I tell you, you're wasting your time."

Fletcher rose. "I'll go talk to Doc."

"He's feeling right poorly, isn't he?" Slaughter asked.

Fletcher nodded. "When he has a real bad coughing fit like he had earlier, it wears him out. Drains him, I guess."

"That man's knocking on death's door," Slaughter said, shaking his head. "And that's a natural fact."

Fletcher turned to walk away, but Slaughter's voice stopped him. "Buck," he said, "when you get to Bisbee, no whores, mind. I don't hold with whores and neither does Viola."

Fletcher touched his hat brim. "That's a thing to remember, John."

Doc was lying on his back in his blankets near the chuck

wagon. When Fletcher stepped toward him he raised a weak hand in greeting.

"Come to see if I'm still in the land of the living, Buck?"

Fletcher smiled. "Something like that." He kneeled beside Doc. "How are you feeling old timer?"

"I'm so far under the weather, the only way back is through hell."

"Can I get you anything?"

Doc shook his head. "I have my bottle close; that's all I need."

Fletcher built himself a smoke, lit the cigarette, then said: "I figure on heading up to Bisbee at daybreak. I need tobacco."

"You think Bosco and Austin are there, don't you?"

"It's a possibility, though John doesn't think so."

"Hell, what does John know? The Utes couldn't find hide nor hair of them."

Doc lifted his whiskey to his lips and took a long, gulping swallow. He wiped off his mustache with the back of his thin hand and said: "I'll come with you."

"Think you can, Doc? You should be riding the bed wagon."

"Don't tell me what I can't do, Buck. Hell, I have so much fun when I'm around you, I wouldn't miss it for the world."

Fletcher knew it was pointless to argue. "I'll see you at first light, then."

He rose to his feet but Doc's raised hand stopped him before he could walk away. "Buck, did I ever tell you about Kate?"

"Can't say you ever did, Doc."

Doc nodded. "A good enough woman, Kate, but full of treachery and a demon in drink. She tried to stab me one time with a Green River knife you know."

"I'm glad she didn't make it, Doc," Fletcher said, feeling uncomfortable.

"Your woman ever try to stab you, Buck?"

"Savannah? No, I don't suppose she ever did."

"Good. I'm right glad to hear that."

"Well, see you in the morning, Doc," Fletcher said.

But Doc Holliday was already asleep, his thin chest fluttering as his shredded lungs labored for breath.

Fletcher stood there, looking down at him for a few moments, then said quietly: "Good night, Doc." He stepped away from the little gambler to seek his blankets, a strange, cold emptiness growing in him.

Out in the darkness the coyotes were calling and by the fire John Slaughter crossed the yellow muffler across his chest against the cool breeze drifting in from the desert.

Slaughter was already up and doing before daybreak. He told Fletcher to get the damn fool Bisbee idea out of his craw, then head west after him.

"When I catch up to those boys, as I will, I won't hang them until you get there," he said, no trace of a smile on his hard, solemn features.

"I appreciate that, John," Fletcher said.

"Just so you know."

Fletcher and Doc rode out a few minutes later, toward the Mule Mountains and booming, roaring Bisbee with its forty-seven saloons, three undertakers and not a single church.

Doc was pale and looked exhausted, but he was as salty as always, pretending an energy and good humor Fletcher knew he did not feel.

Even his mustang looked dispirited, his ugly head hanging low as he plodded wearily along the trail, the usual crop of flies buzzing around his ears.

The sun was still low in the morning sky when they

rode into Bisbee, considered by those who knew, and those who did not, the liveliest spot between El Paso and San Francisco.

The town had grown rich from the gold, copper, silver, lead and zinc the miners had torn from the heart of the surrounding mile-high Mule Mountains and twenty thousand people walked its crowded streets, all eager to grab their share of the wealth by means fair or foul.

Fletcher and Doc headed for Brewery Gulch, the red-light district, with its saloons, dance halls and hurdy-gurdy houses, and left their horses at a livery stable built between Ma O'Reilley's Country Kitchen and the Silver Dollar New York Bar.

"You boys intending to stay long?" the stable hand asked.

"Passing through," Doc said.

"Well, if it's whiskey you want, the Bon-Ton is your best bet. For whores, you can't do better than the Bella Union. No back numbers there," the man said, warming to his task, "just plain talk and beautiful girls. Rates are reasonable too, just a dollar for a lookee, two for a feelee and three for a dooee."

"We'll bear that in mind," Fletcher said, his eyes scanning the barn. But there was no sign of Star Dancer.

Keeping his voice casual, he asked: "Is Bosco Tracy in town?"

"Who?" the man asked, his face blank.

"How about Port Austin?"

The stable hand shrugged. "Mister, there's a lot of people in Bisbee. No telling who's here and who ain't."

"If a man liked both good whiskey and whores, where would he go?" Fletcher asked.

"The Bella Union, like I said." The liveryman grinned. "The whores have lovely tresses, luscious lips and buxom forms and they're always hot to trot. The whiskey ain't all that bad either."

"I'm obliged," Fletcher said, touching his hat brim, ignoring the man's leer and suggestive wink.

He and Doc walked outside where the main street through town was already jammed with people, horses and freight wagons. Bold-eyed whores rubbed shoulders with bearded, booted miners and ragged border riff-raff, drifted in from who knew where, stepped with predatory eyes along the boardwalks or hung around the saloon doors, hoping for a handout.

Even at this early hour the saloons were filled with patrons of both sexes, smoking, drinking, playing poker, all talking at once, yelling at the top of their lungs. From what Fletcher could see when he got an occasional glimpse through swinging doors, most of the women were no longer young and no longer pretty, the men as varied in manners and appearance as leaves in a forest, from ragged miners, fresh down from the Mules, rejoicing in their enormous strength, to pale clerks in shiny top hats and faultless linen. There were a few lanky cattlemen in from the plains, open-handed and good-humored to a fault, and careful-eyed gamblers of both high and low degree shuffling the cards with thin, sensitive fingers. Usually a piano was hard at work in a corner, battling to be heard above the din of drunken men shouting, waiters calling, chairs shuffling, the coming and going of booted feet and the constant clink of glasses and bottles.

It was a riotous cacophony Fletcher had heard many times before in many different towns and in a strange way it pleased him, the assurance that God was still in his Heaven, the Devil in his Hell and all was right with the world.

Doc tore his eyes from the street and turned to Fletcher, his puzzled face framing his question: "Now what?"

Fletcher shrugged. "I don't rightly know, Doc. But I say we start at the Bella Union. If Bosco Tracy and Port Austin are in town, they'll end up there sooner or later."

"And if we find them?"

Fletcher's mouth hardened under his mustache. "Then we'll have it out with them and after that, well, I don't know what will happen."

Doc's eyes slid away from Fletcher's face and over his right shoulder. "We have no need to visit the Bella Union," he said, his voice suddenly flat.

"How come?"

"Because Port Austin is standing right down the street from us," Doc said. "That's how come."

Nineteen

Fletcher turned and followed Doc's eyes. "Where is he?"

Doc nodded in the direction of a tall man in a black broadcloth frock coat leaning idly on an awning post outside a saloon that bore a painted sign hanging from iron chains proclaiming the name, Bella Union.

"Doc, you sure that's him? Is that Port Austin?"

"Of course I'm sure. I've seen him places. Denver for one, Hays for another. A man like that makes his mark in a crowd."

Fletcher studied Austin, seeing a man of medium height, narrow in the waist and hips, thick black hair spilling in carefully arranged waves over his wide shoulders from under a derby hat. His full mustache was well kept and trimmed and his clothes were immaculate, cut in the elegant style of the frontier gambler/gunfighter that had its origins fifty years before in New Orleans and the Mississippi steamboats.

The carefully tailored and groomed style was deliberate, a way of distinguishing a man of the towns from the open-range cowboy, declaring by his appearance that he was a gentleman of substance and standing in the community, not a thirty-a-month laborer on horseback owning nothing but a mustang and a saddle.

Fletcher had expected Austin to be wearing a gunbelt, slung low on the thigh as many would-be gunmen were now doing, but the man carried his walnut-handled Colt almost carelessly stuck in the waistband of his pants.

But this was a deception. When it came down to it, Austin would be lightning fast and deadly accurate as he'd proved so many times in the past.

The gunman stood relaxed and easy, smiling faintly as he smoked a cheroot, knowing the slim significance of his handsome person, like a dark exclamation point of danger on the boardwalk, was drawing its share of eye-fluttering attention from the passing whores and curiosity, not unmixed with a measure of dread, from men.

Doc's blue eyes hardened. "Stay right here, Buck," he said. "I'll take him."

Fletcher shook his head. "No, Doc, not here in the street. There are too many people around who could be hit by flying lead." He hitched his gunbelts into position and in a tone that brooked no argument, added: "Besides, this is my fight. It's something I can't walk away from. I can't stand idly by while you do my fighting for me." Fletcher's smile was faint. "Man can't live with himself, remembering something like that."

Doc thought that through and reached his decision. "How do you want to play this, Buck?"

Fletcher shook his head. "I don't know. We'll watch him and see where he goes. Could be he'll lead us to Bosco Tracy."

"You can't take both of them," Doc said.

"All right, then you can have Bosco." Fletcher's smile widened. "Of course, if Austin beats me, then feel free to kill him."

"My pleasure," Doc said, studying the nonchalant gunman with the glittering eyes of a predatory hawk.

Because of the crowded boardwalk, Port Austin was unaware that Fletcher and Doc were watching him.

But there were someone else's eyes on the gunman—and they belonged to a face from the past that Fletcher recognized.

"Doc," he whispered, "across the street carrying the Sharps. Do you recognize him?"

Doc, always a tad short-sighted, peered across the busy street. "I don't know . . . wait . . . is it Edward James?"

Fletcher nodded. "As ever was."

"What the hell is that low-down, back-shooting skunk doing here?"

"I'd say," Fletcher said, "he has a wanted dodger on Austin and he's here to collect."

At that moment, proving Fletcher correct, James reached into his stained buckskin shirt, took out a folded piece of paper, straightened it out and studied it closely, his pale blue eyes moving from the paper to Austin and back again. Seemingly satisfied, James folded the paper again and stuffed it back into his shirt.

"He's got a dodger all right," Doc said. "And five will get you ten that Port Austin's likeness is on it."

James was a tall man, dressed in buckskins and a battered black hat. A full red beard spread across his chest, ending at his belt buckle, but his hair was cropped very short. He was huge in the chest and belly and Fletcher estimated he must go at least three hundred pounds.

The man was a bounty hunter and sure-thing killer, and the last Fletcher heard he'd been shooting nesters for Wyoming cattlemen at five hundred a head.

If he'd come to Bisbee after Port Austin, then the outlaw must be worth a considerable sum, dead or alive.

Along the boardwalk, Austin finished his cigar, pitched the stub into the street and half turned to step back inside the Bella Union.

Things happened very fast after that.

From across the street James yelled: "Not so fast, Mary Ann!" He threw his Sharps to his shoulder and fired.

Port Austin turned quickly, drawing his Colt. James's bullet smashed into the awning post where Austin had been standing a moment earlier, the fifty-caliber slug chipping a fist-sized chunk out of the dry timber.

People scattered and a woman screamed. A mule team drawing a loaded freight wagon panicked and took off down the street, hooves and wheels kicking up a thick cloud of dust.

Austin fired, very fast. One, two, three, four shots. At a distance of about thirty yards, every round hit James square in the chest. The big bounty hunter staggered a step or two backward, then roared in terrible rage.

Knowing he was hit hard, he stepped off the boardwalk onto the street, firing his rifle from the hip. Bullets hammered around Austin, thudding into the saloon wall on each side of him.

The outlaw steadied his Colt in both hands, took careful aim and fired again. The bullet hit James square between the eyes and the big man fell, dead when he hit the ground.

Austin stepped to the edge of the boardwalk and looked down at the dead bounty hunter. A slight, cruel smile played around his lips, his cheekbones flushing red, revealing the satisfied, almost orgasmic pleasure of the man who lived to kill.

The gunman made no attempt to reload his Colt, a reflex reaction that had long been second nature to him—and that momentary lapse in concentration cost Port Austin, the most feared and deadly gunfighter in the West, his life.

"Five by God!" Doc yelled, to no one but himself.

In the West of those days, a man loaded only five rounds into his six-shooter, the hammer resting on an empty cylinder as a safety measure—especially a man who shoved a Colt down the front of his pants.

Before Fletcher could stop him Doc walked quickly to Austin, his elastic-sided boots thudding loud on the boardwalk. The gunman turned, a surprised look on his face.

"Hello, Port, old fellow," Doc said.

He shoved the muzzle of his gun into the outlaw's chest and pulled the trigger.

Port Austin's breast burst asunder under the crashing impact of Doc's bullet and the flame flashing from the muzzle set the man's vest and shirt on fire. His entire front smoking, scarlet blood splashed over his immaculate white linen, Austin staggered back, his gun coming up. He pulled the trigger again and again, the only sound the mocking *Click! Click! Click!* of the hammer hitting spent rounds.

Austin looked at Doc, his eyes wide, horrified, shocked beyond measure. "You . . . you . . ." he began.

Doc Holliday, no sentimentalist and not much of a one for talk when there was shooting to be done, raised his gun to eye level in the classic duelist style and fired again. The bullet hit Austin in the chest a second time and the gunman staggered a few steps then toppled off the boardwalk into the street.

Fletcher rushed to Doc and stood there for a few moments, looking down at Austin in stunned disbelief. Finally he managed to stammer: "Doc . . . Doc . . . why?"

Unlike Austin earlier, Doc was already feeding shells into the empty cylinders of his gun. He holstered the Colt and said, his voice level: "I got the drop on him, Buck. Ol' Port shouldn't have emptied his gun and he should have reloaded faster."

"Doc," Fletcher said, "that was . . . hell, that was murder. You gave him no chance."

Doc shrugged, unfazed. "You don't give a man like Port Austin a chance. You kill him any way you can." His cold blue eyes fastened on Fletcher. "I've only met two men in my entire life I was proud to call my friend. One of them was Wyatt Earp, the other is you." Doc smiled. "I couldn't let Port draw down on you, Buck. You've slowed so much, he'd have killed you for sure."

"Doc . . . Doc . . ." Fletcher tried, but he couldn't find the words, numbed by what had just happened. Finally he just stood, looking down at Austin's body, shaking his head slowly, trying to come to grips with what he had seen.

Fletcher felt Doc's thin hand on his shoulder. "I told you to leave Austin to me, didn't I, Buck? Well, I took care of him."

When Fletcher did not reply, Doc turned to a miner in the crowd that had gathered to gawp at the dead men and grabbed his arm. "You," he said, nodding toward James's body, "reach inside that man's shirt and bring me the paper he has there."

"Me?" the miner asked.

"Yes, you."

The miner, not liking what he saw in Doc's eyes, did as he was told and got the dodger from James's body. He returned to Doc carrying the bloodstained paper by one corner.

Doc took the dodger from the miner and scanned it quickly. "Somebody," he yelled, "bring the sheriff. That man there is the outlaw Port Austin. He's wanted for murder and bank robbery, and he's worth a thousand dollars to me."

* * *

Two hours later, having seen no sign of Bosco Tracy, Fletcher and Doc rode out of Bisbee and took the trail after Slaughter and his posse.

The two men rode in a strained silence; Doc irritated that his reward money had not been forthcoming, Fletcher annoyed that the duelist code he held so sacred had been so cold-bloodedly violated.

The sheriff, a harried man with a limp and a worried expression, had told Doc that the reward could only be paid by the U.S. marshal since Austin had been wanted on a federal warrant.

Doc had angrily remonstrated with the lawman, but in the end a compromise was reached. The thousand dollars would be sent to Dr. John Henry Holliday in care of the Glenwood Sanitarium in Glenwood Springs, Colorado, where he soon hoped to be girding his loins against his terrible disease.

For his part, Fletcher had lived a considerable number of years of his life in a highly specialized profession, that of the hired gunfighter. In that capacity he had met men who claimed to be his equal in gun battles that were formal and stylized, governed by the unwritten code that you met your enemy face-to-face and after the gunsmoke cleared, the best man walked away and the loser died.

Doc, who lived only by his own code, had killed a man who had no way of fighting back—and had thus spat on everything Fletcher held dear.

He and Doc rode into the late afternoon among ancient mountains that looked down with cool indifference on the petty quarrels of mortal men, a silence stretching long and unbroken between them.

Finally, it was Doc who broke the silence. "Maybe we should make camp, Buck," he said. "We can catch up to ol' John tomorrow." He yawned. "I'm plumb tuckered."

Still smarting, his professional pride badly bruised, it was in Fletcher to insist they keep on riding through the night, but he realized that would be shabby and ungenerous to say nothing of being downright childish.

"As soon as we find a good spot, Doc," he said, fighting down his annoyance. "I could use a bite to eat and some sleep myself."

In the end, as the first stars appeared, they camped by the edge of some aspen near a small stream running down from somewhere high in the mountains. Fletcher had bought a few supplies in Bisbee—a loaf of sourdough bread, salt pork and coffee—and he prepared a quick meal.

Doc took his sandwich from Fletcher, then, chewing thoughtfully said: "Still riled with me, huh?"

Fletcher shook his head. "I'm not angry, Doc. I'm . . . I'm . . . hell, I don't know what I am."

Doc nodded. "Well, I don't know what you are either. I do know this though. I saw Port Austin draw and shoot and you wouldn't have come close. A dozen years ago you were faster, maybe, but not now. Buck, that man would have killed you and it would all have been for nothing. You have a sick child back to home and a wife who needs you. I couldn't let your pride force you into becoming just another notch on a tinhorn's gun."

"That was my decision to make, Doc," Fletcher said, the flickering firelight shadowing the hard planes of his face and his great beak of a nose.

"It was, but I made it for you," Doc said, shrugging his thin shoulders. "I was thinking more clearly at the time."

"You gave Austin no chance, Doc. The man had an empty gun."

"How much chance did he give John Slaughter's puncher?"

Fletcher was unable to frame a reply and Doc went on

quickly: "I gave Port the same chance he gave the vaquero. And that was no chance at all. Judge me on that."

Fletcher finished his own sandwich and built a smoke. He lit his cigarette with a brand from the fire and said: "Judge not and you shall not be judged. Condemn not and you shall not be condemned."

"Who said that? Was it that Judge Parker up in the Indian Territory?"

Despite himself, Fletcher smiled. "No, Doc, it was Jesus Christ."

Doc nodded. "Didn't really think it sounded like Judge Parker. He isn't the forgiving kind."

"Well, what's over is over," Fletcher said, no longer wishing to prolong the thing or dwell any further on Port Austin's death. He threw his cigarette butt into the fire. "Let's get some sleep, Doc. We got a full day of riding ahead of us tomorrow."

Later, Fletcher lay in his blankets looking up at the stars, so close it seemed a man could reach out his hand and grab them like so many diamonds. Sleep came slowly to him and when it did, it was troubled by visions of Port Austin and Hank Riker, coming to him white-faced in the night, their dead eyes accusing, full of hate.

Both men had wronged him—and both had died like dogs.

Fletcher woke to the dawn, wondering as sleep fled from him if the reckoning had gone too far. He had judged and condemned and already five men were dead because of it.

Now, who would judge him?

Fletcher and Doc met up with John Slaughter at Sonoita Creek, fifty miles west of the San Pedro. The little rancher was returning with a dead Ute facedown across his horse, his long black hair trailing almost to the ground, and two other riders, hit hard, slumped over in the saddle.

"We lost Tracy among the breaks beyond the creek," Slaughter said, his face bleak. "Had a running gun battle that took up most of yesterday, and the Ute was killed and two of my men are wounded bad."

Fletcher was stunned. "You giving up on him, John?"

Anger flared in the little rancher's eyes. "We lost him, I told you. He's probably halfway to Yuma by this time."

Slaughter made a visible effort to calm down. "I have a horse race coming up in a couple of days and the Fourth of July celebrations," he said. "There will be hundreds of people arriving at the ranch and I can't disappoint them. I can't disappoint Viola either." He shrugged. "Anyhow, I got a feeling I'll meet up with Bosco Tracy again. He won't escape me next time."

Slaughter opened his mouth to speak, hesitated, then said: "Buck, I've got some bad news for you."

"What is it?" Fletcher asked, fear spiking at him. Had Slaughter heard something about Ginny?

The little rancher's eyes were troubled. "I don't know how to tell you this, so I'll say it straight out—your horse is dead."

"Star Dancer?" Fletcher asked, unable to comprehend what he was hearing. "Star Dancer is dead?"

"He was caught in the crossfire," Slaughter said. "I don't know who shot him, us or Tracy. He took a rifle bullet in the cannon of his right foreleg that completely shattered the bone. He was in a lot of pain and I put him out of his misery." The rancher put a gloved hand on Fletcher's shoulder. "I'm sorry, Buck. He was a fine animal and he would have given even my Big Boy a run for his money."

Fletcher's shoulders slumped and his chin sank to his chest. It was over. Star Dancer was gone and so was all hope for Ginny. Without the ten thousand dollars his daughter would die and now there was not a damn thing he could do about it.

Unless . . .

He could rob a bank.

Twenty

It was Doc, with his uncanny ability to read people, who saved Fletcher from himself.

He kneed his horse alongside Fletcher's buckskin and said quietly: "Buck, I know what you're thinking, but we'll find another way."

"What the hell am I thinking, Doc?" Fletcher asked, a slow-burning, impotent rage tearing at him.

"You need ten thousand dollars for your daughter. A man who needs that kind of money to save his child's life comes up with all sorts of wild schemes, most of them dishonest. That isn't you, Buck. Maybe in the old days it was, but not now."

"Then what do you suggest?" Fletcher asked, his anger riding him hard. "Maybe you're telling me I should take off my boots and run in the race myself."

"We'll find another way, Buck, trust me."

Fletcher turned to Doc, his eyes hardening to the color of cold gunmetal. "Then let me know when you discover it, Doctor Holliday."

He spurred his horse after Slaughter and the others and did not look back. Behind him, Doc waved his hand back and forth, shooing away a cloud of flies from around his mustang's shaggy head, his face gloomy and troubled.

Fletcher and Doc avoided each other until the morning of the Fourth of July, as people from the surrounding ranches poured by horse, wagon and buggy into Slaughter's ranch.

Texas John's cooks had begun to barbecue three yearling steers and half a dozen pigs over open fires the night before, and the entire ranch smelled of burning mesquite and roasting meat.

Beans, thick with pork fat, bubbled in pots in the kitchen alongside enormous stacks of tortillas and out in front of the house Slaughter had set up ice-packed barrels of beer and kegs of whiskey, which dozens of guests were already enthusiastically sampling.

Fletcher saw Doc, as enthusiastic as any, fill a couple of glasses and look around. He saw Fletcher and walked toward him. "Good morning, Buck," he said, grinning as he handed Fletcher a brimming glass of whiskey. "This will get the old heart started."

"Bit early isn't it, Doc?" Fletcher asked, prepared to let bygones be bygones now his anger had cooled.

"Sure is. A man should always do his serious drinking on an empty stomach. Those are words of wisdom." He waved a hand toward the slowly rotating steers. "Food and whiskey don't mix."

Fletcher took the glass and sipped. The whiskey was good Kentucky bourbon and obviously John Slaughter did not believe in stinting on his guests.

"I'd say we're in for one hell of a party," Doc said, looking around.

"I'd say we are," Fletcher agreed.

Over by the corral a group of Mexican musicians was

already playing and out on the flat beyond the house some of the race entrants were exercising their horses.

"Some fine-looking animals out there," Fletcher said.

Doc nodded. "Twenty entries so far, and ol' John is giving odds of ten to one on his Big Boy to beat any of them."

"His horse is that good?" Fletcher asked, remembering Star Dancer.

"Big American stud. Runs like the wind they say. Of course, the question is, can he stay the five miles?"

That took Fletcher by surprise. "Five miles?"

Doc nodded. "They've marked off the course already. Pretty much, it's a mile around the ranch house and each horse has to do that five times."

"Star Dancer was a miler," Fletcher said, realization dawning on him that his horse would have stood no chance even if he had lived. "He was a sprinter. He wasn't bred to run five miles."

"Takes a horse with a lot of bottom and stamina to go that far," Doc allowed. "John thinks his stud has what it takes."

Fletcher shook his head. "It was all for nothing, Doc. Even if I'd gotten my horse back, he wouldn't have stood a chance."

Doc sipped his whiskey in silence, apparently finding no reply to Fletcher's comment.

"It was all for nothing," Fletcher said again. "All of it. Every damn moment of it."

He thought of Ginny and then of Savannah. He had given his wife false hope, a hope that he now knew had been doomed from the start.

Soon he would face the task of riding back to the cabin on Two-Bit Creek and telling Savannah it was all over, that the whole thing, the clinic in Switzerland, saving Ginny's life, had all been a worthless pipe dream.

Over by the corral the Mexican band was gallantly struggling with the Camptown Races and John Slaughter and Viola were moving easily from guest to guest, greeting an old friend here, slapping a back there, an affable, smiling pair, generally making themselves available to everyone and anyone.

Vaqueros in short jackets and tight pants, wearing huge straw sombreros, danced with Mexican women with gardenias in their hair who swirled with the music, their colored petticoats opening up like flowers, showing a generous amount of shapely ankle. The Anglos, mostly somber and bearded ranchers, smoked cigars and talked to Slaughter of drought and cattle prices while their wives, in staid cotton dresses, took no part in the dancing but stood to one side, clapping their hands to the beat, their eyes alight.

A cheer went up from the crowd as Pablo, the slender boy who had ridden with the chuck wagon, led a beautiful sorrel with a white mane and tail from the corral and sprang into the saddle.

"Everybody!" Slaughter yelled. "This is Big Boy, the horse who will win the race today!"

The crowd cheered again and the sorrel went up on his toes, arching his proud neck, his glossy hide catching the sun, touching it with liquid fire.

"That's Big Boy," Doc said. "Magnificent creature, isn't he Buck?"

Fletcher studied the big horse with unhappy eyes. Finally he nodded. "He's some race horse all right."

"Beautiful," Doc said, his voice full of wonder.

Fletcher had thought not to drink so early, but now he drained his glass in a single gulp. The whiskey warmed his belly but did nothing to lift his gloom.

"Hey Doc!" Slaughter yelled. "You want to withdraw your bet?"

Doc laughed. "A bet's a bet, John. I'll let it stand."

"Your funeral," Slaughter laughed and the assembled guests laughed with him.

"What bet?" Fletcher asked. "Did you bet on another horse?"

Doc nodded. "Put five hundred on him at ten to one."

"But you don't have five hundred dollars," Fletcher said.

"I know that," Doc smiled, "and you know that, but ol' John doesn't."

"Doc," Fletcher said, alarmed, "when you can't pay up John Slaughter will hang you for sure."

"Won't happen, Buck."

"Why?"

"Because I don't intend to lose."

"Doc . . ." Fletcher shook his head. "I don't know what the hell you're talking about."

Doc tapped the side of his nose with a thin forefinger, his eyes twinkling. "But I know. All you have to do is empty that money belt of yours and give me the five hundred dollars entry fee."

"Entry fee? Doc, Star Dancer is dead. You don't have a horse to ent—" He stopped, realization suddenly dawning on him. "No, Doc, no. Tell me what I'm thinking isn't true."

"If you're thinking that I plan to enter my own horse," Doc said, "then what you're thinking is true enough."

"Hell, that old mustang of yours is barely alive," Fletcher said, choking on the words. "He can hardly stand, let alone run five miles."

"Oh, he'll run five miles all right," Doc said. "And five more after that and maybe another five after that."

"Doc," Fletcher said, suddenly wishful for more whiskey, "you're crazy."

"Listen, Buck, I bought that little feller from a smooth-talking gent in a fancy frock coat with a lead goldbrick in his pocket who often had reason to get out of town fast. He says he was chased by more necktie parties than you could shake a stick at and never once got caught. And do you know why?"

Doc waited for an answer, didn't get one, and said: "Right, I'll tell you why—because he was forking that ugly little bronc. Hell, Buck, that's why I paid a thousand dollars for him. I knew there might be days when I wanted to get out of town in a hurry my ownself."

"That goldbrick artist saw you coming, Doc," Fletcher said bitterly.

"I don't think so. As it was, he wanted two thousand but I got him down to one."

Fletcher shook his head, knowing he was desperately clutching at a very slender straw. "Can that broken-down nag really run?"

"He'll run fast and do it all day. Hell, Buck, you saw how he was when we crossed the Divide."

"I saw how he was and he didn't impress me much."

Fletcher thought it through for a while, grabbed Doc's half-full glass from his hand and gulped it down. What did he have to lose except his money? He handed back the empty glass, unbuttoned his shirt and untied the rawhide laces of the money belt.

"I must be as crazy as you are," he said. "No, even crazier, because I should know better." He handed Doc the money belt. "Now you have your five hundred—and God help us all."

Doc took the belt and said: "The race starts in an hour. I'd better go get Thunderbolt ready."

"Thunderbolt?"

"He has to have a name to be entered in the race and I just thought that one up," Doc said. "It's crackerjack, isn't it?"

Fletcher, unable to reply, groaned. Something was giving him a headache—and it wasn't the whiskey.

Doc's mustang had been banished to a small corral behind the cookhouse, Slaughter having declared that the sorry sight of the animal could give his ranch a bad name and make folks doubt his horse sense.

Fletcher and Doc saddled and bridled the mustang and tried their best to get rid of at least some of the flies buzzing around his head.

Doc led the horse to the front of the house, saw John Slaughter who was standing talking to his segundo and yelled: "Hey, John, ready to race?"

Slaughter, thinking that Doc was joking, laughed and waved a dismissive hand, but Fletcher said: "John, believe me, he is not speaking in jest." He shook his head. "I almost wish he was."

That last caught Slaughter's attention. He and the segundo, a tall, lanky man with yellow hair and mustache, stepped up to Doc and Slaughter said: "This is the horse you bet five hundred on, the one you want to enter in the race?"

"Sure is," Doc said, brushing back a stray wisp of gray hair that had fallen over his forehead. "This here is Thunderbolt."

"Doc," Slaughter said, shaking a finger at the little gambler, "you must have money to burn."

"Do you want to see a bill of sale for his hoss, Mr. Slaughter?" the segundo asked, taking the five-hundred-dollar entry fee from Doc.

"Bill of sale, hell!" Slaughter roared. "I bet somebody paid you to take this horse off his hands. Ain't that the case, Doc?"

Doc nodded, his smile thin. "Something like that, John."

"Did the flies come for free, or were those extry?" the segundo asked.

Slaughter walked away, shaking his head. He raised a hand and without looking back said: "See you at the starting line, Doc," and he and his segundo laughed and they were still laughing as they told the story to Viola, pointing at Doc and Fletcher, and soon the woman was laughing with them.

"Doc, you had already told John you were entering Thun—I mean the mustang, even before you asked me for the money," Fletcher said, his pride taking another beating.

"Sure I did. I knew I'd be able to talk you into it."

"I'm crazy," Fletcher said. "Hell, I should be locked up."

"Too late now, Buck." Doc grinned. "Now, let's go get ourselves a drink."

"Wait," Fletcher said as a thought suddenly struck him. "Who's going to ride Thu . . . Thu . . . that damn horse?"

"I am, of course. Who else?"

And again, hearing a reply he did not care for, Fletcher groaned.

Including Doc's mustang, twenty-one horses lined up at the starting line.

A puncher stood at each end of a rope wrapped in red, white and blue bunting, holding it waist high. They would drop the rope to signal the start.

There were a few American horses in the group—a couple of flashy Morgans and the rest were cowponies—but these were tall and big-boned, obviously Wyoming- or Montana-bred, and they looked like they could run and stay the course.

Only two horses stood out—Slaughter's magnificent sorrel and Doc's fly-blown mustang, head hanging so low, his ugly Roman nose was almost in the dirt.

The riders were mostly Mexican boys, small and skinny, chosen for their weight and riding ability. Among the crowd betting was brisk, some of the smart money being laid on a rangy paint that had come down in a Southern Pacific boxcar all the way from Nebraska.

As far as Fletcher could see, the only money placed on Thunderbolt was Doc's fictitious five hundred dollars.

As the starter, Viola Slaughter stood to one side of the nervous, jostling line of horses, a large white handkerchief in her hand. Some of the Mexican boys had their hands full controlling their high-strung mounts, and here and there a horse reared and whinnied, not liking the gaudy rope or the tight-in closeness of the other animals.

Doc's mustang seemed oblivious to it all. He looked to be dozing, only waking up now and then to shake his ill-favored head against the flies.

Dust kicked up from churning hooves billowed in a yellow cloud over horses and riders, and the jockeys were yelling angrily at each other, fists flying as they bumped and pushed to clear some room around their mounts, all eyes on Viola Slaughter.

Doc had removed his frock coat and rode in shirtsleeves, his suspenders down over his skinny hips. His eyebrows and mustache were thick with dust and Fletcher saw him quickly put his handkerchief to his mouth.

Then he started to cough.

The breeze came up, creating devils that swirled wildly around the prancing horses, spinning among their dancing hooves, only to collapse moments later in puffs of yellow dust.

Doc was coughing harder, longer, the dust getting into his tormented lungs.

Viola stood with her handkerchief raised, enjoying her moment, letting the tension build as close to a thousand men, women and children crowded eagerly around the starting line.

Fletcher pushed his way to the front where he could still see Doc. The little gambler was lying over his mustang's neck, his thin body racked with terrible, hacking coughs, the handkerchief in his hand stained bright scarlet.

"Doc!" Fletcher yelled, trying to be heard over the roar of the crowd. "Forget it! Let it go!"

He did not know if Doc heard him. Maybe he was beyond hearing anything.

The big Nebraska paint, the kid riding him battling for a better spot in the lineup, sidestepped and crashed heavily into Doc's mustang and the little horse lurched to his left, hooves scrabbling in the dirt to stay on his feet.

Doc, hanging over the horse's neck, tumbled off and thudded into the dirt. Viola dropped the handkerchief.

From somewhere Fletcher heard John Slaughter yell: "They're off!"

The punchers dropped the rope and the horses thundered over it, leaving a thick, choking dust cloud in their wake.

The crowd, seeing Doc fall and his mustang content to hang his head and stay right where he was, laughed and pointed, thinking this was all part of the show.

Fletcher ran to Doc and kneeled by his side. "Doc," he said. "Hell man, are you all right?"

Doc's face was pale. His skin was caked in dust and blood flecked his lips and mustache. "Help me back up on him, Buck," he said, his voice weak, breathless.

"Doc, you're in no condition—"

"Help me into the saddle, damn it."

"I'll ride him, Doc. You stay put."

Doc shook his head. "You outweigh me by seventy pounds, Buck. I'll ride him." Doc rose on one elbow. "Now help me up, like I told you."

"The others have gone," Fletcher said. "They're halfway round the first lap."

"We'll catch them. Now help me."

Fletcher pulled Doc to his feet and pushed him into the

saddle. Doc coughed again, a sudden gush of blood splashing down his chin and over his shirtfront.

"Doc—"

The little man's boot heels thudded into the mustang's bony sides. But the horse refused to move. The crowd roared with laughter. Doc tried again, harder this time. Nothing. The spectators yelled and jeered and Fletcher heard John Slaughter laughing louder than any of them.

"Ride 'em cowboy!" Slaughter yelled, and the crowd roared.

In the distance, the field was coming fast, and Doc was in real danger of being lapped.

His heels thudded into the mustang again. This time the little horse broke into a shambling trot. Then an ungainly lope. His ears pricked, swiveling this way and that, and the mustang caught the sound of horses coming fast behind him. He shook his head, a cloud of flies scattering into the air, and got the bit in his long, yellow teeth.

His haunches lowered and suddenly he was gone, galloping fast, his neck stretched straight out in front of him.

Fletcher watched the horse go, his spirits sinking. Doc and Thunderbolt had a lot of distance to make up.

Too much distance.

The field was closing fast on Doc, Big Boy, running strong, a hundred yards in the lead. Twenty horses thundered past the starting line, the Mexican boys lying over their mounts' necks, yelling at the top of their lungs, urging them on.

"Funcione caballo! Mas rapidamente! Mas rapidamente!"

Fletcher saw Big Boy gain quickly on Doc's mustang until only a couple of hundred yards separated them.

Doc was going to be lapped!

John Slaughter stepped beside Fletcher, grinning from

ear to ear. "Damn it all, Buck," he said, "I'm right glad I never hung Doc. He makes me laugh."

But somewhere in the recesses of Thunderbolt's dim brain must have come an echoing memory of his wild days on the open prairie, when to be the fastest horse in the herd was to survive. Only the slow and the sick fell to predators, the quick, smart wolf and the stealthy cougar. It was the stragglers that died.

The little mustang's stride lengthened and he flung up his head and flew. The distance between Thunderbolt and Big Boy opened. Two hundred yards. Three hundred. Four hundred.

Doc rode through the starting line. He had not been lapped but he was still half a mile behind the remainder of the field.

By the time the rest of the horses passed the start to begin the second mile, Thunderbolt was only a quarter mile behind them and the ugly little mustang was still galloping strong.

Doc caught up with the rest of the field midway during the third mile.

The sprinters had already dropped out, pulled over by their riders as they felt their mounts stumble and falter, but the two big American studs and one of the Morgans were still in the race, as was Big Boy, now well in the lead, and the lanky Nebraska paint, plus several others.

Doc was slowly making his way through the remaining horses as the fourth mile began.

One by one he passed the Americans and the Morgan and now only had the paint and Big Boy in front of him.

Watching from the yelling crowd, Fletcher's pulse was pounding. Doc's mustang showed no sign of slowing and was gaining on Big Boy with every passing quarter mile.

But the sorrel was running easily, puffs of dust kicking up

from his pounding hooves, the sound like a distant, driving drumbeat.

When Big Boy passed the starting line and began the fifth mile, he was three hundred yards ahead of Thunderbolt, the paint trailing badly.

John Slaughter ran to the edge of the track and waved his horse on. “Ride him, Pablo!” he yelled. “Ride him!”

The dry, dusty ground had been churned up by the passage of hooves and the going was now much softer.

Fletcher saw the sorrel slow, struggling with the soft dirt, and gradually Doc began to gain on him.

Doc was now lying flat across his mustang’s neck, his white hair flying in the passing breeze, drumming his heels into the little horse’s slat-sides.

Half a mile to run.

Big Boy and the mustang were now neck and neck.

The soft going seemed to have no effect on Thunderbolt. He looked even stronger and faster now than he had at the start.

Three hundred yards to the finish.

Shouts went up from a thousand throats, cheering on the underdog.

“Run, Thunderbolt! Run!”

Beside him, Fletcher was aware of John Slaughter’s jaws working furiously, chewing on his unlit cigar, his face stricken.

“Faster, Pablo!” he yelled. “Faster, damn you!”

A hundred yards to go and Thunderbolt was leading the sorrel by a length. Fletcher saw Pablo kick the sorrel in the ribs, urging him on, screaming into his ear.

Fifty yards.

Doc was holding the lead, concentrating on the ride, his lips peeled back from his clenched teeth.

Forty yards . . . thirty . . . twenty . . .

Thunderbolt was flying, his short legs churning, dust throwing up and away from his hooves in spurting, yellow Vs.

Ten yards . . .

Fletcher heard Doc give out a wild rebel yell, then he was past the finishing line.

Big Boy finished three lengths behind him, eating the mustang's dust.

Fletcher threw his hands into the air. "Huzzah!" he roared, grinning. "Huzzah!"

Slaughter wrenched off his hat, tossed it on the ground and jumped on it. Then threw down his cigar and jumped on that too.

When he turned to Fletcher his black eyes were blazing. "Beaten by a sheep by God!" he yelled. "Big Boy beaten by a damned sheep!"

"Baa," said Fletcher.

"That wasn't funny!" Slaughter snapped, then he stomped away . . . toward the nearest whiskey keg.

Twenty-one

When Fletcher caught up with Doc, the little man was leading his mustang around, letting him cool down, surrounded by a grinning, hollering crowd of well-wishers.

Fletcher, never a demonstrative man, nevertheless ran up to Doc and hugged him close, lifting him off his feet. "Damn it, Doc, you did it!" he yelled.

Doc looked down at Fletcher from his lofty perch and said: "I didn't do it, Buck. It was Thunderbolt who did it."

The mustang was taking no interest in the proceedings. His head, with its accustomed cloud of flies, hung even lower than usual and the only sign of his recent run was a damp patch on his back where Doc's saddle had sat.

Fletcher lowered Doc to the ground and scratched the mustang's forehead. "You did good, boy," he said. "Mighty good."

The little horse tossed his head, his bit jangling, and Doc said: "He likes you, Buck. That's a sure sign."

Slaughter's usual good humor had apparently reasserted itself, because the little rancher came stomping toward them, a fresh cigar glowing between his teeth.

"Doc," he said, holding up his hand, "before you say a

single word, I'll give you a thousand dollars for that horse, cash in hand."

"He's not for sale, John," Doc said, smiling.

"All right, Doc, you always were a horse trader. Two thousand. Right now, this very minute." Slaughter took out his wallet from his back pocket, held it up and looked at Doc expectantly. "When do I start counting?"

But Doc shook his head.

"Not at any price, John. This little feller isn't for sale."

Slaughter sighed and shoved his wallet back in his pants. "Well, if you should change your mind . . ."

"You'll be the first to know, John."

Doc raised an eyebrow. "But while we're on the subject of money, John . . ."

Slaughter shook his head, but he was smiling. "Damn it, Doc, I knew I should have hung you."

As day shaded into night and Chinese paper lanterns were lit around the ranch, the party continued.

The ranchers and their wives were now dancing along with the Mexicans, Slaughter's good bourbon and food working its magic, melting their natural reserve.

Fletcher and Doc found a quiet corner where they could hear the music and watch the dancers. Doc had a glass of whiskey in his hand while Fletcher made do with a schooner of ice-cold beer.

Doc, richer by fifteen thousand dollars, had recovered from his earlier coughing fit and was now in high good humor, though he looked deathly pale and very tired.

"Nice people," Doc commented, his eyes wandering over the dancing couples, the Mexican band now temporarily replaced by a fiddler.

"I'd say they are," Fletcher agreed. "Seems to me John would invite no other kind."

Doc was silent for a few moments, then said: "So, Buck, I guess it's over."

Fletcher thought that through for a while, then answered: "There's still Bosco." He shrugged. "Maybe someday I'll catch up to him."

"What will you do now?"

"Go back to the Two-Bit, I guess. That's where I belong."

"There's this," Doc said, handing Fletcher his money belt.

"Heavy. What's in it?"

"The entry fee. The winner was to get his entry fee returned along with the ten thousand prize. Of course, ol' John didn't expect that would happen."

Fletcher took the money belt, opened his shirt and tied it around his waist.

"And you, Doc, what will you do?" he asked, buttoning the shirt again.

"That's an easy call. I've got money now so I'll ride the rails to Glenwood Springs and die in style." Doc's smile was faint. "I didn't tell you, but I never did much cotton to being a charity case."

"Maybe it won't happen, Doc. Maybe you'll get better," Fletcher said, knowing the lie as soon as he spoke it.

Doc recognized it as such. "I've got weeks, Buck. Maybe a month or two. But I won't ever get better. I'm too far gone."

Fletcher hunted around in his mind for the right words, couldn't find them, and covered up his confusion by quickly taking a slug of beer.

Doc reached into the pocket of his frock coat and pulled out another thick wad of bills. "And there's also this," he said.

Glancing at the money, Fletcher said: "That's your prize money, Doc. You sure as hell deserved it."

"I want you to have it," Doc said. "It's for the little girl."

"I can't take that," Fletcher said, his pride stung. "It's yours. You won it fair and square."

"Then if it's mine I can do with it what I want and I want to give it to you. Use it to send Ginny and Savannah to that Swiss clinic you told me about."

Fletcher shook his head. "Doc, this is more than kind of you, but I can't accept it."

Doc sipped his whiskey and turned away from Fletcher, watching the dancers. Without turning around, he said: "You're willing to let your daughter die just to preserve your stupid, stiff-necked pride?"

"Doc," Fletcher began, "I can't—"

His eyes blazing, Doc spun around quickly. "Listen, Buck, I'm not doing this for you. I'm doing it for a child who has a terrible disease and I don't want her life to become the living hell mine has been."

Doc's white hand, blue veins popping out thick on the back, reached out and grabbed Fletcher's shirt. "Do you know what it's like to cough your lungs piece by piece into a handkerchief and wish for a merciful death that seems such a long time in coming?

"Buck, I've stood up straight in gunfights, hoping the next bullet fired will be the one that kills me. It never happened. For whatever sins I've committed in the past, I was damned, double damned, to go on living."

Doc dropped his hand and smoothed Fletcher's shirt. "Now it's in my power to help a child avoid my fate—and you're telling me, as her father, you're too proud to accept my help." Doc looked into Fletcher's eyes, his gaze hard and searching. "I wonder what Savannah would say to that? I wonder what Ginny would say?"

Fletcher was silent for long moments. He knew exactly what Savannah would say. And Ginny. He swallowed hard.

It took a tremendous effort of will to choke down what the years had made of him, but he slowly nodded his acceptance. "Doc, I guess when a man is all wrapped up in himself, he makes a pretty small package, doesn't he? I'll accept your money for the sake of my child and my wife." He hesitated. "And me. You have my gratitude."

"I'm glad, Buck, glad you're letting me have this. It's about the only decent thing I've ever done in my life and maybe I can die thinking about it, thinking about Ginny getting well again. That can comfort a man."

He handed Fletcher the money. "Buck, one other thing I have to say—this has been one hell of an adventure. Damn it, being around you has made me feel young again." He grinned. "You're a straitlaced, fussy old puritan by times, but I tell you, I wouldn't have missed a single, wild moment of the weeks I've spent with you."

Looking embarrassed, Doc seemed to realize he'd opened up too much. He turned and glanced over at the dance where the fiddler was busily scraping out, "Oh I'm a Good Old Rebel."

"Now," he said, "what do you say you and me go join the party? I've got a hankering to dance."

Fletcher took his leave of Doc the next morning.

Doc said he was in no hurry to head for Colorado but would go back to Tombstone for a few weeks to remember old times.

"And some mighty recent ones," he added.

For his part, Fletcher rode for Tucson, there to pick up a train heading in the general direction of home.

He crossed the Sonoita and swung north, riding through a wide valley, hemmed in on each side by high mountain peaks, the aspen on their lower slopes giving way to scattered stands of spruce and towering spires of granite.

The mountains always seem timeless and unchanging, yet to Fletcher they were never twice the same, the trees and grass on their slopes shifting color, the shadow patterns made by sun and cloud always moving, subtly altering the shapes of the ravines and deep gullies.

He was two days out from John Slaughter's ranch when he camped for the night in a grove of stunted oak near Keystone Peak, the trees watered by a small creek that meandered between their gnarled trunks.

The bed of an old spring wagon that had been abandoned years before, probably by settlers heading south, provided dry wood for the fire and Fletcher boiled up coffee and ate the last of Slaughter's roast beef and tortillas.

He had been reunited with the calico kitten and the little cat went off to hunt for bugs and lizards among the tree roots, looking back every now and then with pretended indifference to make sure he was still there.

The coyotes were yapping to each other out in the darkness and once a lobo wolf howled, much closer.

Fletcher rolled a cigarette and lit it from the fire, hoping that the wolf's natural curiosity might bring it close.

He was not disappointed.

The wolf emerged from the darkness like a silver ghost and stood beyond the circle of the firelight, watching him, its eyes reflecting red in the darkness. The kitten sensed danger and quickly scuttled back to the fire and slid between Fletcher's legs like a snake, it lifted nose peeking out now and then to test the wind.

Fletcher smoked and watched the wolf until the animal grew bored and melted back into the darkness. Above him a crescent moon, surrounded by a blushing halo of violet and blue, rode high in the sky and one by one the night stars were making their appearance.

The breeze was from the north, smelling of pine and

sage, rustling among the leaves of the oaks, whispering tales of where it had been, of cold places where icebergs as big as castles drifted in gray seas and white bears hunted the sleek, naked seals.

Fletcher closed his eyes . . . lulled by the silence of the night and the murmur of the trees. The kitten climbed onto his chest and began to purr. . . . The darkness drifted in on him, crowding around his camp, heavy with the promise of sleep, and the coyotes were no longer calling.

"Hello the camp!"

Fletcher woke with a start, the kitten jumping off his chest in alarm.

"Hello the camp!"

Conscious of the ten thousand dollars in the money belt around his waist under his shirt, Fletcher rose and picked up his Winchester.

"Come on ahead," he yelled. "Real slow and easy."

Out in the darkness a man laughed. "I'm not hunting trouble," he called. "I'm riding in."

Slowly, a horse and rider emerged from the darkness and stopped just beyond the firelight. Fletcher saw the man reach into a pocket, then pin a star onto his shirtfront.

"Name's Henry Graham," the man said. "I'm a Deputy United States Marshal and I'm a known man in these parts."

"Not to me you're not," Fletcher said. "Ride closer, let me see you plain."

Graham did as he was told and Fletcher saw a tall man, gone to fat in the belly, a huge walrus mustache adorning his top lip, his several chins free of beard.

"I was looking for a place to make camp when I smelled your coffee," Graham said. "I thought, 'What the hell, might as well be sociable,' so I rode on over."

Now that he could see the man better, Fletcher noticed that the walnut handle of the Colt that rode his hip and the stock of his rifle sticking up from the boot were well worn, indicating a lot of use.

U.S. marshal or not, fat or not, this man was no pilgrim.

"Step down and set," Fletcher said after a few moments, making up his mind about the stranger. "I have no grub, but there's coffee and you're welcome to it."

"I'm right obliged," Graham said.

The man quickly unsaddled his horse and staked the animal on a patch of good grass. He retrieved a tin cup and a small, brown paper package from his blanket roll, then strolled over to the fire. He was light on his feet, as many fat men are, moving with an easy, fluid grace that belied his great size.

Graham helped himself to coffee and opened the package. "Widder woman a piece south of here made this up for me," he said. "It's a boiled chicken sandwich. Got some dill pickle on it too." Graham hesitated, like a man who dreaded the answer to the question he was about to ask. "Maybe you'd care to share it with me?"

Fletcher shook his head. "Thanks, but I just ate."

Graham looked relieved and took a huge bite. He chewed thoughtfully for a few moments, studying Fletcher from frank, dark brown eyes, then said: "Right unsociable of me I'm sure, but I don't recollect your name."

"I didn't give it," Fletcher said.

"Ah, then that's the explanation," Graham said, taking another bite of his sandwich while at the same time taking no offense.

Fletcher smiled. "It's Buck Fletcher. I'm from up Two-Bit Creek way in the Dakota Territory."

"You've traveled a fair piece," Graham said. "And I heard your name quite recent and maybe a time or two before that."

Fletcher saw the man frown, obviously studying what he

was going to say next, trying not to give offense. Finally he said: "Heard you and another feller got into a shooting scrape in Tombstone. Two of the Tracy boys gone."

"The other feller was Doc Holliday," Fletcher said, building a smoke. "Earl and Luke Tracy came at us with drawn Colts, meaning to kill us." Fletcher lit his cigarette. "They didn't make it."

Graham took time to absorb this information, then said: "The OK Corral livery stable man . . ." Graham hesitated. "I can't recall his name . . ."

"Clem," Fletcher supplied.

"Yeah, that's it, Clem. Well, anyhoo, he tells it different."

"He's a liar," Fletcher said, his voice flat, without malice.

Graham nodded. "He ain't much, that's for sure."

The lawman let it go at that, stuffed the remainder of his sandwich in his mouth and licked his fingers. "I was surprised to hear Doc Holliday's name after all these years," he said, swallowing, his chins bobbing. "I was told he'd passed away a spell back."

"Not hardly," Fletcher said, prepared to dislike this man.

Graham nodded. "No, I guess not. He was pretty lively in Bisbee. Has a thousand dollar ree-ward coming for gunning Port Austin. Bad man, ol' Port, and mighty handy with the Colt."

Fletcher did not comment, the memory of Austin's death still rankling. Out in the night a restless owl made its presence known to the darkness and something rustled in the dead leaves at the base of a cottonwood. A stick fell in the fire, sending up a small shower of sparks toward a sky where the crescent moon was horning aside a solitary cloud and the scattered stars were playing a silent nocturne.

"Nice kitten you got there," Graham said, nodding toward the calico.

"He rides with me," Fletcher said. "He isn't any trouble.

Finds his own grub mostly, though he'll eat bacon and he's right partial to milk when he can get it."

"Cats like milk," Graham said. "And that's a natural fact."

He leaned back and reached into his pants pocket, rustled around and brought out a small paper bag that he opened and extended to Fletcher. "Broken up stick candy," he said. "Peppermint. Helps settle a man's stomach."

Fletcher shook his head and Graham said: "No? Well, if you don't mind, I'll just help myself."

The lawman took a chunk of candy and popped it in his mouth. He sucked the candy in silence for a while, then said: "Can I call you Buck?"

Fletcher shrugged. "Sure. One name's as good as another."

Graham nodded. "You can call me Hank. Only my mother called me Henry." He sighed. "She's gone now. The croup took her at last a year back. She was called Henrietta, though that wasn't really her given name, but she named me Henry after her ownself anyhow."

Graham's shrewd eyes searched Fletcher's face. "Now," he said, "you talk about names, I was told one a few days back and that name is why I'm here." He leaned forward, the candy bulging his cheek. "Might interest you too, Buck."

Fletcher was sleepy and only half-listening. "What name would that be?" he asked.

"Bosco Tracy."

Now Fletcher was all attention. He jerked upright, his elbows on his knees. "What about Bosco Tracy?"

Graham grinned. "Thought that might wake you up." He shifted the candy in his mouth, sucked on it for a few moments, then said: "About a week ago Bosco Tracy and two other bad ones robbed the Nogales stage. Killed the driver and stole watches, rings and paper money and coin from the passengers to the tune of three hundred dollars." The lawman leaned forward, pinning Fletcher with his eyes. "Bosco now, he was mighty part'iclar about questioning those passengers, said he was hunting a man and needed information."

Graham sat back, a look of smug satisfaction on his face. "He give them the name of that man, and it was your name, Buck." The lawman noisily shifted the candy in his mouth again and said: "The telegraph has been real busy, spreading the news of the Tracy killings all over the territory. You take Bosco now, I reckon he was bound to hear who it was that gunned his kin."

"Where is Tracy now?" Fletcher asked.

The fat man looked disappointed at Fletcher's lack of reaction. "He's heading north. I've been on his trail now for three days, but so far all I've done is bring in a dry hole. I reckon maybe he and them two others could be headed for Tucson. That's where the whiskey and the whores are and Bosco Tracy has money to spend."

Graham rustled in the paper bag and found another piece of candy. "Say, how did you get involved with them Tracy boys in the first place anyhow?" The man rubbed his star with the heel of his hand. "I'm asking this in my official capacity as Deputy United States Marshal, you understand."

Fletcher had told the story many times before, and now he made short work of it.

". . . and the ten thousand dollars Doc Holliday gave me is in a money belt around my waist," he concluded. "I'm on my way back to the Two-Bit, figured to catch a boxcar in Tucson."

"I'm right sorry to hear about your little girl, and your hired hand and your horse," Graham said. "A whole heap of miseries like that can really hurt a man."

Fletcher nodded but said nothing, deflecting any inclination the lawman might have to extend more unwanted sympathy.

"I have a proposition for you, Buck." Without waiting for a reply, Graham forged ahead: "Why don't we ride north together? We both have our reasons for finding Bosco Tracy and two guns are better than one, especially now that Bosco has Lonnie Eaton and Josh Ivers riding with him."

"Who are they?" Fletcher asked, avoiding the question by asking his own.

Graham shrugged. "A couple of small-time rustlers and tinhorns, but they're both gun handy. Lonnie killed a man in Douglas about a month ago and another across the border in Santa Cruz. Josh now, he was raised by an elderly aunt and uncle. When he was fourteen he murdered them both with a wood ax for the money they kept in a tin box and the old man's horse. That was ten years ago and I'm told his disposition hasn't improved any since."

Fletcher shook his head at the lawman. "Graham—"

"Hank, Buck, please."

"All right, Hank, you didn't ride into my camp by accident, just because you smelled my coffee, did you?"

Graham smiled. "Ah, you've caught me out, Buck. John Slaughter told me where you were headed and I've been following you ever since."

"I didn't see any dust on my back trail."

"No, well you wouldn't, would you?"

Fletcher suddenly found a measure of grudging respect for this man. Hank Graham came across as a fat buffoon, but that was far from the truth. He was an expert tracker and Indian enough not to make his presence known.

"I'll ride with you as far as Tucson," Fletcher said. "After that, I have pressing business on the Two-Bit."

"Fair enough, Buck." Graham extended his hand across the fire. "Let's shake on it to seal the bargain like."

Fletcher took the man's hand, expecting it to be fat and flabby. It was neither. The palm was hard, the fingers strong, the grip firm.

There was, Fletcher decided, hidden steel in this man.

Graham sat back and rustled in another pocket. He brought out a second paper bag, offered it to Fletcher and said: "These here are lemon drops, Buck. Do you like lemon drops?"

Twenty-two

Fletcher and Graham rode into Tucson two days later.

Graham checked with the local marshal, but the man had not seen anything of Bosco Tracy or the two other riders, all three men being known to him.

They kicked their heels in town for another day, Graham spending most of his time exploring the restaurants, and the urge to get back to the Two-Bit began to gnaw at Fletcher.

The way her illness was getting worse, the sooner Ginny got to Switzerland the better.

At breakfast on the following morning he told Graham this much. The lawman had a plate piled with food in front of him but took time to put down his fork and say: "Well, I don't blame you none, Buck. We're on a cold trail sure enough and I reckon ol' Bosco has us bumfuzzled."

While Graham ate, Fletcher rolled a smoke and drank his coffee. Outside the streets were becoming alive and there was a constant coming and going of feet on the boardwalk.

The restaurant door swung wide and the town marshal stepped inside. He was a tall, bearded man wearing a gray suit, flowered vest and a cravat of the same material. As far as Fletcher could see, he did not carry a gun.

"Have some news for you, Hank," the lawman said. "Just got it in on the wire."

Graham spoke around a mouthful of flapjack. "Tell me all, John."

"Ain't much to tell except a man answering Bosco Tracy's description just robbed a bank north of here in San Manuel. Killed a teller and then gunned a local deputy while making his escape. The man is in bad shape but is likely to recover."

Graham tore the checkered napkin from around his neck. "Which way is Tracy headed? Does anybody know?"

"He and two others were seen just west of the San Pedro, riding north toward the Black Mountain country. A posse out of San Manuel chased them for a few miles, but had a man wounded and a horse killed and turned back."

Graham lifted his plate to just under his bottom lip, wolfed down his remaining food by stuffing it into his mouth with a fork, then slammed down the plate and rose to his feet.

"I'm riding," he said. He turned to Fletcher and stuck out his hand. "Been nice knowing you, Buck. Have a safe trip back to the Two-Bit."

Graham grabbed his hat from the rack and stomped toward the door, his spurs ringing.

"Wait," Fletcher said, cursing himself even as he said it. "I'll go with you."

"You've no call to do that," Graham said, surprised. "You need to get home."

"I know, but if Tracy is that close, I'd like to get a piece of him. He owes me and mine big time. Besides, like you said a few days ago, two guns are better than one. I can't just stand by and let you ride out of here alone."

"Right glad to have you along, Buck," Graham said, smiling, his relief evident. "Now, let's hit the trail."

* * *

Fletcher and Graham rode through a green, fertile valley west of the San Pedro, the looming bulk of the Santa Catalina Mountains to their east shaded purple by the lifting sun, the first rays touching the tips of the pines and spruce with gold.

Ahead lay the towering, flat-topped spire of Black Mountain, its slopes cut through with deep ravines and gullies, and beyond that the wide, swift-flowing Gila, surrounded by grass-covered mesas that here and there rose into high, rawboned ridges of rock.

Tom turkeys called from the aspen, a sound that set Graham's mouth to watering. "Maybe we can shoot one of them for supper, Buck," he said. "I'm right partial to a nice bait o' roast turkey."

The Apache menace was gone, but the land around them was still mostly unsettled, and for hours Fletcher saw nothing but mountains and sky, the grass of the valley stretching away in front of them, carpeting the long miles. Here and there ocotillo cactus still maintained the scarlet blossoms that had appeared in spring, growing in clusters of straight, thorn-covered poles, ten to fifteen feet in height. In the desert south, where there was always a shortage of wood, the poles were used to build fences and the vaqueros swore that they were stronger than timber and lasted longer.

At noon, they made camp at the mouth of a shallow arroyo in the Santa Catalina foothills and boiled coffee, frying some of the bacon they'd brought with them, then took to the trail again.

Graham constantly scanned the ground as he rode, a bent blade of grass or a broken greasewood twig speaking volumes to him that Fletcher could not even guess at.

"They came this way all right," Graham said. "Three riders, taking it mighty easy if you ask me."

Late in the afternoon, Graham shot a couple of quail that had been pecking around the roots of a yucca, setting a cloud of white yucca moths to dancing like tattered pieces of paper around the plant.

"See that," Graham said. "Neither the yucca nor its moth can live one without the other. When the plant's flower appears in late June, the female yucca moth visits, gathers up a ball of pollen, then flies with it to another flower which she pollinates. The yucca repays the favor by allowing the moth to lay her eggs on its flower. When the larvae hatch, they feed on the seeds at the base of the blossom."

"How do you know all this, Hank?" Fletcher asked.

The fat man shrugged. "My ma taught me. She knew these things, being Jicarilla Apache an' all."

As the long day shaded into a pale twilight, they had seen no sign of Bosco Tracy and his men.

"We'll catch them tomorrow, Buck," Graham said. "I reckon we'll run 'em down this side of the Gila."

"I sure hope so," Fletcher said with feeling. "I still have to get back to the Two-Bit."

"A laudable ambition." Graham nodded. "Of course, that's if we're both lucky enough to survive this thing."

They were just south of Black Mountain, looking for a suitable place to camp, when they found the cabin.

It had been built in against the slope of a low foothill that pointed like a sloping finger away from the mountains toward the valley. No smoke came from the chimney and oil lamps had not been lit against the gathering darkness.

"Abandoned, you think?" Fletcher asked.

Graham nodded. "Maybe so, and maybe for a long time."

"Good place to camp," Fletcher said. "There must be water close by."

"Maybe," Graham said. But his dark eyes were wary, searching the cabin and the crest of the hill. The marshal slid his Winchester out of the boot and nodded to Fletcher to do the same. "Let's just ride in real slow and easy," he said. "There's something about that there cabin I don't like."

Fletcher smiled. "You spooked, Hank?"

The man did not smile in return. "Yes I am," he said.

They rode closer, Graham stopping every now and again to study the ground. At one point he kneeled, nodded to himself, and swung heavily back into the saddle.

Graham's horse walked on careful feet, knowing this land and its dangers, and the fat man's eyes were everywhere, watching, examining the lay of the ground in front of him.

They passed a high outcropping of red, sandstone rock and a deer bounded away from them, its upraised tail flashing a warning as it ran. Fletcher's grip tightened on his rifle, his knuckles growing white. Like Graham, he now had a premonition that something here was badly amiss. His buckskin, feeling the sudden tenseness of the man on his back, began to act up, tossing his head against the bit, trying to side-step away from the cabin where he sensed the danger lay.

"Easy now, Buck," Graham said, his voice low and urgent. "Easy now."

The cabin showed signs of having been recently occupied. There was a vegetable garden out front, and a well-built pole corral off to one side. Beyond the corral were an outhouse and a small shed with a tarpaper roof.

They found the first dead man in the vegetable garden, his body partly covered by the papery stalks of brown, sun-scorched corn plants.

Graham swung out of the saddle and examined the body. The man had been shot several times, at a range close enough to have set his shirt to smoldering. His arms had been folded across his chest and his eyes were closed with flat river pebbles.

Fletcher found a half-grown boy with freckles and a shock of yellow hair over by the pole corral. He too was dead, shot once in the back, obviously while trying to run away. Unlike the older man, his body had not been touched.

The cabin door was ajar, the interior dark, and Fletcher felt a mounting dread of going inside, already guessing at what he would find.

Graham stepped closer to the cabin, rifle at his hip. He motioned to Fletcher with the barrel, indicating that he should go inside.

Swallowing hard, Fletcher walked to the cabin door and stepped through it into the dark interior, his Winchester ready. It took a few moments for his eyes to become accustomed to the darkness, but gradually he saw a small, well-kept room, with a woodstove on the opposite wall. There was a table and a few chairs and an oil lamp hanging by a chain from a roof beam. A small organ with some sheet music still in place stood in a corner, a vase of wildflowers on its mahogany top.

Fletcher thumbed a match into flame and lit the lamp, Graham stepping quietly beside him.

A door to the left that must lead to a bedroom was partly open. Fletcher took the lamp and walked on cat feet to the door. He pushed it open with his rifle and stepped inside, holding the lantern high.

There was a woman on the bed, naked, her legs spread wide, and she'd been stabbed in the chest and belly many times. Flies buzzed around the blood-splashed body as Fletcher stepped closer. The woman was not pretty, no longer young, with gray showing in her black hair. Her shoulders and breasts were covered in bites, the angry red arcs of human teeth, and her face was badly bruised.

Graham took in the scene at a glance, his face stricken. "I reckon all three of them raped her," he said. "Many times. Then, when they'd finished with her, they murdered her." The lawman shook his head. "The dead boy outside once called this woman ma. Hard to believe that now."

Fighting down a wave of nausea, Fletcher asked: "What makes you think this was Bosco Tracy's work?"

"Tracks outside are the same as the ones as we've been following. There's one that's unmistakable because the horse has a special rear shoe built up on the right side." Graham's face was bleak. "It was Tracy all right, and Lonnie Eaton and Josh Ivers." He spat as though the names had left a sour taste in his mouth. "Low-down bastards."

Graham turned to Fletcher, his eyes blazing. "Buck, I'm a duly appointed officer of the law, but I want to find these men, find them and kill them."

"That will have to wait," Fletcher said. "Right now we have a burying to do."

The marshal shook his head, his chins shaking. "This is cattle country. Ground around is too hard, just an inch or two of soil covering bedrock. We'd be at it all night and it would wear us out. No, we'll bring the other bodies inside and see if we can find some kerosene."

Fletcher and Graham carried the two bodies into the cabin, then Graham said he was going to make the woman decent. When he returned from the bedroom he and Fletcher laid the bodies of her husband and son on the bed beside her. The marshal had done what he could. He had closed the woman's legs and pulled the sheet over her face.

They found a can of coal oil in the shed and Graham poured it over the bed and the walls and floor of the cabin. Both men stepped outside and Graham threw the oil lamp through the open door. The cabin was set ablaze immediately and soon roaring yellow and orange flames began to cartwheel through both rooms.

Fletcher stood with Graham for a few minutes, watching the place burn.

"Dear Lord, these poor folks didn't have much, didn't expect much, but they deserved better," Graham said after a while, turning his eyes toward a dark, uncaring sky. "And I reckon that's all the prayer I have in me."

In silence, he and Fletcher swung into the saddle and rode away.

Behind them the fire still blazed, staining the deepening night a dull scarlet. They did not look back.

Twenty-three

Fletcher and Graham rode on through the darkness, each man aware that they were still twenty miles south of the Gila, and beyond lay the peaks and deep canyons of the Superstitions, a maze of brush-choked gulches and arroyos where they would lose all chance of finding Tracy and the others.

They paused briefly in the early morning hours to drink coffee and eat, seeking their blankets for a hasty hour's sleep before taking to the trail again. Graham, who seemed to have eyes like a cat, dismounted every now and then to study tracks, occasionally crumbling horse droppings in his fingers.

The crescent moon was dropping low in the sky when Graham stopped and pointed to the ground ahead of them.

"They swung northwest," he said. "Right about here."

The flat valley had narrowed, sloping upward toward grass-covered foothills that rose to meet table land and then higher, reaching away to mountains covered in pine, cedar and oak, green arrowheads of juniper growing thick in the higher reaches. Among the pines, wild grapes, cherries, strawberries and blackberries were ripening and Fletcher smelled sage and the sharp, lemon tang of creosote bush.

He built a smoke, thumbed a match into fire and lit the cigarette. "Any idea where they might be headed?"

Graham shrugged. "If memory serves me right, the Gila heads up that way and meets the Santa Cruz near an old, abandoned Pima village. There's nothing there that would interest Bosco Tracy. But thirty miles beyond that is the Salt River and Phoenix, a fair-sized town for these parts." Graham leaned over in the saddle and spat. "They've had their appetite whetted for what a woman can give them, and there are whores in Phoenix."

"Seems logical, Hank," Fletcher allowed. "I guess we ride up that way."

Graham nodded. "That we do." He turned to Fletcher. "Ride wakeful from now on, Buck. If Tracy is scouting his back trail, he and his boys could be laying for us."

Fletcher and Graham swung to the northwest, riding over a succession of low-lying hills, many of them cut through by narrow, bubbling creeks coming off the mountains.

As night shaded into dawn, a whispering wind rose that in other years would have heralded rain. But the air was dry and the hooves of the horses kicked up little plumes of dust, the drought that had lasted since January showing no sign of ending.

Vireos sang their sweet song among the aspen and buntings, jays and grosbeaks quarreled in the branches, sending down showers of bright yellow leaves.

Around ten in the morning, by Graham's watch, they found the body of Lonnie Eaton.

The man lay on his back, his pants and long johns down around his knees, his genitals severed and stuffed into his mouth.

Eaton was young and at one time might have been handsome, but the bullet that had entered the back of his head had exited at the bridge of his nose, blowing out one of his eyes. The remaining eye, a light, clear blue, was wide open, staring into the bright sky but seeing nothing.

Graham and Fletcher both swung out of the saddle and stepped beside Eaton's body.

"My God," Graham gasped, "that's a hell of a thing to do to a man."

Fletcher looked around him, the short hairs at the back of his neck rising. "Who would do this? Was it Bosco Tracy?"

Graham shook his head. "Not Bosco. He wouldn't have any cause to kill one of his own men and . . ." Graham pointed the toe of his boot to Eaton's grotesquely stuffed mouth, ". . . and as sure as hell no cause to do that."

The marshal studied the ground around Eaton's body, then rose, his face troubled.

"Eaton was shot from a distance, then Tracy and Josh Ivers dismounted and inspected the body then rode away. But there is a third set of prints, belonging to whoever . . ." Graham nodded to Eaton, ". . . did that."

"Show me the third print you're talking about, Hank," Fletcher said.

Graham squatted and pointed out a depression in the dusty ground. "Right there. Boot heel."

Fletcher studied the print and nodded. "I'm not the tracker you are, but I'd say that was made by a high-heeled boot."

The marshal nodded. "Cattleman's boot, sure enough."

"But who?"

"Your guess is as good as mine," Graham said, rising to his feet. "Whoever did it was not in a forget and forgive frame of mind, I can tell you that. He was an excellent marksman because he near blew Eaton's head clean off his shoulders."

Fletcher stood and looked around him. There were plenty of places where a hidden rifleman could have set up an ambush, then scampered to safety before Tracy and Ivers got to him.

"Well," Graham said, "like I told you before, Buck, ride real careful. Now we got another killer to contend with and there's nothing to say he's any friendlier to us than he was to Lonnie Eaton."

"Want to bury him, maybe?" Fletcher asked.

"Nah," Graham said, his face hard and unforgiving. "Let him lay there."

The two men swung into the saddle and took to the trail.

That night Fletcher and Graham camped at the edge of a timberline. The ground sloped away from the trees, ending in a rock-strewn spit of sand sticking out into a small, shallow lake no more than ten acres in extent.

The lake water was alkaline and bitter, but it boiled up just fine for coffee and the nearby pines provided plenty of firewood to broil the quail Graham had shot and a few strips of bacon to go with them.

After they'd eaten, Graham rustled in his pocket, found his candy and popped a lemon drop into his mouth. His lips puckered under his huge mustache at the sourness and he nodded in Fletcher's direction. "That necklace you wear is Apache."

Fletcher nodded. "An old prospector gave it to me a spell back. Said it would bring me luck."

"It might. My ma set store by things like that, said them beads were powerful medicine." Graham shrugged. "Never knew my pa, so I don't know what he thought. He was an Irishman, worked on the railroads Ma said, and he was just passing through I guess."

"A boy should have his pa," Fletcher allowed. "Lost mine early too."

"You know, when you first gave me your name, I figured

I'd heard it before," Graham said. "It only came to me yesstidy or the day before."

The marshal spit his candy into the fire. "Damn, but that one was sour." His dark eyes angled to Fletcher again. "I recollect that back in the old days you rode with some wild ones, made your mark from Texas to Kansas and beyond."

Fletcher nodded. "Sold my Colt to whoever was paying gun wages. In those days I was too young to care on what side of the law I stood or maybe too young to know any better. I've worn a star now and again if that's where the money was, and I've seen my face on a reward poster." Fletcher smiled. "Once or twice at the same time."

"You had a rep, a big one. There were them as said you were faster than Hardin or Thompson or any of them, maybe the fastest that ever was."

"Maybe," Fletcher said, remembering Doc Holliday, "but I've slowed up some. Getting old I guess."

Graham poked around in his paper bag and found another lemon drop. "I don't hold with revolver fighters," he said, palming the candy into his mouth. "It's just as well those days are about over. Ah," he said, "this one is better. Not near so tart."

"I'm glad those days are over too," Fletcher said, taking no offense. "Living on the dodge is no life at all, and gunfighting is a truly lousy way to make a dollar."

"Well, let bygones be bygones, I always say," Graham said. "A man changes, takes a different path in life."

"And what's your path, Hank?" Fletcher asked.

The man shrugged. "Don't know. I don't think much beyond marshalin'. Wouldn't mind a woman though, if she was nice and fat and could cook. Woman like that can give a man plenty of shade in summer and keep him warm in winter. Nothing warmer than a fat woman in a feather bed an' that's a natural fact."

Fletcher thought about Savannah, seeing her smile, remembering the fresh sweet smell of her. "Man should have a steady woman, Hank. You should try it real soon."

"Well," Graham sighed, leaning back on his upturned saddle, drawing his blanket around his several chins, "I'll sleep on that, Buck, I surely will."

Soon Fletcher too sought his blankets, the calico kitten snuggling close to him, and around both men the darkness of the night deepened and the breeze whispered through the pines, stirring the surface of the lake into shallow, restless ripples. . . .

Around midnight, Fletcher sat up with a start. A single, booming gunshot in the distance had wakened him.

Now as he strained his ears to listen to the night, he heard three, four, five more shots from a different weapon, fired very rapidly; the harsh, staccato bark of a well-handled lever-action rifle.

Then silence.

Graham was snoring softly, his mouth open, and Fletcher shook him awake. "Shots," he said as Graham blinked at him like a quizzical owl. "To the northwest and a fair piece from here."

"Hunters," the lawman said, still full of sleep. "Must be coon hunters."

"Hank," Fletcher said, shaking the man harder. "Wake up! Two rifles firing. One of them could belong to the man who killed Lonnie Eaton."

Graham rose to a sitting position and shook off his sleepiness. "Are you sure? Maybe you dreamed them shots."

"I wasn't dreaming. Now saddle up and let's go take a look-see. Maybe Bosco Tracy is already dead."

* * *

Fletcher and Graham rode into the darkness, the far-flung stars twinkling hard and bright above them.

Around them the mountains loomed like sleeping giants and hunting coyotes were calling from the blue shadows of the ravines and arroyos.

They rode steadily north for half an hour, then cut northwest at a lightning-split cottonwood on the edge of a dry creek bed, Graham spotting horse tracks in the soft ground.

Another half hour's riding brought them to the bottom of a shallow, humpbacked rise that stretched up and away from them for several hundred yards, its slope covered in mescal and soap weed.

Fletcher topped the rise and looked down on a narrow valley cut through by a wide creek, both banks lined by thick stands of cottonwood, sycamore, ash, walnut and a few stunted elder.

At a sharp bend in the creek, a campfire glowed like a candle flame in the darkness and Fletcher's straining eyes could make out two horses standing among the trees.

"They're down there," Graham said, kneeing his horse alongside Fletcher's buckskin. "How do you want to play this?"

"Well," Fletcher said, "we could mount a good old-fashioned cavalry charge down the slope and into their camp."

Doubt creased Graham's face. "Would it work?"

"No, we'd both be shot out of the saddle before we got halfway there."

"Then, I've got a better idea," the marshal said, smoothing his bristling mustache with the back of his hand. "We leave the horses here and Injun up on them, rifles in hand."

Fletcher nodded. "Sounds better than a cavalry charge."

"Anything sounds better than a cavalry charge," Graham said.

Both men swung out of the saddle and slid their rifles

from the boots. Fletcher levered a round into the chamber and Graham did the same, then, crouching low and stepping on careful feet, aware of the danger, they made their way down the slope.

As Fletcher got closer to the camp, he saw a man lying sprawled by the fire, his arms and legs spread wide. A distance away, sitting on a fallen cottonwood log, another man sat, his face buried in his hands.

The fire had died down to a dull, orange glow, red at the center, a few ashy sticks sticking out here and there.

Graham stepped out of the surrounding trees and Fletcher followed.

"Take them hands off your face and raise them!" Graham yelled. "I'm an officer of the law."

The man on the log lifted his head and his eyes flickered warily from Graham to Fletcher and back again. He rose slowly, his hands going up to shoulder height.

"Higher," Graham said, motioning with his rifle.

The man raised his hands higher.

But this was no man, Fletcher saw. He was a slender, tow-headed boy, no older than eighteen, dressed in the sun-faded hat, shirt, jeans and high-heeled boots of a ranch hand.

By the fire lay Josh Ivers. Like Eaton, he'd been shot in the head and, again like Eaton, his pants were down around his ankles, a bloody mess at his crotch where his genitals should have been.

But they were not missing, they had just been moved—into his gaping mouth.

"Did you do this, boy?" Graham asked. "And to the other one?"

The kid nodded. "I would have done it to all three if the third one hadn't got away from me in the dark," the boy said. "He had a better horse than mine."

"Who are you boy?" Graham asked, his voice softening.

"I'm a Deputy United States Marshal mind, so answer me true. I don't want no lies."

"My name is John Sprague. These two killed my ma and pa and my brother."

"Were those your kin back yonder in the cabin by the foothills?" Fletcher asked.

The boy nodded, saying nothing, tears standing in his eyes.

Fletcher looked at the dead man by the fire, an eerie echo of his own past coming back to him.

He'd been younger than this boy when he had taken his own vengeance ride, going after four Sioux warriors who had murdered his mother and father. He had killed all of them. But he had cut off the hands of the one who had carried his ma's scalp so that the man would be maimed in the next world, doomed to wander forever among the misty lodges of his people, unable to hunt or make war or hold a naked woman in the trembling firelight.

It had been a reckoning. And, like Fletcher, this boy had ridden with hell in his heart and had exacted a terrible revenge.

"John is it?" Graham asked.

The boy nodded.

"John, you should have laid out your ma decent. We were strangers passing by and had no call to see her like that."

"I did right by pa, but I knew I was spending too much time and meanwhile these men were getting further away. In the end, I just left everything as it was and went after them."

"Where were you when Bosco Tracy killed your folks?" Fletcher asked.

"Was that his name? Bosco Tracy? I never knew." John Sprague dashed the back of his hand over his eyes. "I was out making a tally of our herd. We didn't run many, longhorns mostly, but they were scattered far and wide. Pa wanted me to locate them and then haze them closer to the cabin where he could cut out the yearlings for sale. When I got back I saw . . . I saw . . ."

"This," said Graham, interrupting, pointing with his rifle muzzle at Ivers, "is a terrible thing to do to a man, John Sprague."

The boy nodded. "I know. But I also know what they did to Ma."

"Buck, get his rifle and belt gun," Graham said.

"I don't have a belt gun," the boy said. "Never had much need to own one."

The youngster's rifle was good, a single-shot .45-70 Winchester Highwall rifle, model of 1885, and it was well maintained and oiled, obviously the only firearm kept at the Sprague ranch.

"I'm taking you back to Tucson with me, John Sprague," Graham said. "It's not for me to argue the right or wrong of what you did. That's for a judge to decide."

Fletcher caught a flicker of fear in the boy's eyes and he smiled and said: "You'll be all right, John. No one will blame you for what happened."

Relief flooded the boy's face and Fletcher, wise to the men and manners of the West, had not been making an empty promise.

What this boy had done was expected and indeed condoned by Western men, and no judge or jury would convict him.

There were some who argued that this was wrong, and maybe it was, but that was the way of it and it would never change, Fletcher decided, at least not in his lifetime, or this boy's, either.

"Buck," Graham said, "are you heading back with me?"

Fletcher shook his head. "I'll keep on Tracy's trail. If I lose him, I can catch a train in Phoenix headed north and make my way back to the Two-Bit." Fletcher smiled, as though remembering. "I have a sick little girl and a wife depending on me."

"So be it," the marshal said. "You done right by me and I won't fault you for parting trails and heading home."

"Marshal, I want to bury my folks," Sprague said, his smooth young face earnest.

"We took care of your folks," Graham said. "Put all three in the same bed then burned their cabin down around their bodies."

The boy looked surprised, then shocked, and Fletcher said quickly: "The cabin became their funeral pyre, boy. It was as good a burying as any other."

Sprague thought that through, then nodded. "I'm beholden to both of you. That was decent." He glanced at Ivers's mutilated body. "What about him?"

"Let him lay," Graham said. "He'll just rot away to nothing on account of how even the buzzards won't touch him."

"One thing, Hank," Fletcher said. "I've been hunting Bosco Tracy for months now and I don't even know what he looks like."

"Big blond feller, good-looking." Graham traced a finger down his left cheek. "Has a scar right here. El Paso whore did that to him with a razor."

The lawman's eyes were suddenly shifty. "Buck, I guarantee that ol' Bosco has your description by this time . . . big, homely man in wore-out range clothes with a great beak of a nose and a raggedy mustache. Wears two guns, one of them in a crossdraw holster." Graham smiled. "Does that fit the bill?"

Fletcher's fingers went to his sweeping dragoon mustache. "Mostly, I'd say. I usually keep this trimmed you know."

"Well, anyhoo, my point is you won't have to go looking

for Bosco Tracy." Graham's smile slipped. "I got a feeling he's gonna come after you."

The fat man stuck out his hand and Fletcher took it. "Ride alert with an eye to the skyline, Buck Fletcher," he said. "And good luck to ye."

Twenty-four

Phoenix in 1887 was a bustling community that had the staid, quietly prosperous look of a farming town. Longhorn herds had never been trailed down its main street and there were no cattle pens shouldering next to the railroad track.

There were a scattering of false-fronted saloons, but these were quieter and more subdued than the opulent and noisy sin palaces of Tombstone and Tucson.

Graham had said there were whores in Phoenix, but if they were they were well hidden because the city had no red-light district, no roaring Hide Park full of drunken punchers and miners.

The main street was busy, crowded with spring wagons and buggies driven by somber, bearded farmers and their wives, but there were no ranch hands and none of the usual frontier riffraff on the make that drifted into boomtowns.

Fletcher saw nothing of a man answering Bosco Tracy's description, nor did he spend time searching for him.

At the station he bought a ticket on a train heading north into Utah that would pull out at nine that evening. In Salt Lake City he would pick up another train for southern Wyoming, and once there would catch yet another and cross the Divide into the Dakota Territory. It was a long trip across some of the most rugged and beautiful country on earth. He would have to kick his heels in lonely depots at the ends of spur lines, waiting for connecting trains, and for at least some of the journey he would have to depend on his buckskin.

But the railcars promised a swifter trip to the Two-Bit than riding all the way, and now that he had the ten thousand dollars for Ginny, time was pressing hard on him.

Fletcher put up his horse at a livery stable and ate a good meal at a restaurant, then killed time by walking around town to take in the sights, carrying the calico kitten, alert and inquisitive as ever, with him. As the day shaded into evening, he slept for a couple of hours in the hayloft of the livery stable, then saddled the buckskin and rode downtown to the station.

The lights were coming on in Phoenix, the oil lamps along both sides of the dusty street casting dancing pools of yellow light on the boardwalks. The town was quieter now, the farmers and their families having gone home for supper, but a lone piano played "Beautiful Dreamer" in one of the saloons and Fletcher heard a woman try to sing along, her voice flat and tentative as she groped for both words and tune.

The crescent moon was rising in the night sky and it had grown noticeably cooler after the long heat of the day.

A train consisting of two passenger cars, a flat freight wagon loaded with farm machinery, a single boxcar and a caboose was waiting at the station, the locomotive hissing like an angry dragon. The lamps had been lit in the passenger cars and already several dozen people were seated, looking out the windows into the gathering darkness.

Fletcher led his buckskin up the ramp of the boxcar, unsaddled him and threw him some hay from a bale standing in a corner. There was another horse in the adjoining stall, a glossy black with a star on his forehead and four white stockings, but no sign of the owner.

Because of the reassuring closeness of the other horse, the buckskin settled quickly and began to eat. Fletcher scooped up the kitten, slid his Winchester from the boot and walked back down the ramp.

The conductor was consulting his watch and a few more travelers were stepping up into the passenger cars. Behind him, Fletcher heard the ramp being lifted and he stopped at the first car, intending to board himself.

That's when he saw Bosco Tracy.

There was no mistaking the tall, blond man with the scar on his cheek who was watching him closely, a look of pure, malevolent hatred on his handsome face.

Tracy, dressed in black frock coat and pants, a gunbelt showing at his waist, was smoking a cigar and his eyes were blazing.

Fletcher stopped where he was, looking at Tracy, wondering if the man would make his move. His hand moved closer to the Colt in the crossdraw holster. There were a lot of people between them, men and women bustling into the passenger cars, carrying all manner of hand luggage. If Tracy drew and the bullets started to fly, innocent people would get hurt.

Fletcher stepped away from the train, trying to get a clear view of the outlaw without the intervening crowd.

Tracy didn't move.

He glared at Fletcher for a few minutes longer, then took the cigar stub from his mouth and contemptuously flicked it in Fletcher's direction. Fletcher followed the glowing arc of the cigar butt until it landed close to his feet, scattering sparks. When he looked up, Bosco Tracy was already stepping into the passenger car.

So, Tracy would not make his fight here.

Then where?

Fletcher stepped into the car. One way or another, before this train reached its destination, it would be carrying a dead man.

That Fletcher knew with a growing certainty.

Fletcher took a seat at the rear of the car, his back to the wall. He set the kitten down beside him, drew one of his Colts and loaded the empty chamber under the hammer then did the same with the second gun.

Only then did he give some study to his fellow passengers. There were about two dozen people in the car, husbands and wives mostly, and a couple of nondescript men in broadcloth suits who could have been drummers. One man, in the plaid shirt and pants of a miner, dozed on one of the seats, mouth open, his head against the window and a young nun in a gray habit sat primly behind him, a small pair of round glasses perched on the end of her nose.

As the train chugged away from the station, Fletcher sensed no danger here. He would have liked to close his eyes, lulled by the rocking motion of the carriage on the rails. But there would be no sleep on this trip.

Bosco Tracy was in the other car. The man was a killer and he could make his move at any time.

The train rolled north, rocking and swaying along its cast-iron tracks through rugged hill country, heading for the high trestle bridge over the Hassayampa River. After it cleared the river, it would swing west, following the line of the pine-covered foothills of the Weaver Mountains and then head due north again to cross yet another river, the swift-flowing Santa Maria.

After an hour, a black porter, gray hair showing under his cap, stepped along the car with practiced ease, adjusting easily to every jolt and sway. His eyes traveled over the passengers and fixed on Fletcher. He walked toward him, a wide smile splitting his face.

"Sir, would you be Mr. Fletcher?" he asked.

Fletcher nodded.

"Then Mr. Tracy, a passenger in the other car, wished me to give you this with his compliments." The porter held out a long, slim cigar and Fletcher took it.

"Will you give Mr. Tracy something in return?" Fletcher asked.

"Of course, sir." The porter smiled.

Fletcher reached down and slipped a cartridge from a loop on his gunbelt. "Give Mr. Tracy this, with my compliments, and tell him I have five more for him. Oh, and one thing more." He broke the cigar in half. "Return this to him."

The porter's smile slipped and he looked confused as he tried to make sense of what was happening.

Fletcher took the man's hand and dropped the .45 round and the pieces of the cigar into his palm. "Go tell him word for word what I just said."

"Yes, sir, whatever you say, sir," the porter said. He turned quickly away and stepped back down the car, turning every now and then to look at Fletcher, his eyes wide and puzzled.

Fletcher nodded and, only to himself, whispered, "I guess it won't be long now."

But another ten minutes passed and there was no sign of Tracy.

The locomotive hissed steam as it slowed and Fletcher felt it lurch as the engineer pulled it into a sidetrack off the main line. He looked out of the window but it was difficult to see anything in the darkness. But, as the locomotive screeched to a stop, he made out the looming bulk of a water tower and nearby a huge coal pile.

The locomotive up front burned around a hundred pounds of coal a mile and sometimes two hundred, depending on the grade of the fuel and the skill of the engineer. And railroad rules stated that an engineer must never pass a water tower without filling up his reserves, which meant a stop every forty to fifty miles, no matter the location or the weather.

Fletcher stood and told the kitten to stay put. His instinct was clamoring at him, telling him that this was when and where Bosco Tracy would make his play. He opened the carriage door, stepped onto the small steel platform and looked both ways along the track.

Up by the locomotive, the fireman was swinging the water tank's rigid hose over the boiler. Fletcher heard the engineer yell, then laugh, but could not make out what he said.

Steam hissed from between the wheels of the big locomotive, sending up swirling white clouds that quickly vanished in the darkness. High above, the horned moon reached out to the only visible star and the sky was dark blue, as though the day was lingering, unwilling to give way to the night.

Where was Tracy?

Fletcher stepped from the carriage and hopped down onto the gravel beside the track.

The fireman was pumping water into the engine's reserve tanks and he saw a pinpoint of red light in the cabin as the engineer puffed on his pipe. The shadowed land around him, stretching out beyond the shallow railroad cut, was hushed, expectant, as if waiting for what was to happen next.

Where was Tracy?

Fletcher had been sure the man would strike now, while the train was stopped in the middle of nowhere. Had he been wrong? Maybe the gunman was sitting in his seat even now, looking out the window, laughing at him.

Fletcher stepped away from the track where he could see the entire length of the train. Nothing moved, the passengers staying inside out of the darkness and the cool night air.

He'd been a fool. Bosco Tracy would strike, but at a time and place of his own choosing—and that could be anywhere between here and Two-Bit Creek.

Fletcher walked back toward the carriage. Then stopped.

A man was getting off the train, dropping on silent feet to the ground.

The man was tall, wearing a frock coat and flat-brimmed hat, and he was stepping purposefully toward him.

It was Bosco Tracy.

When Tracy was fifteen yards from Fletcher he stopped.

"Fletcher!" he yelled. "You've been pressing me mighty hard and you killed my brothers. I'm going to end it right here."

Fletcher nodded. "Suits me just fine, Tracy."

Fletcher caught a glimpse of people crowded to the windows as they realized that men were moving out there in the darkness and that something must be amiss. Windows opened and now heads poked through, looking curiously at him and Tracy.

"You should have stayed away from the Two-Bit, Tracy," Fletcher said, loud enough that the passengers could hear. "You murdered my hand and stole my horse."

"Fletcher," Tracy said, "you talk mighty big for a dead man."

"One of us will soon be dead," Fletcher said, his smile thin. "That's for sure."

The conductor was hurrying along the track toward them. "Here," he yelled, "that won't do!"

"Go to hell," Tracy said over his shoulder. And he drew.

The man was fast, very fast on the revolver draw.

His gun came up, the muzzle leveling at Fletcher's belly, just as Fletcher's first bullet hit him.

The heavy slug took Tracy high in the chest and the outlaw, shocked, took a step back. Tracy's gun barked and Fletcher saw the sudden starburst of orange flame from the muzzle.

Tracy's bullet buzzed past Fletcher's head like an angry bee and Fletcher fired again. Hit hard, Tracy staggered back against the side of the car, his gun spurting fire.

Another miss.

Fletcher fired, saw another hit, steadied himself and fired again.

This time Tracy slid to the ground, his handsome face very white, stunned, unable to believe what was happening to him.

Fletcher stepped beside the fallen outlaw, his Colt at the ready, no mercy in him.

"You weren't supposed to be that fast," Tracy gasped, blood spilling over his chin. "I was advised you'd gotten old and slow."

"You were advised wrong," Fletcher said, his eyes hard, unforgiving. "On my oldest and slowest day I'd still be able to shade a cheap, no-good tinhorn like you."

"This can't be . . . it can't be . . ." Tracy's eyes opened wide and scared, the horror of his death spiking at him.

Then he was gone.

Fletcher holstered his gun.

Bosco Tracy had been the last of them and the worst of them and now it was over.

He felt drained, empty inside, as people crowded around, pointing to the dead man, asking questions. The nun kneeled by Tracy, her rosary beads clicking through her white fingers, whispering prayers for the dead. Now and again she glanced up at Fletcher, her eyes accusing, understanding only the wrong of the thing and not the right.

"He's going to need those prayers," Fletcher said, remembering the woman in the cabin.

The nun did not reply. She dropped her eyes and went back to her prayers, her prim mouth moving tight and white-lipped, murmuring the ancient words.

Fletcher sighed deeply. He looked up at the night sky and the bright, waxing moon.

It was time to go home.

Back to the cabin on the Two-Bit.

Epilogue

Christmas Eve had come to the cabin on Two-Bit Creek.

Outside, the land was hushed, covered in snow, the bitter legacy of yet another hard winter, almost as severe as the one that had gone before, the months of November, December and January 1886 said to be the coldest in recorded history.

In October, Fletcher had dug out his mackinaw and sheepskin gloves and as the temperatures plunged to twenty below zero, he was out every day and night, hazing his cattle back from the rivers with their dangerous air holes and open channels in the ice to the shelter of the protecting hills around the Two-Bit.

Drifts as high as a tall man on a horse were filling the cut banks and arroyos, and throughout December no sooner had one blizzard spent itself than it was followed by another.

And through it all, Fletcher's cows drifted like white ghosts, steam rising from their nostrils, icicles hanging from their ears and eyes and muzzles. A thin layer of ice covered the snow like boilerplate, stopping the cattle from getting to the grass locked below and out on the open range the cows were dying of starvation, Fletcher's among them.

And still the blizzards blew cold and merciless from the

north and there was no sign of a Chinook, the snow-eating winds that would warm the range and end the terrible dying.

That Christmas Eve only the wolves and coyotes were prospering . . . and the buzzards.

Restlessly Fletcher paced the floor of the empty cabin. He stepped to the door, opened it and looked outside.

The snow had stopped for now and the night was bright with stars. Around him the silent hills reflected the pale moonlight and snow lay thick on the branches of the green arrowheads of pine.

Fletcher's breath smoked in the air as his spotted dog, old now, and increasingly infirm, rubbed against his leg and lifted his nose to test the wind. Detecting nothing of interest, the dog turned and went back to the warmth of the stove, where the calico cat lay staring at the glowing logs with mad, unblinking, hazel eyes.

The dog and cat had formed a bond since Fletcher returned from the Arizona Territory, often hunting bugs and lizards together among the underbrush at the base of the pines. The dog, stalking gamely on three legs, never caught anything but was content to stop and snap loudly at flies buzzing around his head.

The calico cat would often pause and look at him, his pitying glance seemingly tolerant of the fact that canines, not blessed with the feline brain, were poor hunters and not to be blamed for their misdeeds.

Fletcher closed the cabin door and sat at the table. He drew the oil lamp closer and picked up the two letters that he'd read and reread and would now read again.

Doc had died on the eighth of November in Glenwood Springs and this was his last letter, though written in another, female hand.

Fletcher read through the letter, mostly an account of

Doc's arrival at the sanitarium and the excellent, though futile, treatment he had received.

"Buck," it ended, "I can look down to the bottom of the bed and see my bare toes. This is funny."

An addendum was added in the woman's fair copperplate and said only: "Dr. Holliday dictated this letter a few minutes before he passed away. He died with his Savior's name on his lips, his mind on the salvation of his immortal soul." And it was signed: "Sister Mary Joseph."

Fletcher smiled. He suspected that Doc's last-minute conversion was a pleasant fiction concocted by Sister Mary Joseph to ease the sense of loss felt by Doc's many friends and admirers.

Though when he thought it through, Fletcher decided that Doc had mighty few friends and less admirers.

Even he, proud to count himself as one of the former, did not come close to being one of the latter.

Now Doc was gone, Fletcher would not grieve for him. He remembered him once saying: "Buck, to grieve over a death is all wrong. Any sorrow is a selfish, misinformed sorrow. Hell, you're grieving for your own loss, not for the poor son of a bitch who just went over the river."

Fletcher carefully folded Doc's letter and sat there for a few moments holding it in his hand, smiling, remembering, seeing Doc laugh, hearing him cuss, picturing him astride his ugly little mustang, writing the man's epitaph in his heart. Doc Holliday had been a man of unquestioned courage with a fierce, almost obsessive loyalty to those he considered friends, but the world was little poorer for his passing.

There was, however, an empty place inside Fletcher that Doc had once filled. Now he was gone, it would always remain that way.

The sense of loss that Doc had talked about was strong in

Fletcher, and it could be he was being selfish, but he owed Doc much, as Savannah's letter had made him realize.

Now he picked up that letter and read it, for maybe the hundredth time. It was dated November fifth and was short, Savannah never a woman to waste words.

My Darling Buck,

I hope this letter finds you as well as it leaves Ginny and me.

Our daughter grows stronger every day and just yesterday spent the entire morning out of bed! The doctors here are wonderful and they say they expect Ginny to make a full recovery.

Buck, we could be home in as little as three months!

Ginny says to send you her love, and, of course, you know all of mine goes with hers.

My darling, we both miss you so much, but I know our parting will soon be over.

Please, please, take care of yourself and remember to wear your muffler and gloves when you go out. You know how chesty you can be in cold weather.

Once again, my darling,

All my love,
Savannah.

Fletcher read the letter again, pressed it gently against his lips where he calculated Savannah's hand had rested while she wrote, then carefully folded it up and placed it on top of Doc's.

He rose and threw a couple of logs on the fire, the restlessness tugging at him, refusing to let him be.

No man should be alone on Christmas Eve, even a man like himself, grown to loneliness, used to its forlorn ways.

But one means to overcome loneliness is to seek out one lonelier still, and Fletcher's thoughts went to the widow woman on Bear Butte Gulch.

The last time he had ridden over there, he had been coolly received.

Christmas or no, would this time be any different?

Fletcher's inclination was to dismiss the thought from his mind. Why risk being snubbed and made to feel a fool?

He rolled a cigarette and sat at the table again, the spotted dog and calico cat regarding him curiously, perhaps wondering why he was not content to remain still and enjoy the warmth and the flickering firelight.

Fletcher lit his cigarette and picked up Savannah's letter again. He read it through, then set it down.

He had made up his mind.

The snow had stopped, the night was clear, the moon bright; it was time to go calling. Maybe this time the woman, drawn by a mutual need for company, would tell him to set a spell and take a load off.

Maybe she would. It was worth a try.

He was taking a chance, but it was a sight better than remaining in the cabin by himself. More than anything, after months of solitude, he needed to hear another human being's voice.

His mind on the woman's youngsters, Fletcher found a small burlap sack and into this he put some things he had bought in Deadwood for Ginny, figuring he now had three months to replace them.

There was a rag doll in a blue print dress, and four gaily striped candy canes, each wrapped in its own piece of wax paper.

"I can give you strawberry," the storekeeper had said.

"Or cherry, peppermint or blueberry. That's a new flavor just in from Cheyenne. Think your daughter will like blueberry?"

Fletcher, to be safe, had taken all four.

After one last glance around the cabin and a strict warning to the dog and calico cat to behave, Fletcher picked up his sack and stepped outside, into the harsh cold and snow.

Buck Fletcher rode south under a full moon, past Pillar Peak, heading for ice-covered Lost Gulch.

What remained of his cattle were now in the arroyos and deep coulees in the hills just north of the gulch, where he could feed them with the hay he had spent weeks cutting on his return from Arizona.

But unless the Chinook came soon, the hay would all be gone and once again the cows would have to fend for themselves.

It was a worrisome prospect, and Fletcher glanced at the sky as if to find his salvation there, seeing only an endless expanse of darkness; here and there the hard glitter of a frosty star.

His breath smoked in the air as he drew his muffler and the collar of his mackinaw up around his ears. The buckskin, annoyed at being taken from his warm barn, tossed his head, fighting the bit, the bridle jangling.

Fletcher leaned down and patted the horse's neck, muttering a few soothing words. The buckskin calmed down a little, but pecked badly now and then as he plowed through deep snowdrifts, piled breast high by the wind.

The Black Hills, so named by the Indians because the pines on their slopes looked black from a distance, were covered in snow, an endless expanse of white relieved only by green spear points of spruce and juniper.

Around Fletcher as he rode, the land was hushed, the

long, silent miles stretching out before him, the peak of Dome Mountain lost in the darkness. To his east rose the frowning rampart of Bear Den Mountain. This too could not be seen in the gloom, but Fletcher sensed its brooding presence and the towering majesty of its rawboned ridges and deep ravines.

From somewhere close to the mountain a wolf howled, a long, drawn-out wail, just once, then it fell silent.

Fletcher rode into a line of scattered aspen at the base of a shallow hill and built a smoke, arguing with himself. Was he being a fool or not?

That Yankee widow woman could keep him at the door, slam it in his face and send him on his way. If that happened, he would have to ride back to the Two-Bit with his tail between his legs.

Fletcher finished his cigarette.

Well, after all, it was Christmas Eve, so that was a chance he would just have to take.

The woman's cabin lay at the southern end of Bear Den, among the rolling foothills and narrow valleys where Bear Butte Creek met Strawberry Creek.

It was a lovely spot, green with buffalo grass and wildflowers in summer, but too unpredictable and harsh for farming country as her husband had learned to his cost.

As Fletcher rode closer, he saw lights in the cabin windows, the soft yellow and orange glow of oil lamps, welcoming beacons in the gathering darkness. Smoke rose from the chimney and Fletcher caught an elusive whiff of frying bacon.

When he was twenty yards from the cabin, Fletcher reined in the buckskin. His practiced eye studied the place. A man had worked hard here and he had worked well. But that had been a time ago. The cabin, of hewn logs, had been raised with an eye to keeping out the worst of the north winds and the corral had been built solid by a man who had taken much pride in his work.

It seemed the woman had tried to keep the place up, but it was obviously a losing proposition. The roof of the shed sagged under the weight of its canopy of snow and behind that, closer to the slope of a hill, a small barn tilted badly to its right, snow banked up against its sides of peeling pine board.

The whole place, cabin, shed, corral and barn, looked run-down, neglected, held together by string and rawhide, a woman's desperate attempt to make do when what was needed was a man's strength.

Fletcher nodded. If she was still here come spring, he would ride over and do what he could to help her.

That is, if she would let him.

Well, there was one way to find out.

Swallowing hard, Fletcher rode closer. As Western etiquette demanded, he kept to the saddle, but called out: "Hello, the cabin!"

After a few moments, the door opened a crack, a slender rectangle of yellow light spilling across the blue darkness of the snow.

"Who is it?"

"Me. Buck Fletcher. I'm your neighbor." Fletcher hesitated, then added: "I live to the north of here. Up on the Two-Bit."

A moment's hesitation, then the woman said: "You've been here before, I think."

"Yes ma'am," Fletcher said, not wanting to go into his last visit too deeply.

"What can I do for you?"

This is not going well, Fletcher thought.

Aloud, he said: "Being Christmas Eve and all, I thought I'd drop by and visit for a spell. See, my wife and daughter are in . . . well, they're not to home and won't be for quite some time." Desperate now, he added quickly: "I guess it's not good to be alone on Christmas Eve, but if you're not receiving company . . ."

The door opened wider and the woman stepped out onto the snow, two young children crowding close and shy, holding on to her skirts.

"Mr. Fletcher," she said, "Christmas Eve is pretty much like any other night around here." She stood silent for a few moments, then seemed to make up her mind. "My name is Mary Anderson." She laid a hand on each of the kids' heads. "These two young 'uns are mine. This—" she patted the girl's yellow curls, "—is Kate. She's seven. And this one is Jacob. He'll be nine next month."

Fletcher touched his hat brim and smiled. "Right pleased to make your acquaintance, ma'am. All three of you."

Fletcher was pleased. The children were quiet and well behaved and that spoke volumes about the parents.

"Well, step down and set for a while," Mary said. "We were just about to eat. We don't have much, but what we have you're welcome to share." The woman nodded behind her. "You can put your horse in the barn. There's some hay back there."

The barn was empty but comparatively warm, and Fletcher led the buckskin to a stall and unsaddled him. He forked a small amount of hay to the horse, picked up his sack and walked back to the cabin.

The door was open and Fletcher stepped inside.

The cabin was warm, sparsely furnished with a table and a few scattered chairs, but the place was well kept, the dirt floor swept and clean. Logs flamed in a stone fireplace with a pine mantel and an oil lamp burned over the table, now set for supper.

Mary Anderson waved to a chair at the head of the table,

manners dictating that the guest should have the place of honor. "Please be seated, Mr. Fletcher," she said.

"Call me Buck, ma'am, please," Fletcher said.

Mary gave one of her rare smiles. "Then Buck it is. Please sit."

As the woman served supper, boiled winter potatoes and fried bacon, and not much of either, Fletcher got his first real chance to study her.

She was plain, with not even a tenuous claim to beauty, her brown eyes set close together over a nose that he recognized was as large and unlovely as his own, her teeth small and white in a wide mouth that gave way to a receding chin.

Her dress was of plain blue wool, much worn and darned, her figure lumpy, without shape.

Mary Anderson looked very tired, strands of gray streaking her brown hair, a woman who was probably no more than thirty yet had grown old before her time, worn out by work that was too hard in a hard and demanding land.

Fletcher's heart went out to her, but he kept his feelings to himself. The last thing this woman would want was his pity.

Likewise with the food. He ate all she gave him without comment except to say how good it was. He knew that in doing so, she and the children were making do with less, especially Mary, whose portions were the smallest of all. But to have refused the food or to suggest that only she and the kids eat, would have been a grave breach of manners. All he would have done was throw her poverty in her face and offend her terribly, and that was something he would not do.

After they ate, Mary cleared away the plates and sat back at the table. Fletcher reached into his shirt pocket, took out the makings and asked: "May I beg your indulgence, ma'am?"

"Please do. My husband smoked a pipe and I came to very much enjoy the smell of tobacco."

Fletcher rolled a smoke, lit the cigarette, and asked: "Do you plan to stay on here? I mean after the winter is gone."

Mary shook her head at him. "No, I'm giving up, heading home."

"Where is home?"

"Back east. I have a sister in Boston. Her husband is prospering in the hardware business and she says we can stay with her for a while until I find a job and we get settled."

"I don't suppose anything can make you change your mind about that?"

"Nothing, Mr. Fletcher. This farm was my husband's dream, not mine. Without him, the dream has gone and I don't wish to hold on to what's left of it any longer."

Fletcher knew argument was useless and would serve no purpose.

"Right," he said, looking at the children. "Then we must make your last Christmas in the Dakota Territory one to remember."

These children never had much and did not expect much, looking at Fletcher with wide, uncomprehending eyes.

He drew on his cigarette, leaned across the table and said: "All over the country, just about now, little kids are hanging their stockings on the chimney wall."

"But why would they do that?" Kate asked, her face puzzled.

"Why? Because good old Saint Nicholas brings presents and he puts them in their stockings."

"No, Mr. Fletcher," Mary whispered, panic in her eyes. "No."

"And they also have a Christmas tree," Fletcher said,

ignoring Mary's warning. "Everyone should have a tree at Christmas."

"Can we have one?" Jacob asked, his eyes suddenly excited.

"Of course we can. All we need is an ax and I bet there's one in the shed out there."

"Mr. Fletcher," Mary said, "please don't take this any further." She turned to the children. "Saint Nicholas won't be visiting us this year."

Fletcher saw disappointment cloud the kids' eyes. "I suppose that's true, because he didn't come last year either," Kate said.

Fletcher sprang to his feet, smiling. "I've got a feeling this year will be different." He ruffled the girl's hair. "Now, what say we dress up warm and go get ourselves a Christmas tree?"

The children cheered this announcement, but their mother's eyes when they turned to Fletcher held a warning, and something else, regret, Fletcher guessed, maybe for allowing him to visit in the first place.

"You too, ma'am," Fletcher smiled, refusing to be intimidated. "This is a family outing, you know."

Reluctantly, the woman shrugged into an oversized mackinaw that Fletcher guessed must have belonged to her husband. She put a gray woolen muffler over her head and tied it under her chin.

She did the same for the children and Fletcher grabbed his hat and led everyone outside. He found an ax in the shed as he'd predicted. The blade was rusty and dull, but it would do the job.

After ten minutes scouting around at the base of one of the surrounding hills, Fletcher found a stunted spruce growing in an aspen grove. The tree was small, but it had a good shape and its needles were green without a trace of brown.

"This," he told the kids, "is ideal."

Mary, stepping forward to examine the tree, slipped on a patch of ice and with a thump sat down heavily on her butt. The children ran to her, waving their hands, full of panicked concern. But when the woman rose to her feet, brushing snow off her mackinaw, she was laughing, her face flushed, cheeks and nose red from the cold, and Fletcher caught a brief, pleasing glimpse of the young girl she had been not too many years before.

Helped by the children, Fletcher carried the tree to the cabin in triumph. He found a bucket in the shed and managed to loosen enough frozen dirt from the abandoned vegetable garden at the back of the cabin to fill it. Into this, he set the slender trunk of the spruce and then placed the tree in a corner beside the fire.

Mary, caught up in the excitement of the moment, said: "Now we have to decorate it."

She stepped into the bedroom and returned with a pile of colorful cloth patches.

"I always intended to make a quilt with these, but never got around to it," she said.

Fletcher nodded. "I reckon they'll dress up our tree real nice."

And they did.

Fletcher, Mary and the children covered the branches in the bright patches, and when they were finished, all four of them stepped back to admire their handiwork.

Kate clasped her hands together, put them against her cheek, and gazed at the little spruce in wide-eyed admiration.

"This is the prettiest, most beautiful tree in the whole world," she said.

"I reckon it is," Fletcher said. "I can't think of another that would be prettier."

"Ma," Jacob said, "do you think there are prettier trees than this in Boston?"

Mary shook her head. "I don't think so. I think this is the prettiest Christmas tree ever."

Later, after the children had gone to bed, full of wide-eyed excitement about the imminent arrival of good old Saint Nicholas, Fletcher took down the stockings they had hung on the chimney wall.

"I really wish you hadn't told them about the stockings, Mr. Fletcher," Mary said, her eyes troubled. "I have nothing to give them."

"But I have," Fletcher said, his smile wide under his mustache.

He dug into his pocket and into each stocking he dropped a silver dollar. Then he opened his sack and produced the candy canes, two for each of the children.

"I gave Kate blueberry," Fletcher said. "It's a new flavor just in from Cheyenne. Do you think she'll like blueberry?"

Mary looked dazed, unable to believe that Saint Nicholas had arrived in the shape of a big, homely man with a ragged mustache under a great beak of a nose.

"Neither she or Jacob have ever had a candy cane," she said. "But I'm sure she will love it."

"And now there's this," Fletcher said, producing the rag doll with all the flair of a medicine show magician pulling a rabbit out of a hat.

"Mr. Fletcher," Mary protested, "surely you bought that for your own daughter."

Fletcher nodded. "I did, but I have time to get her another."

He stuffed the doll into Kate's stocking, then asked: "Do you think Jacob is responsible enough to have his own folding knife?"

Mary nodded, unable to speak.

Fletcher produced his beautiful Sheffield knife with the ivory handle and dropped it into the boy's stocking. Then, while Mary watched in stunned amazement, he went back to the fireplace and hung up the stockings again.

When he stepped back to the table, the woman said: "You didn't have to do this, Mr. Fletcher. It's too much to give."

Fletcher shook his head. "I love children and this has pleased me, maybe more than you realize." He smiled. "You know, I was pretty lonely earlier tonight and feeling mighty sorry for myself. Well, now I don't feel so lonely anymore."

"Neither do I, Mr. Fletcher," Mary said, her eyes softening, her fingers lightly touching the back of Fletcher's hand. "Not now. Not at this very moment."

Embarrassed, Fletcher turned away. "I still have one last present to give," he said finally. "And this one's for Ma."

He untied the bead necklace from around his neck. "This is for you, Mary. It's Apache and it will bring you luck."

The woman made no protest, accepting the gift graciously, knowing how kindly it was meant and that her refusal would hurt this warm, generous man badly. "Will you tie it for me?" she asked.

Fletcher stepped behind Mary and tied the necklace around her neck.

She smoothed it into place with her hand and said: "It's beautiful. Thank you. I've never had anything quite so pretty."

When Fletcher sat again, Mary said, her eyes downcast, voice barely a whisper: "I have nothing to give you in return."

"Mary, you've given me a great deal," Fletcher said. "You, and Kate and Jacob, and I surely do appreciate it."

Without looking up, the woman said: "I'm sure the children would love for you to be here in the morning." Now she lifted her head and her eyes met Fletcher's. "You can stay the night . . . if that would please you."

The invitation was sincere, a woman giving what she could when there was nothing else to give, and Fletcher recognized it and accepted it as such.

"That's more than kind of you, Mary," he said. "But I have a dog and cat back at the cabin and a fire burning low by this time. I guess I ought to be getting back."

The woman looked neither hurt nor relieved. "Wait," she said. "There is something else."

She rose and stepped to a small sideboard and returned with a bottle. "This is Hennessey brandy," she said. "My husband brought it with us all the way from Boston. He said we'd keep it for a special occasion, but that occasion never came." She smiled. "But I believe it's here now."

Mary laid the bottle on the table and went to the sideboard again. She returned with two small china cups and into each of these she poured a generous shot of the Hennessey.

The woman passed a cup to Fletcher and raised her own. "Happy Christmas, Buck Fletcher," she said. "Happy Christmas."

Later, when Fletcher rose to leave, Mary stepped close beside him.

"Buck," she said, "will you do one last thing for me before you go?"

"Of course," Fletcher said. "Anything."

"Just hold me close. Hold me close for a very long time."

Fletcher took the woman in his arms and held her tight, her head on his shoulder.

A log dropped in the fire, sending up a shower of sparks, and outside a rising wind whispered around the walls of the cabin. A few flakes of snow began to fall and the branches of the pines on the slopes of the hills stirred in the breeze.

Fletcher and Mary stood in a close embrace for many minutes, two worn, life-scarred people with no claim to beauty or sophistication, bonded only by their loneliness and their need for the closeness of another human being.

And when it was over, Fletcher got his hat and stepped out of the cabin, no fair parting words coming to him.

As he rode away he looked back.

Mary was standing in the doorway of the cabin, watching him go. She did not wave but she watched him for a long time until he was swallowed up by the darkness and the distance and even then, she watched a little longer. . . .

The blizzard struck with terrible, shrieking fury when Fletcher was still but halfway home.

A solid wall of snow cartwheeled toward him, driven by a howling wind, and the temperature took a sudden, terrifying plunge.

The snow hit, each spinning, swirling flake stinging like an angry wasp, a vicious white shroud that blocked out the night sky and the land around.

Fletcher, his mustache white with ice and snow, swung his muffler over his hat and tied it under his chin. Because of the storm, hemming him in on every side like walls of cold iron, he had lost all sense of direction. Now he would have to depend on the buckskin's instinct to lead him home.

But, as the blizzard's ferocity grew and the temperature continued to plunge, even the buckskin's great strength began to falter.

Fletcher felt the horse stumble, floundering badly now as the drifts grew ever higher. He leaned over and patted the buckskin's neck, yelling above the screaming wind: "We can make it, boy. We can make it."

Fletcher glanced around him and saw nothing but the thick white curtain of the driving snow. His breath smoked in the air as he bent his head against the awful, mindless violence of the wind.

Under him, the buckskin stumbled, then stopped, unwilling or unable to continue.

"We can make it, boy," Fletcher yelled again. "Don't give up now."

He was very cold and suddenly deathly tired.

And it was still a long, long way from the cabin on the Two-Bit.

Historical Note

In Ralph Compton's proposal for *Vengeance Rider*, he said the novel would be loosely based on the exploits of Texas Ranger John Reynolds Hughes.

At the age of fifteen, Hughes had his right arm shattered in a brawl, causing him to switch gun hands. He taught himself to become a skilled and deadly southpaw marksman, and on August 10, 1887, he enlisted in the Rangers.

A year earlier, rustlers stole nearly one hundred horses from ranches in the Liberty Hill area of Texas, including eighteen belonging to Hughes.

Over the next twelve months, Hughes rode after the rustlers, killing three, capturing two others, and returning with the herd.

During his vengeance ride, Hughes traveled twelve hundred miles, used up nine mounts and spent all but seventy-six cents of the forty-three dollars he'd started out with in his jeans.

Texas John Slaughter, War Between the States veteran, trail-driver, cattle king, professional gambler and finally sheriff, cleaned up the mess left in the Arizona Territory by the Earp brothers after the street fight in Tombstone.

Slaughter imposed law and order in the Territory with his Colt, repeating shotgun and Henry rifle, and among those who openly admired his guns and courage were well-known shootists like Wild Bill Hickok, Ben Thompson, Big Foot Wallace, King Fisher, Sam Bass, Billy the Kid and Pat Garrett.

Although Slaughter was only a few inches over five feet, outlaws often gave up without a fight after taking one look into his hard, black eyes. When Slaughter told a man, "Lay down or be shot down," his lips barely moved—and he meant every whispered word he said.

Like John Hughes, Slaughter was tireless in his pursuit of outlaws, riding anywhere across the six thousand square miles of Arizona's Cochise County and never returning until he could place his quarry on the list of permanently absent friends.

Slaughter, who hanged, shot or jailed more outlaws than any other lawman in Western history, finally crossed the river at the age of eighty-one in 1922.

The last months of Doc Holliday's life have not been documented.

His last recorded shooting scrape, of a minor sort, happened in Leadville, Colorado, on August 19, 1884, and thereafter Doc disappears from the newspaper record until his death in Glenwood Springs, Colorado on November 8, 1887.

In *Vengeance Rider*, Ralph Compton describes the final months of Doc's life, probably not as they were, but as they should have been.